tHE VoiCE of The bUtteRfly

tHE VoiCE of The bUtteRfly

JohN NiChoLs

CHRONICLE BOOKS
SAN FRANCISCO

Library of Congress Cataloging-in-Publication Data:

Nichols, John Treadwell, 1940 –
The voice of the butterfly / John Nichols.
p. cm.
ISBN 0-8118-3201-5
Express highways—Design and construction—Fiction. 2. Butterflies—
Habitat—Fiction. 3. Habitat conservation—Fiction. 4. Environmentalists—
Fiction. 5. Middle-aged men—Fiction. 6. New Mexico—Fiction. I. Title

PS3564.I274 V65 2001
813'.54—dc21   00-047438

Printed in the United States

Design by Vivien Sung
Composition by Suzanne Scott
Typeset in Vendetta.

Distributed in Canada by Raincoast Books
9050 Shaughnessy Street
Vancouver, British Columbia V6P 6E5

10 9 8 7 6 5 4 3 2 1

Chronicle Books LLC
85 Second Street
San Francisco, California 94105

www.chroniclebooks.com

TO
Kathy Anderson
Marian Wood
Jay Schaefer

. . . and anyone else who ever helped an endangered butterfly.

How can we save ourselves before we self-destruct?

ANY IMPLAUSIBLE story worth its salt begins with an alarm going off.

"Shit!"

Arise, ye prisoners of starvation.

I woke up in a panic and started humping it because I had already slept through three ten-minute snooze alarms and time was running out. Today, September twenty-eighth, was National Feline Leukemia Prevention Day, so I scrambled about madly, grabbing cats and shoving them one atop another into my cardboard Cat Caddy. Last one in (Tommy), whom I crammed atop Elroy, Oopboop, Ginger, and Carlos, squirmed, mewed, hissed, and clawed defiantly, but a pumped-up Charley McFarland is nothing if not determined when the chips are down, so I stuffed Tommy in among the others with a contemptible lack of sympathy for their claustrophobia. Why would a guy like me, who is not naturally a cat man, be taking such good care of that raggedy bunch of misfits? Because they were Kelly's cats when we were still together, that's why. And she had loved them dearly, liberating them all from Death Row at the Animal Shelter. In fact, they were the only "sane" part of her that remained, even though her proclivity had been to adopt the hard-cores, the pirates, the one-eyed toms with half an ear missing who'd as soon piss on your bedspread just for the inbred thrill of it. But hey, they'd made Kelly "happy," and I would *never* have argued with that.

Then I hopped into my beater Buick convertible (circa 1976) and headed north on Willow Road, creating one pound of carbon dioxide for every mile traveled. I'm supposed to be an environmentalist and I actually cringed as blue smoke billowed out grotesquely behind me, mugging a flight of evening grosbeaks in a box elder tree, scorching the petals of wild sunflowers, and laying a thin film of poisonous fallout on the foreheads of two Appaloosas staring benignly at my junker wheels.

"I'm sorry!" I shouted miserably. "I don't have the bread for a catalytic converter!" ("You're a pathetic guilt freak, Charley," Kelly used to harp. "You're not happy unless you feel miserable for killing every stupid frog on the planet and enslaving all the starving coffee workers in Honduras by buying a jar of Maxwell House freeze-dried instant java once every three years.")

Yeah, yeah, yeah. But what I *really* felt sorry about on this particular grim morning were the plans to eradicate my beloved Willow Road, the last relatively untrammeled artery (and land) in our valley. Come November, in the election, a local mill levy proposition on the ballot (Prop X), if passed, would tax all of us befuddled citizens in order to build a highway bypass, an industrial park, and other assorted travesties on bucolic Willow Road. Coincidentally, the bypass would flatten my oldest friend and rabble-rousing cohort, Lydia Arlington Babcock, and in the process demolish a rare and endangered butterfly, the Rocky Mountain Phistic Copper, which called Lydia's property (at the end of Willow Road) its home. Enraged by this shortsighted, environmentally terracidal project, I had recently decided (almost too late!) to form an organization whose purpose would be to derail Proposition X. This would only be about the two hundredth such dysfunctional coalition that I had spawned over the last twenty years, but today the stakes were higher than ever and the resources to draw on nearly nonexistent given the attrition rate during the Nineties on serious social activism in Suicide City. I didn't care, though, I'm a maniac. I mean, ever since the anti–Vietnam war movement, my role in life has been to *fight*. I also *remember* Chico Mendes.

When I turned off Willow Road onto Bayview, the modern world—the *real* world—hit me full in the face like a gigantic lemon meringue pie traveling at ninety miles an hour: *Poomph! Splatter! Glub!* First, in the Clarence Fagerquist Mobile Court hundreds of bloated doublewides were lined end-to-end in an orgasm of aluminum siding and Astroturf WELCOME mats. Then came those wonderful Poddubny Estates, which featured about eight hundred pre-fab lookalike hermetically sealed Monopoly houses with an air conditioner in every window (*love* those CFCs!), and an ornamental maple blazing golden in the middle of every Weed Free® lawn with a skull and crossbones dwidget on it warning about herbicides, fertilizers, and gopher baits made of coumadin. *Yum.* After that, I turned left at the highway, out of Dante's Inferno and into Hieronymus Boschville.

"Neon and freon!" I gabbled insanely, squinting against the glare. On the radio, atavistic WPNX disc jockey Randy Featherstone screamed, "HERE COME THE STONES!" and before you could shake a stick, Mick Jagger—Mick *Jagger? Still alive?*—was bellowing that he couldn't get no satisfaction.

Me neither, girlfriend. So I gritted my rotting teeth and snarled, beeped at all the confusion, and passed on the right, pebbles flying. The usual assholes honked back, fired the required birdies, and shook their fists at me, but I told them all to blow it out their overweight fannies, squared. Of course I couldn't *see* half of them because they were hidden behind darkly tinted windows, anonymous voyagers on the road to hell in an autocentric America where thanks to voice mail, e-mail, caller IDs, Internet-shopping Web sites, and frosted auto glass, actual Human Contact has become an unnecessary luxury and a true impediment to the final total alienation of humanity from the universe. Kelly once went on one of her sprees, shooting the windows out of a half dozen tinted Camaros on the lot at Copernicus Motors. No ma'am, I do not approve of firearms, but Kelly certainly understood the concept.

When traffic finally thinned out, I hit the gas to make up for lost time and promptly the Southern Rocky Mountains' answer to agents Scully and Mulder, Johnny Batrus, tripped his siren button and pulled me over. This had happened to me often, but I'm Pavlovian and almost shit in my pants *and* had a heart attack.

Even before his ridiculous self-important macho ball-bulging saunter had carried him (and his filthy, alienating, one-way Mercury shades) to my door, my terrified motor mouth was off and running:

"Yo, Johnny, I'm sorry, I'm late, I'll get fired if I don't make it to work on time and today's the only day they can fit in Kelly's cats for shots, I didn't mean it, I promise I'll never speed again, listen, I'll give you guys a donation to the PAL this summer so you can buy baseballs made in Haiti by kwashiorkor vic—"

Great spiel . . . but it cost me thirty bucks anyway, it always does.

"That's just for going twenty over the limit," Johnny said. "I shoulda gave you another fifty for no seatbelt. Does this piece of crap even *have* a seatbelt? Well, you better get one, and then you better buckle up, because next time I catch you, bub, I'm gonna throw the book."

Yada, yada, yada.

Before I could split, however, a mud-spattered dyspeptic '88 Toyota pickup missing the right front fender pulled over behind Johnny's cruiser, and a scrawny popeyed female dingaling jumped out, camera in hand: *click!click!click!* Then she skipped toward us, a ballpoint clamped between her teeth, flipping the yellow pages of her notepad.

"Hiya gang," this quirky zealot piped cheerfully. "Am I in time for a salacious tidbit? Hey Chaz, honey, what do I hear about the Butterfly Coalition?"

Susan Delgado, *Sentinel-Argus* cub reporter, and the least popular carcinogen in Suicide City. She measured five feet nine inches and weighed about sixty pounds and her blue eyes bulged froglike through inch-thick lenses set in bold black Buddy Holly frames. Her punker hairdo looked like terrified cat whiskers Superglued onto a pink balloon. But I actually enjoyed her because Susan was on *our* side, and the reporter *loved* me, or so she liked to tease, claiming I was a "kindred spirit."

"Beat it, Susan," Johnny said, heading back to his squad car. "Or I'll bust you for arrested development."

To me, he added, "By the way, I hadda escort your wife out of Smith's the other day. She tried to steal a Mickey Bigmouth six-pack and a family-size bag of pork rinds."

As an afterthought he yelled, "Why don't you *drown* the cats?"

Susan sighed, "Aww, gee . . ." Then she just stood there, pigeontoed, inhaling my exhaust. I felt bad, but I was in a hurry: *Ciao, baby—gotta book*, save the scuttlebutt for later.

And anyway, the Butterfly Coalition was still supposed to be under wraps, and once Susan got on the case it would be like bloodhounds in Bangladesh, searching for disaster.

WOULDN'T YOU know it, though, but the only person (sic) in Buddy Hawthorne's execrable animal clinic waiting room when I arrived was Eleanor Poddubny, the fourth wife of Manjo Poddubny, a local septuagenarian entrepreneur who owned a funeral parlor (The Body Shoppe), an insurance agency, the Hot Rod Motel, Eagle Savings and Loan, that Poddubny Estates development I had driven by, the *Sentinel-Argus* (which was edited by his rotund daughter, Edna, who hated her mom-in-law, Eleanor, like cows hate meat), and a number of other shady operations that kept him rolling in megabucks. Manjo himself, who lived in a grotesque rococo nouveau chateau among our town's other elites atop Nob Hill, was one of those old-fashioned gigolo pencil-thin moustache fuddy-duddies who slicked back his graying locks with enough coconut hair oil to grease a Mercedes bus. His anorexic bride of six months, on the other hand (who ran an ad agency on the Plaza), was thirty-two years younger than Manjo and—according to local gossip—a real hot tamale with sado-masochistic sexual pro-clivities and a tiny Sam Peckinpah in her hormone glands calling all the erotic shots. Apparently Manjo adored Eleanor even though she was the most totally messed-up, coke-tooting, flashback-crippled, therapist-dependent manic depressive he had ever known.

Eleanor had boyishly short hair, and in her lap (at Buddy Hawthorne's Doggy Dachau) she clutched one of those irritatingly snippety white toy poodles I love to despise, name of Mitzi. Kelly called Eleanor "That Placenta from Planet Zilch."

Naturally, when I unlatched my Cat Caddy door to grab Tommy, the other fat cats—Oopboop, Elroy, Ginger, and Carlos—also leaped to freedom and went haywire in the waiting room, literally scrambling up the walls and flying upside-down across the ceiling while Buddy's parttime assistant, Tallulah Moe, and I tried to recapture them: It was a true "Kelly McFarland moment." Mitzi leaped clear of Eleanor's arms to attack Oopboop, who swatted her across the linoleum into a pyramid of Science Diet sacks and cans of dolphin-free weight-watcher tuna for obese felines. *Go, Oopboop!* Eleanor screamed, Buddy lumbered out of OR to try and stem the chaos, and dogs in all the corridor holding pens launched an appropriately noisy hullabaloo as a parakeet cage, knocked off its stanchion by a flying Tommy, rolled across the floor, tripping up Eleanor P. just as she rescued her beloved Mitzi.

By the time I had bulldozed the last recalcitrant (Carlos) back into my box, Buddy was bleeding profusely from one elbow (through a shirt half-ripped to ribbons), Tallulah was staring, shocked, at puncture wounds in both her palms, and Eleanor Poddubny, minus both fuck-me pumps, and with her seamed mocha panty hose in shreds, clutched Mitzi to her flat chest and fired daggers at me from seething eyes. Yet her voice, when she spoke, seemed remarkably self-contained (if a trifle icy):

"You're Charley McFarland, aren't you?"

Trembling, embarrassed, appalled, frightened, and gasping, I nodded affirmatively.

"You're the father of that twenty-year-old Road Warrior prepubescent piece of hyena scat who slings hash at Burger Boy and was busted three months ago for skateboarding on the Plaza?"

Yeah, but I'm supposed to *admit* it? (She was talking about my son, Luther.)

"Also Lydia 'The Red Menace' Babcock's friend?"

Hey, Eleanor was starting to grate and make me feel *defensive.*

"And your wife is that infamous red-headed homeless dipso-
maniac who took her shirt off in a July town council meeting to
protest the lack of local option Sunday liquor sales?"

If the shoe fits, deny it. And anyway, I was riled up by now so I
jutted my jaw and stared at her, feeling faint because my heart was
locked into atrial fibrillation. I *hate* confrontation.

Never a person to mince words, Eleanor said, "Sweetie, you're a
fool and an idiot to think you stand even a half-assed chance
against mighty FAGERBAN."

FAGERBAN. Jesus Christ. Call out the eco-cavalry! FAGERBAN
was the acronym for Fagerquist/Bannerman: Clarence Fagerquist,
Jack Bannerman. Clarence being the gnarly old prince of uncon-
scionable developers in our scrofulous burg, a real John Wayne/
Charlton Heston sack of reactionary horse manure. And Jack was a
young upstart philandering go-go banker stud determined to butt-
fuck what was left of Suicide City the way Keating had buttfucked
Arizona (to put it mildly).

The delightfully terracidal FAGERBAN project, an offshoot of
the highway bypass and totally dependent on the passage of Proposition X on November eighth, was ". . . a multidimensional growth-
oriented commercial endeavor based on an enterprise zone concept
of low-income, tax-abatement financing measures already poised for
enactment by Mayor Sam Clendennon and the city council, which
was comprised of an industrial park and shopping malls, modular
neighborhoods for low-income workers, an airport runway extension program tied into blanket tourism promotion, and—"

But why go on?

Just call it our festering, eager-beaver hamlet's Final Solution.

Trying to control the fearful quaver in my voice, I indignantly
replied to Eleanor Poddubny: "Maybe you people are in for a surprise. Don't forget, mighty oaks from tiny acorns grow."

She gave me a really superior scornful snort. "FAGERBAN already
has a base of commitments for the industrial park from reliable
cross-pollinating industries that comes along only once in a lifetime,"

she said. "Jack Bannerman is a genius, everybody is for it, and polls indicate we're already guaranteed ninety-five percent of the vote."

"Oh yeah? Whatta you think'll happen when the Phistic Copper is granted endangered status?"

Eleanor uncorked a withering smile: "When do you think that will take place—in the year two thousand and fifty?"

I said, "We've already submitted an application, and the evidence, to Peter Lithgow at Fish and Wildlife in the Capital."

"'Peter Lithgow?'"she chortled, hugging Mitzi in glee. "'Lithgow the Lunatic?' Lithgow, the chief proponent of the 'Adolf Eichmann School of Environmental Management?'"

I hadn't much of a riposte to that—Eleanor had him pegged. Nevertheless, scaredy cat though I may be, I am also a *very* stubborn man, I will hang on like a bulldog, a snapping turtle, or a tick with Lyme disease. So I said, "We'll go over Lithgow's head. We'll get Bo Hrbyk of the Comptroller's Office up here to classify every loan in Mr. Bannerman's jug. Even if Prop X passes and FAGERBAN gets a green light, we'll see that you have to pay an exorbitant impact fee on every dwelling that goes up, which'll make the project prohibitive, for sure."

She smirked, "And what, pray tell, is an 'impact fee?'"

"A tax to offset depredation of endangered species habitat. Sometimes it's as high as two K an acre for private homes. And a lot worse for commercial endeavors."

Her eyes narrowed. "Who's your lawyer?"

"Farragut Wallaby."

Eleanor cracked up: "*That* geriatric bumblefuck?" She joked to Buddy, "You better give this delusional eco moron a distemper shot before he bites somebody. As for Bo Hrbyk and Farragut, they couldn't tell a C & D from a D & C, I promise."

I clamped my mouth shut, then, because, like, I'm a *pacifist*. Yup, in the age of Pol Pot and Slobodan Milosevic, Gandhi and Martin Luther King are my true heroes. Don't laugh, but I also sincerely believe that with dignity and careful organizing democratic principles *will* prevail. Granted, it's not easy to stay sane, calm, and focused in today's chaotic world. But that's my job. And it's the *only* way to win.

"Tallulah," Buddy said, cordial as always, The Friendly Vet With A Permanent Grin (who doubled as County Coroner), "do me a favor and don't tickle his file when the next four cats are due."

"Maybe I should only bring two at a time," I mumbled, scribbling a check that would probably bounce to the moon and back as Tallulah typed my cat info into her computer.

Buddy said, "Why be rational? Bring eight, bring ten. We're here to serve you." His scathing sarcasm trailed me out the door: "Have your wife do the honors next time. *These cats are her legacy.* WE MISS HER!"

WELL, I GOT KELLY'S renegade felines home lickety-split to my trailer, fed everybody, threw a rock at an emaciated cow eating mildewed peavines in my organic garden, then I answered the phone and told Mary (at the library), "I *know* I'm late, but I'm on my way so hold your water, okay?" Yeesh! That accomplished, I slammed my middle fingertip in the driverside door, took out the Buick's bottom six times on my way down the (seriously) potholed driveway, stopped once on the way townward to glurp another quart of 10-40 and a pint of STP Oil Treatment into my ravenous crankcase, then hit a *real* traffic jam two hundred yards shy of my destination and screeched to a halt.

Gridlock. The American Way of Death right here in Suicide City. Welcome to the Twenty-First Century, you clowns: *honk! honk!* We build fast cars with slick wind-resistant spaceage bodies and speedometers reading up to 130 whose average speed over a lifetime of what is jokingly called "travel" is approximately 12.3 miles per hour. But hey, don't knock it, rocket, most of the social life in downtown Suicide City took place in traffic jams. Yo, there's reactionary Marcia Stonebutter Crawford in her aluminum-green 1993 hermetically sealed Dodge Shadow, with Alex and Gwyneth in their kiddie-proof Allstate-approved car seats and crash helmets in back, talking on the cell phone to Patty Gusdorf up ahead, our town's only certified puppy psychiatrist, looking right smart behind the wheel of her white 1998 hermetically sealed Lexus with tangerine leather grill bib and "Alligator Eye" recessible headlamps. And here's Billy Joe Bob Fagerquist, a buck-toothed surveyor (and second born of Clarence and Willa's I.Q.-challenged boys) in his 1996 hermetically sealed lobster red Ford Dynamite X8 with extended bed, vanity cab, booster shocks, and oversized "concrete" demolition bumpers (with Gitzo winch attachment), talking on his cell phone to pert, fresh, and lively Kathy Gaverdine, the Christian (town pump) daughter of Gladys and Elton Gaverdine (the business manager and corpse prepper at Manjo Poddubny's Body Shoppe) next door in her maroon Honda Accord (1996) about the latest Mookie Dirigible CD Randy Featherstone has just played on WPNX, his *Mein Kampf Trilogy* album, especially the hit "Voodoo Homage to Wagner," winner of this year's Tipper Gore Seal of Disapproval. Behind Kathy sits the mayor's silicone wife, Tammy Sue Clendennon, in her snazzy '99 Mustang convertible; she's wearing a skimpy aluminum pink bando top so full of tits it oughtta be declared illegal or a Living Treasure. And down the line is that insane malevolent grifter, Billy Watrous jr, in his firegreen Chevy S10 boombuggy lowrider amped to the max with the late rapper J.J. Crave at eight thousand shuddering eardrum shattering decibels driving everybody within earshot crazy—

They're all sucking up ten thousand liters of carbon monoxide every twenty minutes like it's Zyklon-B, but so what? La de dah. The whole *bunch* of them is oblivious.

Half an hour later my Buick had moved forward in sclerotic ecstasy about ten feet, and on his mouldy golden oldy show Randy Featherstone had gone through the entire collected hits of Oingo Boingo. So what else could I do?—I flipped out, pulled onto the shoulder, grabbed my Jansport knapsack with all its Lifetime Guaranteed zippers totally kaput and—the irony! the *irony!*—I abandoned my wheels, hightailing it to work on foot.

But Murphy says that when a day begins like that, it can only get a whole lot worse, so about eleven seconds after I had slunk into my desk at the library (fifteen minutes late), the boss, John Spoffard, called me back to his inner sanctum. Mary grinned at me and made a slashing motion across her throat. Fuck Mary. She was a plain Jane without any distinguishing features and absolutely no personality who'd just gotten pregnant again through immaculate conception.

Sad to say, I didn't much like my boss. At forty-two, Spoffard was a decade younger than me, and so far right Jerry Falwell would've blinked. A moderately sized bachelor from Iowa, he hated sports and carried in his vest on a gold fob his grandfather's old pocket watch that he liked to click open and peer down his nose at for emphasis during critical conversations. Clean to the point of looking scoured, the man took great care of his fingernails and massaged Rogaine into his scalp every night before beddy-bye-low. Kelly had him pegged for a spastic Highlander, but in my book he was just a plain old servile fop.

To me Spoffard said: "Charles, as you know I am a liberal and conscientious man. I am even planning an elaborate greenhouse addition to my dwelling so that I can heat with solar energy. However, I think it would probably be in the best interests of all parties concerned if the Rius comic book, *Marxism for Beginners*, quietly ceased to be one of the seminal textbooks in the literacy program you are running for underprivileged, impoverished children from the ghetto who might find themselves somewhat confused by the message of Rius. Some of the more distinguished—which we may translate in private among ourselves as meaning more 'wealthy'— matrons in the Friends of the Library have told me they feel your approach is inflammatory, humanistic, and—"

I interrupted: "They're probably uptight because of the Butterfly Coalition."

"What's that?"

"Lydia Babcock and me are starting an organization to fight Proposition X and the highway bypass. Wanna join?"

He appraised me in vacuous horror. "You're going to publicly go up against Clarence Fagerquist, Manjo, Sam Clendennon, and

Jack the Flak *again?* The Nob Hill Mobsters? Have you finally lost all your marbles?"

"Somebody has to. Hey, I *live* on Willow Road."

"You're crazy. They defeated you on the ski valley expansion; they stuffed you major on the mine Superfund petition; they riddled you on the variance to build Wal-Mart in the historical zone. On this one they'll chop you up like chicken livers and make McFarland Pâté. They always do."

"Tell me something I don't know."

"It isn't worth it," my boss said. "Particularly not for a stupid butterfly. As for Lydia, how old is that nasty old battle-ax now, anyway?"

"Ninety-two."

"Senile and sick as a dog, I understand."

"True enough."

"She'll be dead in two weeks," he argued. "And the butterfly is meaningless."

"As a metaphor it's priceless," I insisted brashly. "There's only a hundred left in the world, all on Lydia's property. They're like the spotted owl or the Houston toad or—"

"But what does that butterfly *do?*" he interrupted. "What *good* is it?"

My heart sank. Was I doomed forever to prattle ineffectually at decorticated assholes? But here's the rub: If you truly *care* about survival of the planet you cannot tiptoe around like a fainthearted nervous Nellie afraid to lock horns with the Philistines.

"The adult feeds on the blossoms—then lays its eggs on the stalks—of the *Calexis trifida arboretum* plant," I said. "Which is also a threatened species. Its pollination depends on the Phistic Copper. Rub out one and you rub out the other."

John Spoffard eyeballed me as if I was utterly bonkers. No matter, I'm like a diesel once I get wound up, so I plowed straight ahead:

"The Phistic caterpillers eat the leaves of the *Calexis trifida arboretum* plant. The caterpiller feces is absolutely essential for fertilization of that plant. In fact, in autumn the caterpillers also eat the tiny seeds of the *arboretum* and pass them out into the soil in their feces. Believe it or don't, but the seeds will not sprout if they haven't traveled through the digestive system of the caterpiller, where they seem to pick up an enzyme that triggers germination. It's a fragile process, a miracle, but it has endured for millenniums and that's important."

"To whom?" he asked incredulously.

"To me. And Lydia. And our lawyer, Farragut Wallaby."

Spoffard pointed out, "That's only three people among six billion souls on the globe."

"So what?" I fired back defensively. "If you kill a single person, or an animal, or a butterfly, you destroy an entire universe."

My feeble-minded, phony, pusillanimous overseer, always sympathetic, ever compassionate, started playing—with mocking exaggeration—an imaginary teeny weeny violin.

THEN GUESS WHAT happens an hour after Spoffard reads me the riot act? My absolutely irrevocably *worst* nightmare stumbles through the front door of the library and veers sideways across the short hallway leading to the main reading room, waving goofily at me (at the front desk) as it fumfers out of sight, clobbering the Men's Room door—"*Oof!*" The thing struggles with the handle a moment—*rattle!rattle!rattle!*—then I hear the door open and slam shut so loudly even my boss, way back in another time zone at his own pulpit, must have heard the reverberations.

Mary clucked, "Uh-oh, spaghetti-o."

I raced to the bathroom door, kicked it open . . . and stopped dead in my tracks.

Ai, talk about squalid scenes!

My homeless, soon-to-be-ex wife Kelly sat hunched over on a gunmetal gray wastebasket in the corner, face burrowed deeply into her twisted mitts. Naturally, the fingers were all chopped up, the knuckles blue and puffy. Once upon a time this Gorgon had beautiful piano-playing hands, but now they were weak and maimed and nearly useless. The rest of her formerly voluptuous body that I used to avidly photograph in cheesecake poses looked as if it had just (barely) survived a bomb blast: black eye, missing teeth, and wild red hair caked with blood that seemed caught in a cyclone emanating up from her own skull. And her clothes?—she'd probably slept in them for a month. *Two* months. Yet her eyes, her beautiful gray-green eyes, her wonderful bloodshot eyes—not even decades of booze and drugs and cigarettes had extinguished those sensational eyes in which a glimmer of the former lollapalooza still remained, a bright ember in the ruins.

Back during the halcyon days of our marriage Kelly would get tanked up on Kahlúa and Absolut and run Susan Hayward film festivals through our VCR. She must've watched *Smash-Up* and *I'll Cry Tomorrow* a hundred times in preparation for this future. I never understood the attraction of such nihilistic bullshit, but I'll admit I'm also befuddled by Rwanda and Kosovo. Bottom line, of course: There's a lot of people out there calling themselves "sane" doing to the planet exactly what Kelly had done to herself, so it's not like my wife was "unique."

I shut and locked the door and lowered onto the edge of the toilet seat, stymied bigtime. Man, we had been here before, on many divergent occasions, but I must admit that each succeeding confrontation always ripped me a new asshole in my heart worse than the one before. Maybe Tough Love is easy for some bland coprophagist out there, but I ain't him. Kelly was forty-four, eight years younger than me, and a perfect environmental poster girl for our collapsing city.

"Boy, look at you, babe. The human incarnation of shit on a shingle." Sue me, but I felt like crying.

She wiped her bloody nose, saying petulantly, "You'll be glad to hear I'm gonna join your Butterfly Liberation Army."

Very quickly I said, "It's the Butterfly Coalition and I don't want you. You'd like to help the cause?—move to Alaska."

Kelly infused her beautiful eyes with her typical sick puppyish importuning:

"Charley, for fourteen years we have been married—"

"That's eleven too many."

"I supported every cause you championed. Against the airport runway extension; against the conservancy district and the—"

I held up my hand: "Stop, you lousy lowlife liar."

"You can't keep me from joining," she whimpered pathetically. "It's a free country."

I growled in despair, "No way. Go home. Forget it."

Kelly clambered into an erect position, reeled, then caught herself and cleverly veered off on a totally different tack. Stone alcoholics are like Barry Sanders, they just keep bouncing off of tacklers and switching directions on their way toward the End Zone of Life, where a TD is simply an acronym for Tragic Death. And believe me (because I *am* an authority), they're harder than greased pigs to catch.

My wife said, "You know what W.W. told me yesterday? FAGERBAN is running him for the state House of Representatives so he can introduce a Right-to-Work bill in January that'll help grease the development skids."

That caught me by surprise. "W.W." was William Watrous, a major league skuzzball who owned the Topless Au Go Go, a shoddy venereal dive where Kelly liked to drink. I knew Watrous was a candidate; but the Right-to-Work I hadn't counted upon.

"What else does Billy talk about?" I asked morosely.

"He says the biggest corporation slated for FAGERBAN's industrial park is Genetevil, which manufactures Clot-Blocks and Alk-erase, products that use plasminogen activators fermented in mouse milk to aid heart attack victims. And a hundred percent of their plasminogen recepts will be local if—"

The woman could still amaze. Truth is, Kelly used to be a cogent human being, she actually had a college degree, majoring in English, and once upon a time we'd actually been able to share intelligent repartees about existential angst and transcendental utopias. For years we even made love like Kim Basinger and Mickey Rourke, three times daily, no-holds-barred, a real erotic Juggernaut. Before alcohol and untold quantities of interesting chemicals and opium derivates fried her remarkable brain (and libido), Kelly was effervescent and brilliant no matter how shocking or off-the-wall her behavior. She revived me after my first wife, Luther's mom, died in a car accident.

Kelly made me and her stepkid laugh, she gave us *hope*. Hell, it was Kelly who suckered me back into politics when I was depressed and growing cynical. Just to show what an impression she'd once made on yours truly, I took *her* last name at our wedding instead of keeping my own.

"What's a 'Plasminogen Recept?'" I asked glumly.

"A kangaroo rat."

"Aah . . ."

"See, y'all need me," she giggled coyly. "I am a veritable font of pertinent information."

I know, I know, I should've been dialing 911 or calling the State Hospital for the Criminally Insane. After I threw Kelly out last year when she refused yet again to attend AA, I had made a commitment not to "enable" my wife. Unfortunately, Tough Love is like cutting your own heart out and stomping on it if the enablee is truly your Significant Other. Plus, you know the shtick: Alcoholism ain't deliberate, it's a *disease*. Kelly was *innocent*. It's all *genetic*. So in the bathroom I looked at her and I thought a bit, and then suddenly— overwhelmed by "compassion" (i.e., guilt)—I hatched yet another plan that in retrospect seems obviously to have been the airbrained concoction of someone utterly out of touch with reality. A comparable action would be to board a plane with just one wing and a flat tire, presuming it could safely become airborne and carry you to a distant destination. But my problem was: *I still loved Kelly a lot.* I don't mean like In Love, or Infatuation, or Mutual Admiration, or even Mildly Respectful, nothing like that. Nevertheless, you don't go through what we'd been through without becoming permanently attached to the scars . . . and to the sizzle, or to the memory of it, anyway. Yes, this monster Kelly had once been the most *life* that ever loved me and I had responded in kind. Hey, even though we hadn't screwed in two years, I *still* harbored no desire for anyone else.

I said, "Okay, baby, do you really want to join the Butterfly Coalition?"

She raised both paws up under her chin, dangled her scummy white tongue, and panted slavishly (and disgustingly) like an eager puppy.

I warned, "You can't tipple at meetings. I catch you drunk at one official function and you're fired, no appeal. Understand?"

"Bueno," she lied. "Why not?" Her beautiful eyes went positively lopsided with mendacity.

Feeling sick to my stomach, I said, "But this is the *last time ever* I'm throwing a life preserver. Now beat it before the boss arrives, and don't come back here ever again—that's condition number two."

I swear she looked at me with "gratitude," but I'd been-there/done-that dance so often her "sincerity" actually repelled me bigtime. And of course I felt horribly panicked, too, like I'd just committed a felony: *You're not supposed to do this, Charley. You can't save her. She has to save herself—*

Kelly punched off the lock, kicked open the door, bellowed *"Qué viva el* Butterfly Liberation Army!" and fled—encumbered by all her dark secrets—off to another world.

Two steps into that world the dipso spastic collided with Susan Delgado, who screamed, her Buddy Holly glasses hit the ceiling, a ballpoint pen bounced off the drinking fountain, and her reporter's notebook landed on top of the Free Shelf above all our heads. The Scarecrow and the Pickled Blob hit the floor simultaneously with a muffled crunching sound—*"Ouch!"*

I shook my finger at Susan. "You better quit stalking me, girl."

Who knows how Susan could breathe let alone converse from under that mountain of befuddled meat, but damned if she even skipped a beat:

"Charley, honey, if your kid Luther quit Burger Boy and accepted a job from FAGERBAN harvesting Plasminogen Recepts for eight bucks an hour, would you disown him?"

"I'd skin him alive," I assured her. "With no anesthetic."

"Yo, mofo, get this anorexic lollipop offa me," Kelly drawled in her best incest-crippled deep south accent. *"She is ruinin' my makeup."*

NATURALLY, ONCE the Butterfly Coalition cat was out of the bag, Jack Bannerman—the slick, sick, philandering wizard behind FAGERBAN—made an appointment to see my friend Lydia at a meeting slated to take place at 5:15 P.M. on a Thursday afternoon at Lydia's trailer. So I scheduled a rendezvous on Tuesday with my aforementioned irascible child, Luther, in order to discuss Jack's pending visit.

Obviously, my ulterior motive was tied to the cockeyed "plan" that had spontaneously reared its bathetic head in the library bathroom with Kelly: i.e., use the fight against FAGERBAN as a catalyst for family rehabilitation. How many times had I done *that* before? Break out the calculators! Boot up the Tocamak! So why did I persist? You might just as well ask: Why do Ralph Nader and Barry Commoner keep trying to save the planet? It's a *disease*.

I invited my semi-estranged kid over to the trailer for beer and a pizza. The booze and the food lured him into the trap, but as soon as I saw him my heart shriveled (as usual) in pain. Luther was six-one and he weighed one-fifty—not an ounce of fat. Tonight his Mohawk was dyed pink; irradiated skeletons dangled from both earlobes; his black leather jacket weighed about a hundred pounds; and his dungarees were deliberately ripped in eighty-nine places. These days, that sort of old-fashioned retro punk outfit and hairstyle is called self-expression. It's called letting free your inner child. *It's called using your own shit to fingerpaint all over your own clueless body.*

"Luther," I said, trying hard not to sound like yet another Baby Boomer parent intimidated by yet another Generation X bullying kid locked in an extended adolescence, "I called you here tonight to explain that you are now officially a member of the Butterfly Coalition."

"Forget it, Pop. Blow chunks. Not a chance."

"You're twenty years old. It's about time you took responsibility for the earth."

Luther said, "If I join your Butterfly Coalition I'll get fired. Burger Boy has PROMISE KEEPERS stickers on its windows."

"Good. It's about time you stepped up to the plate for your principles."

"I don't *have* any principles."

I said, "And for your first assignment in the coalition, tomorrow you will come with me over to Lydia's trailer when Jack Bannerman pays a call. We need an intimidator."

Luther said, "No way, José. I'm not gonna make a fool of myself and destroy my credit rating for the rest of my life."

"You *are* going to be in our coalition," I insisted. "You *owe* it to me."

"Get out of my face," Luther fired right back. "I don't owe you squat. You don't possess me, I'm not your private property, I am not you—" And, yes Virginia, he actually said this, he had the audacity to mock my politics to my face: "I am *not* your capitalist lackey working class running dog slave of imperial warmongers."

"You owe it to Kelly," I said. "She treated you great for years."

That stopped him. He even blinked. Then frowned, caught between conflicting contradictions. "What does Kelly have to do with it?"

"She's in the coalition," I said quickly. "We can use her brilliant insanity. And maybe the political focus will save her and patch our family back together. At least I need to make one last effort, for her, for all of us. Otherwise, I know she's going to die. And I need you on my side. She loves you. I know you love her, too . . . and you don't want to be responsible for her death."

Yes, the young of Generation X/Y(Z!) are notoriously simple-minded crackheads, death metal freaks, and "whatever" groupies, but that last comment of mine was *such* a reprehensible deed it actually registered in some foggy area of Luther's defective brain and his eyes reacted in hostile confusion. Confusion, because in the beginning no kid ever had a better stepmom than Luther. She'd been his were-wolf den mother at Cub Scouts. She taught him how to raise guppies and eat them. Kelly had taken him to White Zombie concerts where they *both* hung out in the mosh pit. She always shot free throws with him in the driveway until three A.M. For Halloween, they trick-or-treated together on Nob Hill wearing Jason masks and cammy outfits, toting lifesize AK-47 replicas. On various birthdays Kelly had given Luther a BB gun . . . electronic num-chuks . . . and a subscription to *Hustler* magazine. Then she paid for them both to go bungee jumping off the High Bridge and have it videotaped for posterity. The way cowboys venerate unbroke stallions Luther had positively *idolized* Kelly, the only mother he remembered.

But that was then and this was now. So in response to my last comment, Luther exploded: "Kelly's a gonzo drunken *dope fiend*, Pop! Her divorce lawyer, Rollie Cathcart, has tried to castrate me in three depositions over the last ten months. And she almost killed me fifty times in the past thirteen years."

"She was only trying to have fun with you," I said.

"*Fun*," Luther spat bitterly. "I thought you kicked her out last year to save her life. You're supposed to be divorcing her to maintain our sanity and make her face herself. I'm scared of her. *You are too.* She's *extreme*. No *way* do I join your Butterfly Coalition."

Later, as Luther prepared to depart, I asked: "Do you want a ride home?" Maybe we could make amends in the car.

"Thanks, but I like my bike."

"It's dark, pitch black, no moon, you're wearing Levi's, a purple shirt, brown boots, there are no reflectors on the bike. You are a sitting duck."

"Do me a favor, Dad." My sullen child mounted his BMX bike, a tiny stupid thing he looked like an Ichabod Cranosaurus riding.

"All it takes is one accident," I warned pathetically. "Why don't you wear a fluorescent vest or something? Please, I'll drive you home—"

Too late: He popped a wheelie, then Eternity swallowed him up. My dear boy was headed back to Miranda Satan, his bold Wendy O. Williams look-alike, ripped-on-skag, whacked-on-crack, probably-HIV-positive, coke-snorting, dildo-wielding Lolita with a shaved head, a ring in her nose, and a Mookie Dirigible tattoo on her belly: *Born To Catch AIDS.* They would probably spend the night ingesting PCP with JD shooters while having unprotected anal sex to Scorpions, The Pixies, and Siouxsie and the Banshees tapes.

"Be there!" I hollered. "Lydia's trailer! At five-fifteen!"

Yeah . . . sure . . . right . . . *dude.*

A strobe light blared in the dark, blinding me. I backpeddled shielding my eyes and cried out, "Susan, *enough* already!" Mangus, Kelly's huge orange chow, came bounding to the rescue barking insanely. He leaped up, knocked Susan down . . . and then splashed his sticky black tongue amorously against her cheeks. The reporter rolled away over and over shrieking, *"Yuk! Charley! Get him offa me!"*

"Not until you promise to quit stalking me, Susan."

"Okay, babe, I promise, I *promise.*"

Instantly, her nose grew longer by at least a foot.

A T EXACTLY FIVE-THIRTY on Thursday afternoon, Jack Bannerman's debonair silver Mercedes SL 2400-JX pulled up briskly in front of Lydia's trailer, and out stepped Jack himself, all five-foot-eleven, blond-hair-and-steely-blue-eyes of lupine flesh: Picture the more handsome identical twin of Robert Redford without all those doots on his cheeks. He wore a silk suit, a striped shirt, a custom-tailored tie, and brilliantly laquered Cordovan wingtips. The man was athletic to the max, reeking of vitamins, and if you wanted to know how come we live on a planet with a collapsing ecological and social infrastructure, all you had to do was take a look at this impeccably dressed and manicured Caucasian Wizard of the Deal. Our streams were biologically dead from tailings spills, our inverted air was lethally toxic from monoxide, mining dust, and woodsmoke, and the aquifer that supplied our drinking water was drying up, so Jack had decided to pile on more cars, an industrial park, new shopping malls, and an airport expansion. *Go, Jack!*

"Yo there, Mr. Bannerman," I boldly called as I opened the trailer door. My own threads were not quite as uptown as his. I mean, I was decked out in a beige Mao cap with a red star pinned over the visor, a purple fringed cowboy shirt, Black Watch Bermuda shorts, and Taos Mountain Outfitter hiking boots. Why? Because the best defense is always a good offense, *always*, and you never get a second chance to make a first impression. I have a weird beard, too, and a missing front tooth. You look at me, you think: *Oops, here comes a raging bomb-throwing anarchist.* I don't mind saying I like to create that impression, too, because a little fear never hurt anyone. A total wimp (*and* a pacifist) like me needs all the advantages he can get.

Under his breath Jack said, "Shit on a biscuit." Aloud, he boomed, "Hello there, Mr. McFarland."

"When we heard you were coming I rushed right over," I said in my usual scared stiff bombastic manner that people often mistake for obstreperous arrogance.

"Who's 'we'?"

"Our committee to kill the bypass. Otherwise known as the Butterfly Coalition."

"Our town is crying for traffic relief," quoth Jack. "It *has* to have a bypass."

"Not through the only virginal land left in town, it doesn't."

Jack sighed. No doubt I was like some irritating piece of gnat feces he felt he could have simply brushed off his collar with impunity, but he hated to waste the energy. Jack was dealing here (once again) with a timid gadfly who nevertheless during his checkered career in Suicide City had started a gay/lesbian carpenter's collective, briefly stopped the Forest Service from spraying for the Saddleback Rosy Claw Beetle, and screamed every time the ligtonite mine's tailings pipes broke killing five thousand trout in Midnight Creek. Me and my tiny bands of malcontents had put together a grand jury abuse attack squad, and whenever the police smoked another wasted tecato from the ghetto who had flipped them off just for being *marranos,* our gang hit the cop station with two dozen rabid protestors shaking POLICE BRUTALITY placards in their impassive faces: Kelly had been jailed three times for throwing eggs and once for using a paintball gun. It cost McDonald's six years and five hundred thousand dollars to finally land a Suicide City franchise, but at least we forced them to make it "adobe style," with phony tin vigas sticking out just under the soffits and their beige Propanel siding grooved to imitate adobe bricks. That one gave Manjo Poddubny his first heart attack. I had also wrangled an injunction against the ski valley for flushing all its sewage directly into Midnight Creek that put Clarence Fagerquist on beta-blockers. And nobody will soon forget the ruckus we raised to prohibit the Feds from using the North-South Highway as a relief route for their nuclear waste trucks bound from Hanford, Wash., to Carlsbad, N.M. On that one, Kelly dressed up in a bomb uniform and, on a drunken whim, leaped from the second floor spectator's gallery in the Capital City roundhouse into a pod of caucusing solons below, breaking her leg but capturing a LOT of publicity.

Jack said, "Are you a representative for Mrs. Babcock?"

"You bet I am."

"Then I'm sure you have informed her if she doesn't sell out now, the state will condemn her land after Election Day."

I said, "Why don't you come inside and speak to her yourself?"

"With pleasure," that merciless buffalo hunter said.

Then he straightened his tie, shot his cuffs, turned off the cell phone in his shirt pocket, and trotted past me into the ramshackle trailer to hang Lydia on a meat hook and disembowel her with an oversized Bowie knife.

N

OT SO FAST, The Donald!

Picture Eudora Welty, Dr. Ruth, and Eleanor Roosevelt as really *old* ladies.

Then add Mother Teresa.

Lydia's grubby silver wig was tilted at a rakish angle against her bony skull. She reclined in a dilapidated rocking chair wrapped in a filthy yellow electric blanket. Her skinny arms ended in teensy fragile hands whose brittle fingers, clasped over her tiny tummykins, seemed capable of being broken at the slightest touch. Thick-lensed glasses gave her a startled mien: Lydia had one glass eye and the other harbored a near blinding cataract.

But there was a glitter to the old harridan, an almost malevolent elfishness throbbing just beneath her surface that I *loved*. In her lifetime, Lydia had been a child suffragette, a union organizer, a member of the CPUSA, a civil rights worker, an anti–Vietnam war activist, a pro-choice zealot, and even a Green Party candidate for governor. Laugh at those credentials, you cretins . . . but tiptoe *carefully* past the graveyard.

At the moment Jack arrived, my favorite shrew was puffing on a Marlboro cigarette. Lydia's trailer could have been a set for one of those old mutant ninja nightmare movies. No less than eleven morbidly obese cats lay about in obscenely indolent postures, and enormous twisted plants in huge clay pots occupied every corner. At least a dozen cardboard boxes containing Lydia's files stood hither and yon, disgorging yellowed and mouse-eaten flakes of paper; tilting stacks of old *New York Times* cluttered the god-awful rugs. A thirteen-inch black-and-white TV on Mute was tuned to a Patty Duke rerun, and six large Kitty Litter boxes, placed at random like existential ashtrays, were filled to the brim and overflowing because I deliberately hadn't yet emptied them today. You want an edge in this cutthroat game, you've *got* to set the scene.

Then there was that thing on the couch, that pissed-off catatonic coelacanth with a six-inch purple Mohawk and shredded Levi's on its long knobby legs: A skeleton the size of a tarantula dangled from the left ear; a rubber tarantula the size of a parakeet drooped from the other lobe.

"Luther," I said, "meet Mr. Jack Bannerman, a banker."

My son grunted like a thing from some parallel universe.

His stepmom, who sat in a lotus position in front of the TV, lifted her right hand and casually popped the index finger at Jack in greeting: "Yo." Rust-colored crud, shaped like a Gorby blotch, stained her forelocks and forehead. She wore a Spice Girls sweatshirt that seemed fabricated from coagulated blood, and also sported stone-ground cutoffs and red hightop Converse All-Stars held together by duct tape. Her top lip was fattened by the crust of a herpes blister, and small round bruises blotched her calves as if they had been peppered relentlessly by squash balls. I could tell she was sober, but so hungover all her platelets had become clotted in her feet and were probably begging for a shot of Heparin.

But the big bad banker never acknowledged their presence; he was too busy gawking at Lydia. Like, never before had Jack laid eyes upon a similar apparition of frailty. A mere cough might collapse Lydia's sternum; a sudden guffaw would rend cracks in her delicate pate; and how much did she weigh at ninety-two years of age— twenty-eight pounds?

Of course, that financial lizard did *not* know that the medicine Lydia was taking to prolong her life was also killing her. But when we had asked Dr. Lorenzo Jackson to quit prescribing the pills, he'd balked, explaining her lungs would fill dangerously, putting even more stress on the feeble heart. Hence Lanoxin monitored her heartbeat; Lasix cleared her lungs; K-tabs replenished potassium robbed by the diuretic; and Prednisone countered nausea caused by the K-tabs. Lydia could barely eat without throwing up, and, because the pill combination made her constipated, she devoured Ex-Lax by the ton. Some people call this "modern health care"; I call it "protracted euthanasia."

I sucked in my gut, mumbled a silent prayer, and said, "Lydia, I'm sure you remember Mr. Bannerman."

Her voice, though raspy, had a surprising camber: "Like I remember Adolf Hitler."

Jack sat down confidently and replied, "I'm happy to see you again, Mrs. Babcock."

"Sorry I can't say the same about you."

Jack swiped an attractive shock of hair out of his blue eyes. "Be that as it may, let's get down to business."

"State *your* business," Lydia said, sucking in enough smoke to kill a small rhinoceros.

Jack said, "Okay," and unlimbered his silver tongue, a formidable weapon. "As you know, I represent an investors' group which plans to develop land on either side of the highway bypass that's slated to bisect your—"

"Bullhockey." The old lady leaned forward, knocking her ashtray onto the floor. "You people would crawl through an ocean of snail slime to kiss a dollar, but the only way I'm leaving here is feet first and not before."

Jack cleared his throat. "I can understand your reluctance, and I must say I don't blame you. Nevertheless—"

"If I sell this land," Lydia interrupted, "who takes care of my butterflies?"

Jack said, "The preliminary EIS feels they can be successfully relocated to a similar terrain in the National Forest."

"Hogwash, poppycock, horsefeathers."

Fastidiously, Jack readjusted his beautiful shirt cuffs. "Mrs. Babcock, I came here this evening in good faith to—"

"If you understood my butterfly," Lydia gasped, goggled-eyed from a nicotine spasm, "you'd build your poopy highway bypass over Nob Hill instead of through my backyard."

"I assure you I *do* understand your butterfly, Mrs. Babcock. But you can't stop Progress, I'm afraid. You see—"

That's when Kelly suddenly emerged from a stupor and began earning her keep by unlimbering *her* silver tongue. Jack actually straightened up and cocked one eyebrow only ten words into the rant:

"Oh come on, you horse's ass," Kelly said. "I understand Clarence Fagerquist already has options to buy three quarters of the Willow Road properties at ten percent over par. The options are due to be exercised on November ninth. Of course, if Prop X doesn't pass, or if Peter Lithgow at Fish and Wildlife gives us a favorable endangered species listing, Clarence—and therefore by inference you—will be out a king's ransom because the earnest is non-refundable. You'll come a cropper for all his origination plus the gross, and the entire FAGERBAN lease-purchase arrangement will go down the tubes like crap in a hot pipe."

"Bullshit," Jack remarked, no doubt intrigued that our mega-hammered derelict could speak in parsable sentences containing coherent "thoughts."

Kelly sucked in a deep breath and calmly kept on truckin':

"Unless I'm mistaken, it's also probably illegal that the entire package has been collateralized on preselling or preleasing seventy percent of the job. Your 'guaranteed' commitments won't be guaranteed if you lose at the polls on election day. Especially since your money already out on loans is so over-appraised by that schmuck Casper Pilkington that it'll collapse at the first sign of a liquidity crunch. Then the FSLIC will send Bo Hrbyk up to dismantle you pettifoggers like a tornado from Oklahoma."

Jack narrowed his intelligent eyes wondering if Kelly had Asperger's syndrome: "Who told you all this?"

Kelly said, "The same person who says you've already upstreamed fourteen loans worth twenty-six million in order to keep legal with your limit. Which you wouldn't be if it weren't for T. Garth Radesovich's criminally doctored audits. And my bet is if your correspondents don't get their balloons on time, this whole town will be crawling with Fizzlick agents and hungry yuppies from the comptroller's office, led by the irrepressible Bo Hrbyk, and you'll wind up paddling a canoe on Havana Harbor with Bobby Vesco."

The banker flicked a piece of lint off his kneecap as casually as he would have laid off five hundred destitute textile workers organizing to form a union as he said, "Hearsay. Conjecture. False rumors."

I drummed up the courage to point out, "Actually, the Phistic Copper is already protected by several local, state, and federal laws relating to threatened species."

Jack bristled: "So are wolves and grizzlies, but look where it got them."

Lydia said, "Don't tell me you're one of those bloodthirsty krauts who gleefully clubs baby seals to death with baseball bats?"

"No, Mrs. Babcock, I happen to be a humanitarian who believes that when Prop X comes to a vote, the starving people of this valley in line for all those good construction jobs are not going to worry about a few silly butterflies."

Abruptly, Kelly assumed her other persona, the one assiduously cultivated in the back alleys of PMS Hell and Premature Alcohol-Induced Menopause. She snorted, "Get over it, Jack. I have it on impeccable authority that you cornhole Tammy Sue Clendennon in the Gun and Skeet Club library every Wednesday, then pork your secretary, Marbella Tremaine, for dessert."

That did it, Jack finally cracked, he muttered, "Fuck you," and departed our happy little cat utopia in a huff.

Instantly, Lydia fell asleep.

Wow.

"I devour chumps like him for breakfast," Kelly bragged, ahhing proudly on her fingernails, every one of which had a plum purple blood blister underneath it.

Dazedly, I asked, "How the hell do you know that Clarence has options on three quarters of Willow Road at, what did you say, ten percent over par?"

"I don't, but it's logical." She pried a booger the size of a pencil eraser from her left nostril and flicked it at Luther, who ducked.

"What about the whole loan package based on preselling seventy percent of the job? That's true?"

"Who cares? Makes sense to me."

"And the fourteen upstreamed loans worth twenty-six million?"

Kelly brightened like an alpha hyena at a wildebeest carcass. "When in doubt, babble."

"You *invented* all that stuff? You just lied through your teeth?"

"It ain't lies, Charley. It's what they do all the time. They cheat, steal, prevaricate about everything—their equity, their liquidity, the size of their puny dongs. They juggle numbers, cook the books, rob Peter to pay Paul, and wear three-piece suits so we think they're respectable. I spit on their hypocrisy."

That's when Luther got up and adjusted his swollen testicles with a great display of arrogant boredom. Then he mumbled, "She's just doing it to get you to stop the divorce, Pop," and slouched irritably out of there.

F UCK LUTHER.

Tempus fugit.

It's 5:01 P.M. three days after our meeting with Jack and I'm in a hurry to escape my humdrum job and continue the political organizing because now that the gloves are off, time is definitely of the essence. Already it's October, five weeks to go, and not a PAC in our pocket. Unfortunately, at the library's front entranceway I bump right into Eleanor Poddubny, whose skinny arms are clutching a passel of mystery novels that fly off in all directions, tumbling to earth and tearing pages and splitting spines with terrible gut-wrenching sounds.

I exclaimed, *"Oh my God, I'm sorry!"* and stooped to gather them up: Dean Koontz, Elmore Leonard, and James Ellroy—it figured. Give her credit, though: Nobody checks out books, anymore. Mostly it's pre-pubescent retards in there on our computers trying to drive the search engines toward Web sites tumescent with kiddie porn. *Filters?* Don't make me laugh. Coca-Cola would go nuts quoting the First Amendment.

Today, Eleanor's short hair was moussed in tight hydra curls, and she had enough pancake makeup on her face to manufacture four adobe bricks, with change. Though already five-ten barefoot, the giraffe had accentuated her height with black stiletto slingbacks and a gray jersey minidress so lowcut you could see the ribs beneath her tits. The hem of that monstrosity was so high it almost revealed her bush. Her sunken eyes peered at me raccoon style from circles of charcoal, and the garish crimson lipstick on her grim devouring mouth glistened like blood on the cutting edge of a switchblade knife. The effect? A fascinating hag, I reckon, but I felt a sympathy pang for Manjo nevertheless (it's a guy thing).

"Well, well," Eleanor said, "we meet again. I must remember to wear shoulder pads next time I visit the library."

"I'm really sorry," I sincerely apologized, handing back the books after carefully brushing them off. "I didn't mean to do it."

"But you meant to shove a dildo straight up Jack Bannerman's lovely butt yesterday—didn't you?—you hairy snaggletooth bigoted hippy."

That floored me. I blurted instinctively, "I am not a hippy, I'm a—"

"No," she interrupted, "listen up, Charley McFarland. You're a meddlesome brat, a tiny stumpy ego with a Napolean complex and a dumb beard that you probably wash in Tide at the Laundromat. Well, I pity you from the bottom of my heart. Jack has hired me to run the FAGERBAN campaign and you butterflies are going to be thrashed so badly the welts won't subside for a year. Bo Hrbyk?—cut me some slack. We will rip out his dilettante guts and hang them on the handlebars of that ridiculous bike you peddle around town, I promise." She crossed her heart and made a fist: "Now step aside, girl, I am coming through."

I stumbled out of the way, allowing Eleanor to stride by me like the erotic Queen of Hades, and I must admit: That scary gal owned a *fancy* strut.

Naturally, Susan Delgado, Suicide City's ubiquitous alpha snoop, had been eavesdropping from a corner beyond the Free Shelf. "Word is out, darlin'," she whispered conspiratorially. "The reason that harridan is stretched so tight is she's planking Jack Bannerman, who's also doing the nasties with Tammy Sue Clendennon, and if the mayor or Manjo or Jack's wife, Lu Ann, ever twigs, FAGERBAN's goose is *cooked*."

That kind of gossip bores me. I said, "Susan, things are heating up, the Surprise Card has been played, now it will be all-out conflict and I need bodies, a lot of money, and press coverage up the gazot. Let me put it to you bluntly: Will you officially join the Butterfly Coalition?"

She blanched coyly. "Hey, cupcake, I'm a *reporter*. An *objective observer*. I don't take *sides*."

"*Objective?*" I roared. "Ninety percent of that newspaper is corporate advertisements! There's no such thing as an objective reporter in America! Every damn journalist in the country is paid by—"

Susan interrupted: "Nice try, you adorable browbeater—but the answer is ixnay. . . ixnay. . . ixnay."

"I'll *kill* you if you don't join us," I said.

Susan saluted smartly. "In that case, I'm your man, bro'." Then she dropped her camera and yelped.

"What happened?"

"It bit me." Susan began sucking her index finger but did not shut up: "What'd John Spoffard say to you in his office today? How come Mary won't join your group? Will you marry me if I do a good job?"

I ordered her: "Just write something great about the Butterfly Coalition. We need attention. Coverage. Publicity."

"Edna would never print it."

"She has to. We're news. This will be a major campaign."

"She's on *their* side, bubalu. Her blat is a FAGERBAN house organ."

"Subvert her. Undermine the paper. Cheat. Shame the fat crone into submission. The first rule of a political campaign is: *Get the ink.*"

"Okay, sweetie pie—" Susan started to say, but then she ducked. A green lizard going sixty banged her in the head anyway, and one of the spikes in her Edward Scissorhands hairdo got stuck in the walnut paneling like the point of a Korean throwing star.

It's a surreal world we live in, kids . . . but nobody seems to notice.

T HE FIRST THING that Eleanor Poddubny did as Propaganda Minister of FAGERBAN is she put a couple of brand new vans painted red-white-and-blue (with speakers on top) into action, cruising around town spouting the pro–Prop X/Hail FAGERBAN line. Their theme song took after "Battle Hymn of the Republic," only the words had been slightly altered:

> Mine eyes have seen the glory
> of a road around our town;
> We need it to grow strong and rich,
> to live without a frown;
> We know that Progress soon will be
> the diamond in our crown—
> And that Truth is marching on.
>
> Glory, glory, Highway Bypass,
> Glory, glory, Highway Bypass,
> Glory, glory, Highway Bypass—
> Progress marches on!

True to form, *Edna* Poddubny at the *Sentinel-Argus* gave this treacle a front-page box flanked by American flags and photographs of the FAGERBAN principals beside their spanking new agit-prop wagons flashing *V-for-Victory* signs like a bunch of coked-up polyester yokels on a preused car lot hyping a January fire sale.

Fifteen minutes after the first FAGERBAN mobile brainwashing lab hit the streets, I spotted it (piloted by Marcia Stonebutter Crawford) circling around the T-shirt emporiums and rubber tomahawk clip joints on the Plaza blaring out its gung ho message and immediately I outfitted Kelly's blue Dodge van with a roof speaker, a tape deck, and a microphone, declared Dolly Parton's "Love is Like a Butterfly" to be our theme song, and gave Kelly an anti–Prop X rap sheet to read as she drove around town (drunk out of her fucking skull, no doubt) spreading the Insect Gospel. Then I called an emergency meeting of the Butterfly Coalition *and* my Willow Road neighbors at my trailer at six P.M. and that was a *really* successful parlay.

Lydia held court by the TV in her wheelchair, wearing a FREE SACCO AND VANZETTI pin from her collection as she watched *Wheel of Fortune* with the Mute on while chain-smoking Marlboro cigarettes and drooling onto her lobster bib that said *Cundy's Harbor, Maine.*

Though I'd requested her presence at the event, Kelly did not bother to drop in.

Susan Delgado did, however, wearing three cameras around her neck, kinda cute bib overalls, and a MONICA SUCKS button the size of a Frisbee.

Luther, lured by the food, sat in a corner scratching Mangus and eating piñon nuts whose shells he discarded carelessly onto my dusty floor.

And how would I characterize the contingent of Willow Road neighbors who attended that whoop-de-do event? Maybe like this: One dozen primordial Baby Boomers in tweed with 2.1 children apiece and six-figure socially responsible money market accounts congregate to drink expensive gin, plan holistic vacations in Maui and Nepal, and brag about their college-age kids' 4.0s at Reed and Oberlin while also conversing in a genteel manner about crucial subjects like Ya Wananchi, sustainable development, personal home Web sites (e-tweed@yuppie.org), and Deep Ecology. To prove they were PC they celebrated Kwanzaa after Chanukah and Xmas and sent ten bucks a year to Mumia Abu—

(Susan whispered into my ear, "Don't be abrasive, Carlito. That's no way to win converts.")

Included in this tony group of rock climbers, mountain-bike riders, dry-fly trout fishers, cyberinvestors, and sailplane enthusiasts crowded into my cluttered twelve-by-eighteen booklined living room were a New Age lawyer, a sensitive realtor, a herbal proctologist, an angel-based massage therapist, and the owner of a natureopathic pizza joint (Shalom Mozzarella).

The only important Willow Road property owner *not* in attendance was Tristan Griffith, our notorious transvestite stockbroker and the CEO of WPNX, the valley's uniquely dysfunctional all-solar FM radio station, home of Randy Featherstone, the world's most out-of-touch DJ, who among other travesties was still playing Black Sabbath tapes; Blood, Sweat and Tears; and Sly and the Family Stone.

(Susan pinched me—*ouch!* "You better get in a more charitable mood, Charles. Otherwise this meeting will be a washout.")

I'd advertised it as a potluck affair, and among the eats arrayed on my two card tables were a Key lime pie, some tofu enchiladas, chilled scallops in ceviche sauce, and platters of antipasto with provolone, prosciutto, head cheese, and paprika-smothered deviled eggs. While the world starves, America scarfs, belches, visits the vomitorium, then starts all over again, after which we pop a few Cheat & Eat tablets and enter cellulite therapy with—

("Don't be so vulgar," Susan urged through clenched teeth. "You came not to bury these people but to praise them.")

Unfortunately, what happens to me when I feel insecure and out of my element and also a tad hostile toward my auditors is I immediately develop a self-conscious sort of Tourette's syndrome:

"Thank you all for coming here tonight" I said. "I believe we are up against the wall and, if we don't watch out, those cum-bubbles in FAGERBAN are gonna ream us bigtime right up our rosy red little honky rectums."

Too late, as I was lathed in a Gasp Heard Round the Trailer, I realized my lingo was inappropriate to the occasion.

(Susan buried her face in her hands and sobbed.)

Tom Florissant (the Realtor) said, "Really, Charley, I don't think gutter language is necessary to make our point."

His wife, Mildred Olney-Florissant, agreed in her Bryn Mawr accent: "My gosh, there's no reason to lower ourselves to their level."

"What level?" asked Abe Gingivitis, a stocky guy built like a collegiate wrestler who'd made a fortune on organic pizzas. "We have several loans out with Jack Bannerman. He is a trustworthy and accommodating banker."

I said, "Yo. If Mr. Bannerman gets his cheese, everybody in this room will be bulldozed right off the face of the earth."

"'Bulldozed?'" scoffed Tom Florissant, lighting his meerschaum full of British Blends. "Isn't that a bit histrionic? Come come, old sport, no need for such alarmist rhetoric."

Charity Gingivitis, Abe's gazelle-skinny fey helpmeet, added, "They can't just 'bulldoze' you for no good reason. There have to be hearings, environmental impact statements, and referendums on the matter. It's all written down in codes and statutes. We can raise our objections in a courteous manner."

Courteous?

I said, "Sorry, folks, but already the ligtonite mine has ruined our rivers, the ghetto is expanding hourly, our stripmalls are poisoned by fast food and drive-up liquor windows, and downtown is choked by gridlock and air inversions. So I guarantee FAGERBAN will be about as courteous to us as a ten-foot anaconda eating a three-pound spider monkey."

"Spider monkey?" the proctologist chortled—Dale Ethan Chambers, a square-jawed man with a tiny crocodile on his blue knit polo shirt. "Tom here and I coach all the Bannerman kids in peewee soccer. They are very well behaved and intelligent boys."

Hello?

The lawyer, Bob Maelstorm, raised his hand. "Charley, what does a three-pound spider monkey have to do with the price of eggs in China?"

I said, "It's a metaphor. We are *all* a spider monkey."

Bellicose Butchie Maelstorm begged to differ. "I am *not* a spider monkey, sir. In fact, Manjo Poddubny is a good friend of ours. We play golf together at the Nob Hill Country Club. His wife and I are tennis partners."

Mildred Olney-Florissant added, "I don't agree with you at all about the spider monkey. This is a civilized country."

"It was only a *metaphor*," I explained testily. "This is crunch time in Tap City. The FAGERBAN barbarians are going to condemn our precious, still-arable land, pay only twenty cents on the dollar of real appraised value, and rub out Willow Road."

Charity Gingivitis said, "Oh, help help, the sky is falling on my spider monkey!"

Everyone tittered.

I glanced helplessly at Susan Delgado; she winked and her hair ruffled sympathetically.

So I figured okay, theoretically I'm a grown-up, and theoretically all these people are grown-ups, too—let's try another tack. And I suggested we form a committee to at least study the problem. But the Willow Roaders waffled, fumfered, backed away. Mildred Olney-Florissant gave a little speech about not fixing something that wasn't broken. And nobody had the TIME. For example, next week Babette Quicksilver was off on a tour of New England foliage; Adele Symington-Laidlaw had tickets to San Remo, Ischia, and a D. H. Lawrence circle jerk on Sardinia; and Butchie Maelstorm's Feng Shui master was coming in to reposition her furniture and update her personal Web site (on floral arrangements to cure cats from licking all their fur off). Others could free up no windows in their busy schedules of Weight Watchers meetings, Kendo workouts, Night Walking sessions, and classes at the local Junior College in how to eat your way to more creative gout—

On her way out ten minutes later, Susan Delgado gave me a real squeezy hug. "Charley," she said, "you're the Edsel of political organizers, but I love you anyway." I cried "Ouch!" when one of the orange spikes in her Knox Gelatin'd punker hairdo poked me in the eye.

In passing, Charity Gingivitis whispered with impish gleefulness, *"Nous sommes tous des singes araignées."*

Luther, his pockets bulging with exotic tarts and turnovers, remarked snidely, "The bourgeoisie is really gung ho to slit its own throat in order to create an egalitarian and sustainable socialist society, Pop."

I said, "Pick up those fucking piñon shells."

"When hell freezes over," he snickered, and slithered out the warped door just behind the last Willow Roader.

"What about you, Lydia?" I asked belligerently. "Care to add any other helpful comments?"

Tactfully, Lydia observed, "Charles, I don't think you could sell week-old leghorn chicks to a starving boa constrictor."

On that cue, out a window I saw Kelly's blue Dodge van rattling up the potholed driveway, its speaker blaring our theme song. Kelly hit the brakes and skidded to a halt three inches from the rear bumper of my Buick. One of her tires was almost flat, the aerial was bent double, the tailpipe dragged, the side door was riddled by bulletholes, and the front windshield was spiderwebbed left-to-right and top-to-bottom with horrific cracks. Kelly opened the door and fell out, got up and dusted herself off, wobbled to the trailer, stumbled through the front door, tripped over Carlos, banged into a bookcase, staggered sideways, grabbed my favorite rubber tree plant for balance, and fell over backward taking the foliage with her. Terrified cats sprayed in all directions, but Mangus pounced on her, licking and squeaking with love.

"Oh dear, am I a bit en retard?" the besotted mendicant asked, grossly licking ecstatic Mangus back, tongue to tongue. She had a black eye and a blood-soaked bandage over her left ear.

I stated grimly, "Yes you are, Kelly, by about an hour."

"Is there any grub left?" She rolled out from under the dog, who playfully grabbed the seat of her baggy pants and tugged, grrring affectionately while Kelly helplessly pawed the air in front of herself trying to escape.

"As a matter of fact there is," I said.

Standing, I walked to the card tables, latched onto a platter of deviled eggs, sashayed back to my drunken wife and . . . but no, I'm a pacifist, I always have been and always will be, so I did *not* dump the whole mess onto her reeling head.

Instead, I asked sarcastically, "Tell me, Kelly, how would *you* counteract those stupid FAGERBAN indoctrination vans cruising around town spouting their right-wing pro—Prop X jeremiads?"

"Piece of cake," she coughed, selecting a deviled egg and feeding it to Mangus. "Let's start a radio program starring Lydia as a left-wing Rush Limbaugh—type personality and blow FAGERBAN out of the water with spurious sneak attacks filled with lies, half-truths, and pornographic innuendos."

"Excuse me?"

"I'll write the scripts," she elaborated, swallowing another deviled egg whole herself. "Then Lydia can expose the Enterprise Zone and all its tax dodges and the abatements Sam Clendennon will grant to—"

When she had finished her spiel five minutes later I just stared at Kelly the way I bet people gawk at Stephen Hawking, the genius astrophysicist totally incapacitated by Lou Gehrig's disease. Then, with genuine admiration, I asked, "Would you like some apple juice to wash down those eggs?"

"Actually, Charles, I'd prefer a glass of water."

R ANDY FEATHERSTONE said, "For*get* it, dude. You must think I'm crazy."

No, I never thought that. Not openly, anyway. Not out *loud*. "In fact I always felt you were the best damn disk jockey in town," I said in my most unctuous wheedling manner.

"'*Were?*'" The least ferocious person I have ever met, he nevertheless bared his teeth at me like an irate possum. "Excuse me, but I am not yet a past tense. I still have a job, I get paid, I buy food, I'm alive and well and *not* living in Argentina. I also have a wife and three hungry mouths to feed at home. I know I'm a far-out guy, but I am *not* suicidal."

"Cash on the barrelhead, bro'." I plunked down the money. "It isn't a program, it's an advertisement. Surely the FCC has laws about fair play on the airwaves. This is a democracy we live in."

"Where did you get that stuff, Charley?" Randy fingered the crisp bills suspiciously. "You're always broke."

"Lydia took it from her account."

"Yeah, right. The tightest skinflint in America."

"It's her rap, for Pete's sake. Lydia *wants* the publicity. Plus she can't take it with her, anyway, and she's going there pretty soon."

Poor Randy. He glared at me. The deejay wore little rimless glasses, had bad teeth, and affected a scraggly red moustache that looked like a half-drowned mouse clinging to a partially eaten corn-cob. He said, "Manjo Poddubny happens to be a WPNX investor, and he is also on the school board. They'll fire Tiffany."

"No way. It's illegal. There are laws governing discrimination in education."

"Laws? When did that ever stop those maniacs? Last week Tallulah Moe and Gladys Gaverdine threatened to get Tiffany fired for teaching evolution. Clarence Fagerquist is on the board and he's a *creationist*. Tammy Sue Clendennon wants the Ten Commandments to be a part of the curriculum. Those Nob Hill Mobsters are *nuts*."

Patience is *the* virtue of all primo political organizers like myself, so I said, "Yo, Randy, stop being a jerk. It's no big deal, give me a contract, take the greenbacks, run our tape. We need the attention."

"Mr. Griffith will race up here with a sledgehammer and break my kneecaps. Then he'll force me to play Up With People or Donny Osmond CDs."

"He'll do no such thing. He happens to be a liberal human being, also a wimp. I've never had trouble with radio spots in the past."

"Ads," Randy said. "Commercial blips. Maybe a thirty-second blivet announcing a rally to support striking miners, okay. But this garbage you're asking me to run is heresy."

I nudged the jack a wee bit closer so he could catch the glitter, get a whiff of the smell. "C'mon, take it. Nobody cares about The Evil Empire anymore. And I know Whip-Nix is in the red."

"Financially, not politically. But Mr. Griffith has so much dough he wipes his ass on dollar bills. We're not in it for the bread."

Frankly, I liked Randy a lot. He used to be a hippy, a pot-smoking Buddhist love junkie who'd even signed on the dotted line for a number of my crusades, including the gay-bashing forums, the Drug Free Ghetto Chautauquas, and our Take Back the Night marches. When Kelly and he dropped acid together they drove a motorcycle into our chicken coop, killing eleven hens. Then he joined AA, married Tiffany, had three kids, and went sort of straight. His mouldy golden oldie

radio shows were eclectic: Dylan and B.B. King one minute; Randy
Newman and Leonard Cohen the next. And, just when you thought
it was safe to leap back in the water, King Pleasure, The Circle Jerks,
and Mookie Dirigible.

"If you don't call him," I threatened in a jocular but edgy
manner, "I'll drive to his castle, swim across the moat, bang on his
baronial door, and commence screaming."

Deep down, Randy had about as much spine as a housefly. So
he rolled his eyes, finally picked up the phone, punched in a number,
handed me the apparatus, and clicked on the intercom speaker:

"Hello?—"

"Hi, Mr. Griffith. This is your neighbor, Charley McFarland."

""Oh, hello Charley—*Sieg heil!* No, wait a minute, I got that
wrong, I meant: *Workers of the world, unite!*"

Very funny. I waited for him to park *his* motorcycle and brush
off the feathers. Then: "Sir, I'm up here at the station with Randy and
we've got a problem."

"What is the problem, Charley? You want him to roll the best
of Victor Jara for the next two hours? Fine by me. Broadcast whatever he wants, Randolph. The Leningrad Sisters, Paul Robeson, the
Beijing Whiffenpoofs. We must humor the hoi polloi every now and
then. Gives them a pressure relief valve, like Roosevelt did during
the Great Depression. It's the only way to save Capitalism and keep
us honest into the bargain. And anyway, communism has become so
quaint, like Twiggy or *Leave It To Beaver.* And I just love it when
Manjo has a conniption—he beat me in golf twice last week."

Dejectedly, Randy started counting my shekels. I told him, "It's
all there."

"I hate you." He tapped my cassette against his palm. "When
Mr. Griffith hears this, my name is mud. I might as well file for unem-
ployment this afternoon. Tiffany will divorce me. Jamie, Shanti, and
Rainbow will accuse me in district court of parental abuse."

I gave him a bro' grip before he could yank his hand away. "You
worry too much."

"Oh yeah? Charley, don't take this personal, but, everything you touch turns to gruel."

Gruel?

Y UP, I ACTUALLY got to observe the horror on Clarence Fagerquist's gnarly old phizog when that reluctantly aired tape on WPNX tickled his delicate eardrums on October tenth.

I was in Thompson's Lumber Company buying roofing asphalt to repair some flashing on my trailer that a flicker had hammered away. A radio behind the front counter was tuned to one of Randy Featherstone's snide hillbilly programs, "Redneck Alphabet." Just as I started to fork over my sawbuck for the tar to Hank Wattle, Clarence—Mr. FAGERBAN himself—lumbered into the hardware store, damn near crumpled me with one of his thunderhead Jovian glowers, and said (a trifle confrontationally), "Up yours, McFarland, you cheap bag of crap." Then he asked Hank for a five-gallon can of Polytrichlorathion Liquid Plastic Fiber to weatherproof the new widow's walk on the south wing of his mansion where wife Willa's doll-making studio was located.

Hank allowed as how PTC had been discontinued "by order of the EPA."

"EPA!" Clarence roared. "What the heck does that stand for, Egret Poontang Amalgamated?" And to Hank's stoned gopher, Eddie Sparrowfeather, he said, "Go get me some of that goop, Eddie, I ain't got all day."

"He can't," Hank reiterated. "They took it all away. They'd fine me a thousand dollars if I sold you a can."

Clarence scribbled a check for $1,046.95 and slapped it on the counter. "Now, go fetch me five gallons from wherever you got it stashed, Eddie. That's been the best stuff on the market for sixteen years, and I don't aim to go with second best."

"Honest, I don't have any," Hank insisted. "Two guys wearing asbestos zoot suits and gas masks walked in here last week and repossessed my entire stock. Ask Eddie. The fumes cause melanomas in rats."

Clarence reared up, mighty puzzled and irate. He was a big Bunyonesque man, six feet three inches tall, who weighed two hundred and thirty-six pounds naked as a jaybird. He wore size 13 Red Wings, and his Levi's shirts had an eighteen-inch neck. His head did not feel right unless it was protected by a size 9 yellow hardhat. All his life he had smoked cigarettes and cigars, and he drank plenty of Coors beer, even now at age seventy-three. He imbibed Coors because Chicanos had once been on strike against it: *Fuck those Commie spics!* He also sent hefty donations to right-to-lifers and Pat Robertson, and he admired Strom Thurmond and George W. Bush. When Willa brought home a Microsoft computer so she could go online with her doll business, Clarence *shot* it with his Colt .45. He was a main stockholder at the hideous ligtonite mine and First State S & L, he owned a chain of Booze and Butts shacks in the ghetto, had built just about every subdivision and trailer park in Suicide City, and lived in a twenty-thousand-square-foot pre-fab chateau right at the tippy *top* of Nob Hill.

"Shit, Hank," Clarence said. "When did you start eatin' pussy like all the rest of them dang eco mollycoddlers like Mr. McFarland here?" He glared at me so ponderously *my* hair ruffled.

Embarrassed, Hank observed, "The times they are a-changing, Clarence."

"*Fuck* the times!" Clarence was so pissed his massive craggy face inflated and turned crimson. "Used to be a man could do whatever he pleased, but I guess the frontier fell into a toilet. Nowadays, everybody is kissing the environment's ass. 'Endangered Species?'

Pull my tail and call me dogie, *I'm* an endangered species. And you are, too, Hank," he added, banging his fist on the counter: BOOM! A tape measure hopped off, bouncing once on the floor, then Clarence drop-kicked it over Eddie Sparrowfeather and across the store where it knocked the top bottle of Pine-Sol off a five-foot-high display pyramid.

Which is exactly when the odious developer was jolted rudely into a far deeper cafard by a familiar rasping voice on the radio that made his hackles stiffen and sent blood literally *rushing* into my penis.

Lydia croaked, "Hello, Americans, my name is Lydia Arlington Babcock, and I'm proud to say this is the first broadcast of The Voice of the Butterfly. Currently, in our fair city, the forces of good are locked in a life and death struggle with the forces of evil over the survival of a beautiful and innocent little bug, which—"

Clarence frowned: "What the hell is that old windbag talkin' about?"

"I have lived for almost ninety-three years," Lydia continued, "but never have I seen as much skullduggery afoot as now threatens to destroy the very biological capital upon which all life in this valley, and indeed on earth, depends."

Clarence turned on me, put two and two together faster than a rat can shit in a cracker box, and said, "This is one of your stupid pet tricks, ain't it, McFarland?"

Before I could answer, Lydia said, "The gangsters who control FAGERBAN are running scared because the upstream banking con-glomerate, Citi-Mag, which may cough up close to nineteen million in short-term assets to guarantee the project, is asking for a collat-eral check that requires an on-site inspection of the guarantee, plus a line-by-line certified accounting of the structural vigorish justify-ing its risk before it opens the vault and passes on almost twenty double Ms in Jumbo CDs purchased from three credit unions and a Cayman offshore speculation junk bond broker named Joe, who—"

Clarence, who had some anger management issues, laid his rather huge hand on my shoulder, saying, "Fuck you, buster, and the bloated nag you rode in on, too." His hand weighed about twenty pounds and quivered like an octopus.

The aging giant added, "I'll stop by Whip Nix on my way downtown and cancel all our advertising. Tristan thinks he can get away with this, I'll knock his stupid top hat off with a cinder block and stick my uncircumcised dick all the way up his flabby rectum."

Foolhardy to the max, I blurted, "Great. *Do it.* We'll make enough hay out of *that* to drive the price of a bale in this valley down to a nickel!"

The developer's massive blunt fingers dug into my shoulder like a backhoe bucket, but Lydia stopped him again:

"According to our information, Jack Bannerman's already in the minus column when it comes to loan-loss reserves," she said. "He's waiting until interest rates go up another quarter point before he dumps his excess baggage to an upstream participant. The problem is, half his assets are booked as third- and fourth-generation Renewals and Extensions without a cent of interest being paid in—"

For some abstract reason, Clarence raised me up almost above his head and tossed me into the rake and spade rack. The clatter of hoe handles, rake tines, shovel blades, and weed cutters erupting all around my flailing appendages almost drowned out his exclamation, "TURN OFF THAT DAD BLASTED RADIO, HANK!" Then Clarence grabbed my sawbuck off the counter and ripped it in half, yelled "Up yours, you chickenshit eco-faggot!" and, fit to be tied—"I'll cold-cock that old cunt like a glue horse in the stockyards!"—the cumbersome autocrat started toward the door while I settled to earth among clanging and banging garden utensils like an oversize beanbag landing in the middle of a (very) noisy drum solo.

Clarence almost collided with a breathless Susan Delgado, who had a pencil poised above her yellow reporter's notebook and a pugnacious challenge on her pointy face. "'Eco faggot?' 'Glue horse?' Would you care to elaborate, Mr. Fagerquist?"

He barked, "KISS MY RUDDY BUM!" and *SLAM!* went the door behind him. Susan yanked it open, cried, *"Banzai!"* and catapulted off in hot pursuit.

As I lay there tangled up and hyperventilating in a nest of hickory sticks, Hank Wattle said, "People like you and that old windbag oughtta be shot, Charley Mac, and then hung out in the rain to dry."

But he clicked the radio back on just in time for these pearls from the garrulous dowager by way of our talented scriptwriter, Kelly McFarland:

"The mayor already told Clarence Fagerquist he'll be granted an exception and an extension of the water main free of charge providing he hooks the entire commercial subdivision up to city water. Of course, if Citi-Mag discovers this preferential treatment they might take a powder, leaving FAGERBAN up the creek without a paddle. Jack's already holding too many blank notes over a million bucks. He has a clutch of big tickets at two or more points over par. A third of his bookings show no coverage ratios and no cash flows. So if Citi-Mag reneges, every upstream bank could force a buyback, exposing Jack's capital-to-assets ratio for what it is, thus undermining the carryback he thinks will bail him out, causing his wife Lu Ann to pawn her diamonds to buy the kiddies soup."

Hank grumbled, "No way. The commitment fees alone on Citi-Mag will keep everything in order until after the election."

But he was shook up, especially after Eddie Sparrowfeather asked, "What happens if Bo Hrbyk classifies half the loans at First State instead?"

"In a pig's ear." Hank glared at Eddie. "Nobody will believe what that hag says. Everyone knows she's bonkers. Those Butterfly jokers got about as much credibility as a potato in a bucket of camel dung."

T HAT EVENING our charming newspaper editor, Edna Poddubny, summoned Susan Delgado into the main office at the *Sentinel-Argus*. Sissy, Edna's dog, growled until Edna went "*Sssst!*" between her teeth. Sharon Ludlow, owner/manager of The Petatorium, a dog grooming salon just off the Plaza, grabbed her bra, her Birkenstocks, and her Bible and scurried into the bathroom, locking the door behind her: *clack!*

To be polite, I'll describe the editor as short, rotund, and near-sighted. Picture an adult from the *South Park* movie (but ban *all* the scatology!). As my oddball journalist buddy pulled up a chair, Edna dropped a copy of Susan's latest article and photograph onto the desk in front of her topnotch sleuth.

"I take it you wrote this and took the picture?"

"Yes ma'am."

"We can't print it, of course."

Susan became obsequious. "Oh please," she begged. "It's only a little auto accident. Mr. Fagerquist was leaving Thompson's Lumber in a hurry and he backed his Cadillac into the county ambulance, which was parked in front of Celso's Burrito Wagon next door. It's a funny and harmless story."

"Nothing is harmless in a political season, my dear." Edna offered a Tic-Tac, but the reporter politely declined. Tonight Susan's hair spikes glowed purple and she was wearing a camouflage T-shirt, beige cargo pants held up by fireman's suspenders, and an ancient pair of checkered Vans. She looked cute, kind of like the scarecrow from Oz, an updated MTV version.

The boss continued, "In the past five hours I've gotten three calls from downstate editors asking about Lydia Babcock and the Butterfly Coalition. They'd already heard about that atrocious radio program." Vigorously, she hooked a final three peanut M&M's from their package, and, with a downward lefthand palm slap, popped them expertly off her right fingertips up into her gaping mouth.

"What did you tell them?" Susan asked.

"That the Butterfly Coalition is a group of four deranged alcoholics with absolutely no credibility whatsoever." Edna swallowed the candies whole.

"And—?"

"They bought it . . . for the time being. However: no negative ink against us, and no story, no nothing about *them*. That's the way to win Prop X in a walk, I promise."

Casually, Susan said, "Suppose the butterfly gets its endangered status?"

Edna laughed, picking up a cinnamon twist cruller: She licked it. "I saw Peter Lithgow and his wife Sherrilynn at the State Womens' Press Association Convention Banquet last Friday in the Capital. Peter's dumb but not slow: The application for endangered status has been permanently shelved."

Susan blinked. Within seconds, Edna's eyebrows grew bushy, her eyes diminished to half their normal size and turned gaudy pink, sinister long white hairs sprouted from her nostrils, and, when her upper lip curled into a leer, bloody vampire fangs were exposed.

But when Susan ventured a sharp intake of breath, it all went away and Edna became her usual benignly plump self again, the magnanimous reactionary mentor who had no idea that her ward, Susan, was a double agent.

Susan said, "But that isn't fair, is it?"

"'*Fair*'?" Edna pried a salami out of her knick-knack drawer and cut off a chunk with her Swiss Army knife. "Fair in the eyes of the law," she asked mischievously, "or fair in the eyes of God?" Edna swallowed a large chunk of salami without chewing beforehand, and washed it down with a pint of Diet Pepsi. Then the editor rolled up her sweater sleeves and ripped open a bag of Ruffles Potato Chips. Her teeth were soon crunching through the salty treats like a gas-operated mulching machine eating pruned cottonwood branches.

But Susan, who had her own Machiavellian tendencies, replied, "Fair in the eyes of God."

Whereupon Edna's nose—like Pinocchio's—shot out seven inches and a malicious little mouth with very sharp teeth at the tip of it snapped viciously six times—*clickety-click-clack!*—then the nose recoiled back to its normal proportions and the mouth disappeared: *doink.*

THOSE MALEVOLENT developers didn't let us rest, though, not even for a minute. Like: Next Monday FAGERBAN elevated bad taste to Olympian heights by erecting a half dozen billboards (created by Eleanor Poddubny's ad agency) north and south of town that featured the grossly overstated charms of that ineffable hunk of outrageous eye candy, Tammy Sue Clendennon, the mayor's unfaithful wife and mammocephalic slut queen of our feculent burg. In each enormous ad the voluptuous wet dream (in a skimpy polkadot mini-bikini, spike heels, and yellow hardhat) was coyly stepping on a shovel blade poked into some Astroturf, theoretically breaking ground for the new bypass and industrial park:

VOTE "YES!" VOTE PROP X! VOTE PROGRESS!

Five minutes after the last stupendously offensive panel had been glued into place, I knocked on what was left of Luther's front door, ready to rock 'n' roll. When my kid hollered, "Who is it?" I twisted the handle, kicked that sagging disaster open eight inches, turned sideways, squeezed inside . . . and paused for a moment just to *appreciate* his habitat.

How did people (sic) live in a squalid dump like this? The decor mode was black on purple on black, over the windows dark blankets had been nailed, and tasteless posters on the wall were of Joe Camel and Hermann Goering boning Little Orphan Annie doggie style. Other sensitive posters touted the musical virtues of such antiquated performers as The Dead Kennedys, KISS, Limp Bizkit, Korn, and, of course, Mookie Dirigible (the famous shot of him in thigh-high velvet boots, obsidian chaps, frilly silk codpiece, skimpy vest made of human skin, snakehide choker, and bombardier helmet, playing an electric zither in an old-fashioned eagle claw bathtub situated on the main steps of the Palace of Versailles). Lethal implements resembling meat cleavers embedded at random in the walls had humongous rusting chains draped over their handles; a bureau in splinters occupied space at the foot of Luther's mattress; and all his clothes (sic) lay scattered like the aftermath rubble of an Armenian earthquake. On the computer's screen saver garish tropical monsters limped back and forth, and a boogie box somewhere was tuned almost silently to Whip-Nix, the usual Randy Featherstone bombast: Metallica and Black Sabbath screaming at the Foo Fighters, a sort of sado-masochistic blueprint for people bent on murder/suicide pacts. Luther's bald girlfriend, Miranda Satan, was curled up in a fetal position totally passed out, eyes wide open, sucking on a pacifier, with two rings in her nose and a tiny cobra tattoo on her left cheek. The only thing missing here was a drugged Igor strapped to a corner embalming gurney getting a mustard plaster from a zombie.

I gagged and said, "Luther, are you some place in this slag heap of bat guano?"

"Maybe," muttered a reluctant voice among the stalagmites.

"I need you to do a job," I said. "Are you listening?"

A large pile of rags shifted slightly and grunted. I said, "Well, you know how to use a chain saw, don't you?"

He waited.

"Have you seen those new FAGERBAN billboards north and south of town?"

He waited some more.

"They have wooden stanchions."

Silence from that not exactly pumped-up heap. Randy Featherstone had done a 180 on WPNX, now featuring the love ballads of
Englebert Humperdink and Nervous Norvis.

I elaborated, "They could and should be cut down. They're illegal."

My boy finally deigned to speak: "So call a cop, Pop."

"Luther, you're deliberately misunderstanding the concept."

"I thought you were against violence, Pop."

"This isn't violent. People won't get hurt."

"Let Kelly do it, then, Pop. You trust her so much. She's so
responsible, Pop."

"Get off it. Kelly would cut off her own leg and one arm at
the wrist."

"Then why don't *you* do it, Pop, you're so eager to make an ass
of yourself?"

I'm a pacifist, so I counted to five, bypassing the customary
response of my kind of father to that kind of adolescent taunt, and I
said calmly, "Because I'm the *commander*, Luther. I make the plans.
If I went into battle and was killed, or wound up in jail, that would
remove the head of our organization and the organization would
collapse. In his book on guerrilla warfare, Che says—"

Luther's head wriggled into view from among rags that had the
look and texture of rotting autumn mushrooms—slick, black, and
oily. His Mohawk was as mussed up as roadkill atop his bald dome.
Fresh zits across his features, highlighted as if by garish infrared
illumination, seemed to have been caused by shotgun pellets. How
he could sleep still wearing earrings, I don't know, but these were
both swastika pendants as large as yogurt cannisters. And around
his neck?—a wide leather S & M choker studded with aluminum
arrow points. *Neat.*

Luther said, "Pop, you always told me it's a great waste of political time, energy, and money to get busted for stupid crimes, for
example shoplifting, possession, or DWI. Your billboards seem to
fall in that category: stupid crimes."

With tactful restraint, I explained, "Yo, Luther, the billboards are pro–Prop X. They are also obscene. Destroying them will be an important political act. It will give us a lot of publicity. *Ink*. If you're caught, I'll bail you out."

"Yeah, sure. Goodbye, Pop. Have a nice life." He pulled the septic covers over his head.

After counting slowly to five again, I said, "Luther, I *hate* it when you're so superior and snide and hostile and obnoxious. You think you're so smart, but you're really just a cynical pile of punker snot. You don't even have a real idea in your head, anymore. It's like I sired a heavy metal Muppet."

My son went deathly silent inside his rank sleeping bag.

I continued angrily: "*Look* at you, asshole. Do you ever stand in front of a mirror or are you too scared to? 'Progress' is destroying the natural world, we're baking to death from the Greenhouse Effect, there are huge holes in the ozone, the air we breathe reeks of toxic chemicals, but you've got an idiotic bulldog collar around your neck. Why don't you wear a big cardboard nametag that reads *Spike*?"

Deadly sullen vibes came out of his noisome bedding.

"The oceans are dying," I said, gaining momentum in my Tourette's mode, "and the world's forests are being destroyed. Almost all our topsoil is gone or polluted by chemical fertilizers, and over a billion people on the globe don't even have marginally potable drinking water—"

Luther suddenly took the bait, butting into my rant: "I don't *want* to be a political person, Pop. Look at you. It's a miserable life of constant defeat and humiliation. You yell and scream and march and protest and picket and eat organic food and *still* a hundred species go extinct every day and Serbs and Albanians hack apart each other's pregnant girlfriends with battle axes. People laugh at you, Pop. They call you 'Eco-Faggot' behind your back, Pop. I *hate* that."

Tough shit, Luther, learn to deal, and stop calling me 'Pop'! "The Greenhouse Effect can only get worse so long as the industrialized world continues to grow," I harped insistently. "But do you care? Oh no, not my black leather S & M heir to the throne. Antarctica and the North Pole are melting, but my son is saving up his money to buy a Mookie Dirigible CD, featuring the hit song 'Fuck Frank in the Kiester.'"

Luther hunched so deeply into himself under the sleeping bag that if he'd been a turtle his head probably would've been protruding out his anus. On the other hand, Miranda opened one eye and fixed it on me with cyclopean intensity. "Beat it," she whispered. "You are totally jamming my frequencies."

"Everybody on earth contributes to this dilemma," I persisted, locking into cruise control, "but the major problem is us. The United States is only six percent of the world's population, but we consume—"

My boy couldn't resist lip-synching along in a muffled rage: "—fifty percent of the world's resources and energy each year, and we create seventy percent of the solid waste."

"Very funny." I tugged so hard on my beard a great big tuft came out in my fist. "You mock me, Luther, you selfish little toad. But one of these days you'll be grateful. You'll thank me. You'll weep at my grave."

"I'll shit on your grave, Pop."

"*What?*"

Luther snarled, "You make me want to sodomize every environmentalist and vegetarian on this planet and then shove rotten meat down their throats until they choke to death."

That stopped me for a second, I'll admit. And I thought to myself: *Charley, what the hell are you doing?* You're letting personal family issues interfere with your sacred trust to organize the masses to fight for a better tomorrow. So get hold of yourself, *Pop*, and start treating this kid that you love with the dignity and respect he deserves.

Yesss. That was a whole lot better. I took a deep breath. I let it out slowly. Then I leaned over real close to the pile of rags under which Luther was lying beside his pickled moll, and I said, "Okay, you bastard, I'll give you a hundred dollars, cash."

My boy hesitated. But I knew he was only earning minimum wage at Burger Boy. Too, he could hardly make his rent, and Miranda earned zilch from her occasional jobs as a pet sitter for clueless spinsters. Plus one tablet of Mitsubishi "e" must have cost at least twenty bucks—

"Lemme see the dough," he grumbled resentfully.

"I don't have it with me."

Luther readjusted himself with insulting indifferent finality inside his filthy cocoon. Miranda winked . . . and fell into a coma.

Okay, okay. *Jesus*. If he insisted on driving a hard bargain, I could cope. I unzipped my knapsack's pocket pouch, removed my day planner, and carefully extricated five crisp new twenty dollar bills, which I held over the entrance to their blanket heap. One of Luther's hands reached forth and grabbed the loot, retreating quickly lest I renege.

"Deal?" I asked.

What was he gonna say—"No"?

KELLY HAD A chain saw because one of the temporary jobs she'd held in the last four years was working as an apprentice to a street artist, Molochai Burton, who sculpted eagles and grizzly bears with chainsaws in front of the new courthouse during the Farmer's Market gatherings on Saturday mornings in July and August. So Luther pedaled around town until he located the Butterfly Coalition sound van parked conveniently behind Furr's among the overturned shopping carts and stinking green Dumpsters. He dismounted from his bike and knocked on the back doors, asking if he could borrow the chain saw.

Kelly, who lay half-dead among empty liquor bottles, used tampons, cigarette butts, and piles of mold-covered clothes, said, "No. You're my enemy. Beat it." For some reason she wore bright red lipstick that was smeared all over what was left of her teeth as if somebody had smashed a tomato in her face.

Luther said, "He paid me a hundred bucks. You can have half of it if you come along and help."

She lurched into a sort of sitting position. "Why, so I take the rap? Making the divorce inevitable?"

They stared at each other uncomfortably until Luther said, "You're killing yourself, anyway, so what does it matter?"

Kelly thought for a moment, then said, "*Bueno*. I can't argue with that. Let's go, I'm stoked. Where's my vig?"

The kid peeled off two twenties and a ten. "Can we use the van?" he asked hopefully.

"Nope. The battery's dead."

Luther forgot to notify Susan Delgado that our plan had been activated. Then he purchased chain oil from Hank Wattle at Thompson's Lumber (as Kelly bought two doobies from Eddie Sparrowfeather while Hank made change), and they zigzagged south through bumper-to-bumper gridlocked traffic along the Californicated strip with Kelly perched on Luther's BMX handlebars. They were bombarded by fast-food palacios and drive-up liquor silos. Thanks to La Niña it hadn't rained in three months, hence the mid-October dust was pretty oppressive. In a prankish mood, Sweeny Dancebow heaved a Night Train bottle at the odd couple, but missed. Nicolai Joaquín Aragón waved from the Wal-Mart parking lot where he was stalking pigeons for food; sometimes my son and Nick sniffed Wite-Out and played air guitars together in the shadow of the Colonel Buffalo Meat statue in Miller Park. Next, from the hermetically sealed interior of her Ford Explorer, Tallulah Moe crossed herself and brandished the silver crucifix on a chain around her neck at the peculiar duo as they cruised on by. Cathie Bayless, an aroma therapist having an anxiety attack in her idling blue Chevy Elf, popped two ginkgo bilobas and self-consciously buttoned up her blouse against The Devil's prying eyes as she dialed 911 on her miniature Nokia. Beowulf Griffith went berserk inside Tristan's becalmed Land Cruiser, banging his fangs against the closed windows, but all the doors were locked. Pomeroy Gaverdine, the idiot savant son of Elton and Gladys Gaverdine, was practicing his magic act outside the Body Shoppe to amuse the stalled motorists, shaking white doves from billowy silken scarves the color of bright Hawaiian pineapple slices. And Father Benny Wombat, feasting on a pork pocket pita and Milk Duds at Bob's Quik-Fart, made the chakka greeting sign and laughed. He liked Luther, the feeling was mutual: Mostly, when together, they discussed flying saucers and alien earth visitors, a subject endlessly fascinating to my boy.

By the time they reached the first billboard two miles south of town, Luther was exhausted, soggy from sweating, lightheaded from carbon monoxide, and thoroughly pissed at Kelly. En route she had smoked both joints. When Luther braked, Kelly pitched flat onto her face and started giggling. Fuck her. Disgusted, Luther laid down his bike, freed her chain saw from bungee chords on the rear rack, and walked over to the northernmost billboard stanchion, casting his eyes aloft at Tammy Sue Clendennon, twelve feet high by twenty-five feet wide. *Great.* On top of everything else it had to be Tammy Sue, the one superlative bonk in town who had most tormented his adolescence. *Ten thousand times my frustrated, seething scion had pounded himself nearly senseless in some dark corner of his teenage cave while visions of the mayor's delectable helpmeet danced like Salomé in his fevered brain. Nope, nobody gets out of puberty alive.*

Naturally, the damn chain saw wouldn't fire up. "Give it to me," Kelly said. Gladly. However, Luther observed the start of her ensuing pre-ignition ritual with growing awareness that Kelly was sure to lose both hands, her nose, maybe even her large sagging tits into the bargain if he let her proceed. Well . . . *good. Good riddance to bad rubbish,* he always said. Or, in the immortal words of Mookie Dirigible: "Let's choke to death on blood!"

Kelly jiggled the implement to slosh the gas around, spit into the exhaust manifold, pumped the choke knob five times, flipped on the start switch, set the saw on the ground, pressed her toe into the handlebar safety guard to keep it steady, gripped tightly the accelerator flange, then really YANKED the pullrope handle. The engine caught, the chain whined, Kelly stumbled, the blade hit a rock and bucked up the rig in a double somersault four feet off the ground missing Kelly's head by centimeters as she lost her balance and crashed to earth. The saw came down screaming and flip-flopped around, chopping up frantic spurts of dirt like a wounded helicopter, actually bouncing once right over Kelly's belly (shredding through her sweater without somehow disemboweling her in the process), and then clanged into Luther's bike, ripping out thirty front spokes and shredding the tire as it stalled.

Clunk.

Kelly was laughing so hard her stomach ached. Luther, on the other hand, was suddenly so petrified his testicles had lurched back up to where they'd last been when he was eleven. Kelly rolled over and crawled to the saw whooping noisily as she went through the same ritual again while my appalled boy could only gape in terror, absolutely mesmerized. This time, however, Kelly did not lose control. In fact, she actually approached the billboard and began to cut with a blade curved hockey-stick fashion yet with the chain and its cutter links somehow still extant, and inside of eleven minutes she was able to step back and watch in mega-stoned *delight* as FAGERBAN'S mammoth bikini'd babe toppled over. Tammy Sue landed flat with an emphatic *whoomph!* . . . right on top of Luther's bicycle.

"*We are the Butterfly Liberation Army!*" Kelly bawled ecstatically.

Several cars zooming along in the steady traffic honked appreciatively, including one being driven by Paul Sweetwater, a buddy of Luther's once arrested with him in a bucolic Mexican village for throwing beer bottles through the window of a liquor store. Paul worked as a waiter at the Inn of the Sun God Restaurant, and he was also a towel boy and all around weapons gopher at the Gun and Skeet Club. He gave Luther and Kelly a Vulcan "live long and prosper" greeting sign and, even though paralyzed, Luther managed to flash him that Trekkie salute in return.

Then my boy hustled to catch up with Kelly as she strode purposefully a quarter mile south to their next victim. Obviously, now that his conscience had kicked in, Luther should have tackled her, confiscated the chain saw, and subdued her by any means necessary before she killed herself in some gory orgy of psychotic ineptitude and wasted carelessness. But how did you disarm a female of Kelly's heft and instability with an implement of mega destruction in her hands? The answer? Don't even *think* about going there, girlfriend.

So Luther could only watch as the chain sliced into the four supports like a hot knife cleaving through Reddi-wip. My son knew the chain had to break and Kelly would promptly be beheaded, dis-armed, eviscerated. It never happened, though: *God moves in mysterious ways!* But even after a fourth cut the enormous billboard remained aloft. So Kelly tiptoed up to a strut, touched it with her right pinkie, then stepped back, and—slowly—the massive sign keeled over. . . landing right on top of *her*.

The chain saw kept whining, gagging, spitting, coughing, and backfiring underneath.

What did Luther do?

He ran over to the billboard yelling "JESUS CHRIST, KELLY! JESUS CHRIST!" and tried to lift the sign up a little, but it was way too heavy, so Luther cast about frantically for something, anything—a tool!—and his eyes alighted on a jagged stone that he grabbed, and, jumping onto the billboard yelling "JESUS CHRIST, KELLY! JESUS CHRIST!" he began to bash the plywood, which actually splintered rather easily between the two-by-four support struts under his superhuman pounding, until a hole appeared that he smashed wider and wider with each blow—"JESUS CHRIST! JESUS CHRIST!"—and finally Kelly's face appeared, startled, grinning, bloody all over, and Luther kept slamming his rock against feeble plywood, hammering a hole big enough for Kelly, then he pulled her out and rolled her across the billboard onto the ground—SAVED!—just as Johnny Batrus executed a squealing U-turn on the highway so sharply that his cruiser sank onto the left-side shocks low enough for the metal frame to raise sparks and the car almost flipped over. The pint-sized law officer jumped out the door while the car was still rolling forward and he did a somersault, coming up with a service revolver in one hand, his sunglasses in the other, and he hollered at the criminal duo: "Hold it right there, you freaks, or you're a dead man!" Then Johnny jammed on the shades, instantly reeking of much more authority: *"And put your hands on your heads!"*

"You put your hands on your *own* fucking head, you macho pipsqueak!" Kelly shouted right back at him.

Beside her, Luther almost fainted. "Don't shoot!" he yelled. His bloody palms were clapped so firmly atop his nearly bald gourd that the Mohawk wouldn't rise again for a week. *"I don't know her!"* he screamed at Johnny. *"I NEVER SAW HER BEFORE IN MY LIFE!"*

E DNA PODDUBNY said, "Oh, it's you, Charley Mac. Why am I not surprised? Please come in and do sit down." To Sissy—who growled—she went "Ssst," and the big ugly dog shrank like an anti-sponge when the water hits. The bathroom door opened a crack, but shut immediately with too loud a bang. Edna punched Save on her keyboard and the machine said, *"Thank you, have a nice day, earn lots of money"* as she stood up, leaned over the desk as much as her tummy would allow, and extended her sweaty hand. "Now what seems to be the problem?"

"Your coverup, that's what," I said angrily. Yeah, my heart was racing. And I certainly did *not* shake that plump little proffered flip-per, what am I, a hypocrite? A grooming brush, a white plastic butt plug, and a pair of furlined handcuffs seemed out of place and some-how inappropriate on Edna's desk. But I've never been one to judge.

"Coverup?" At 5′1″, 150, and 36 years old, Edna had a prissy habit of tucking in her elbows and folding her hands across her chest as if frozen in mid–Dirty Bird. She kept her black hair curly like Shirley Temple, and preferred cammy outfits and Reeboks. A half-eaten container of chocolate-covered donuts sat on her desk like a box of elephant scat, and her chin was dappled by crumbs.

She said, "Charley, please don't flay me with your self-righteous left-wing hysteria. This is still a free country. And I run a private newspaper, need I remind you? I set editorial policy, not you, not the government."

She reached for another donut, plucking it coquettishly from the box like a giant lizard spearing a katydid as I said, "You have a *mandate*, Edna—how can you ignore it? The front-page slug line under the logo says 'The Light of Freedom and Democracy.'"

"I should hope so, my dear. 'Freedom and Democracy.' We are not yet a forum for pinko demagogues and socialist crackpots like that caterwauling nonagenarian you put on Whip-Nix every Monday and Thursday."

I opened my mouth again, but Edna was as fast as a frog tongue and beat me to the punch:

"Don't tell me, let me guess. You're disappointed we gave no ink, no photographs, and no editorial comment to your puerile desecration of the VOTE 'YES!' billboards?"

"That's right, and why the hell not?" I complained in my best outraged manner.

She snapped right back, "Because in baseball games on TV they never show fans who run illegally onto the field. Nobody from the media in their right mind would condone a criminal act by giving it space or airtime."

Though I felt almost faint from overstimulation, I shouted: "You report *all* criminal acts, Edna! They're news! Chain-saw murders, arson and robbery, sodomy and rape! You stick your filthy meathooks into any old bag of crap if there's saleable gossip in it!"

She replied calmly, "But this wouldn't have been news, Charley. It was done strictly to gain attention. An imprudent article would have been a free paid political advertisement. That's also why Johnny Batrus refused to arrest your demented wife and child."

"Oh yeah?" I lifted my chin and jutted my lower jaw: "People in this town are pissed off, Edna! You can't hoodwink them forever! They're tired of a collapsing inner city, ligtonite-poisoning, substandard housing, and—"

Yada, yada, yada.

While I ran down my monotonous dirge Edna polished off her donut, then reached for another pimple grenade. And as soon as my wad was shot, she said, "I hate to be the one to break the news, Fidel, but you're living in a reality warp that nobody relates to anymore."

"You'll see!" I blurted defiantly. "Bo Hrbyk is gonna slap your crooked dad and all his Nob Hill cronies in jail and then Fizzlick will dismantle FAGERBAN like roustabouts striking a circus tent when all the ballyhoo's over!"

Edna giggled, licking half a pound of chocolate off the deep-fried calorie bomb in her fist. "Thank you for your opinion, Mr. McFarland. Please drop two copies on the front desk as you leave and we'll get back to you. Meantime, why don't you go get a self-alignment from Melba Stallone, kiddo? She could help you breathe, uncover your Inner Essence, perhaps even build up your Personal Congruence."

And as I stumbled backwards, she broke into song:

Glory, glory highway bypass,
Glory, glory highway bypass—

Yuk. I spun around dramatically to storm out the door, but instead I barged face first into *Eleanor* Poddubny and almost broke my nose.

"Charley McFarland, you're dead meat!" Eleanor cried. "You and that grotesque person you call a son, and that butt-ugly manatee pickled in formaldehyde masquerading as your wife."

Oi vez. Today's stirring outfit featured a gray fedora, a black spangled torero vest, tight silk slacks, and red high-heeled Gucci sandals. Blue rouge on her cheeks accentuated the high bone structure, and dark purple lipstick gave her mouth a velvety derisive look. This stressed-out cutie grabbed both my arms and shook me:

"You won't get away with cutting down those billboards, you little red twit! Edna here is going to splash your perfidy all over this newspaper. We will personally see to it that you criminals rot in hell for eternity."

"No I won't," her chubby stepdaughter said.

"Say *what?*" Eleanor let go of my arms, thrusting me backward onto the floor.

"No publicity," Edna explained placidly, chomping into her third donut. "If they blew themselves up with an atomic bomb I still wouldn't give 'em an inch of ink. Out of sight out of mind is our best campaign strategy against those kooks."

"Excuse me, honey." Eleanor marched up to the edge of the desk. "The Butterfly Coalition needs to be (one) in jail, and (two) flagellated repeatedly in the court of public opinion. They fucked with my billboards and they are going to *pay*. I don't care what Manjo and the rest of his peckerhead buddies told you to do, the *Sentinel-Argus* will roast those butterflies on its front page until their assholes pucker up so tightly the poop starts dropping out as tiny as deer pellets."

Slowly, the editor put down her third, partially scarfed chocolate donut and very deliberately sucked dulcet frosting off her tubby fingers as she crossed herself. Sissy growled until Edna went "Ssst!"

Then: "The Lord gives me orders, Eleanor, not you, not my Daddy, not FAGERBAN, not anyone else. We don't say the F-word or any other swear words in this office. And *I* run this paper, so don't you *ever* hint even in a *whisper* that you have a right to tell me what to do."

Cruella De Vil shot her a visual hoagie so pitiless I expected Edna to disintegrate as if etherized by a ray gun. No such luck, however. So Eleanor said, "Why, you obstinate mule. I'll call your daddy on the phone right now if you don't give an order to fry them butterflies in print. I'm a professional, Edna, I know how to sink a ship, and believe me, bad publicity and then more bad publicity are the most devastating cannon balls on earth. So hop down off your high horse, humpty, and let's start kicking ass."

I was there, I actually saw this happen, it's *true*. The editor circled around the desk and placed herself squarely in front of Eleanor, stomach to stomach, nose to nose, bosom to bosom. Then she made a fist of her right hand and drove it about two and a half feet directly *through* Eleanor's abdomen. In an explosion of shocked spittle,

Edna's skinny stepmother doubled over with a grunt, hit the floor, and didn't even bounce.

I released an astonished bleat. Sissy cowered in the corner. The bathroom toilet was flushed. Then Edna swiveled her head in my direction, blew on her sticky knuckles, and sarcastically peeled each one of her fingers back separately until they were unclenched and able to wiggle at me in a toodle-oo gesture: "Good-bye, Charley, weren't you just about to vanish?"

B ENT ALL OUT OF SHAPE, I barreled through Lydia's door
complaining loudly about Edna Podubbny's refusal to recognize
our billboard desecration, but the old bat ignored me because she
was fiddling with her cockamamie will again while Dr. Lorenzo Jackson had her hooked up to a portable EKG machine. On her lapel
Lydia wore an old FREE JULIUS AND ETHEL pin from her collection.
Pages of blotched, corrected, rewritten, and edited legalese were
scattered across the floor like bodies in a London restaurant after an
IRA bomb explosion. Kelly sat nearby in a dilapidated easy chair
scribbling into a notebook as she recovered from six bruised ribs
and a sprained ankle. Her face was plastered with blue cosmetic mud
and occasionally she painted another fingernail avocado green,
dipping the poison out of a tiny bottle shaped like an hourglass.
With a crew like this one manning our barricades, who needed
money, luck, or publicity?

"Lydia," I cried, "what the hell are you *doing*?"

"Don't shout, my man," the lanky doctor said. "You'll mess
up the needle on this magic box." He punched a button to stop the
machine and tore off a thin piece of graph paper with heartbeat
squiggles on it.

Lydia had been using one of those cheap ballpoint pens that
bleed ink, gathering drippy black fuzzballs at the tip and smearing

everything, consequently her right hand, her forearm, and the entire front of her dress were filthy with Rorschach blotches.

When I snatched the pen from her hand, she screeched, "CHAR-leeeee!"

Dr. Lorenzo said, "Oh my, look at this rhythm strip, Lydia. Here's one heartbeat, and, uh . . ." he threaded slowly along the rest of the narrow printout ". . . here's *another* one. Wow, how *exciting*. No atrial or ventricular bumps on either beat, of course, but we beggars can't be choosy."

"You're not supposed to *touch* that will unless Farragut's around," I scolded, gathering up pages from the floor.

"I have more knowledge of the law in my *pinkie* than Farragut contains in either his anus *or* his brain," Lydia said as Dr. Lorenzo prepared an injection in a hypodermic needle the size of a turkey baster.

Kelly groaned, "Would you guys mind keeping it down to a dull roar? I'm trying to invent a new Liberation Army broadside over here."

Dr. Lorenzo rolled up Lydia's right sleeve for the shot and I said, "Yo, doc, what is *in* that freakin' needle?"

"Just a lot of healthy vitamin stuff," he assured me, tapping the syringe's barrel to evenly distribute the liquid inside. "It'll keep her alive for at least another day." His pager tweedled and he checked it.

"What *kind* of healthy vitamin stuff?" I asked.

"Just call it a cocktail of life-sustaining fluids," he said. "No big deal. Now relax and hold your breath—"

He jabbed the needle into Lydia's arm and thumbed home the plunger: She jerked stiffly erect so abruptly her upper bridge popped out, bounced on the floor, and was instantly snatched by a hungry cat.

"I really want to know what you just gave her," I insisted, grabbing the cat's tail as it scooted by and yanking away the teeth.

Dr. Lorenzo rolled his eyes impatiently as he packed up his bag and EKG apparatus. "Okay, you asked for it, Chaz. Five hundred cc's of crystal meth, two hundred cc's of pure caffeine, a four-hundred-milligram mix of epinephrine and theophylline, and six liquified No-Doz gel-caps. Are you satisfied? Bye."

Gone.

When the door slammed behind him, Lydia testified, "I feel *great.*"

Well, right now all I really wanted to do was rage against the *Sentinel-Argus* and that right-wing theocratic tub of lard, Edna Poddubny, who refused to give us ink. But, after I'd reinserted her partial, all Lydia felt like talking about was death and dying.

"If I croak before the election," she said, lighting a cigarette, "don't forget to plant me out back in the Phistic Copper feeding grounds. Then, even if we lose the vote, it'll be hell for those rascals to get legal permission to disrupt a sacred burial site for their rotten road."

Yeah yeah, sure, okay—impatiently I promised. "Now: do you realize that Edna Poddubny just—"

"No undertakers, either, no embalming, no coffin—I don't want Manjo to touch me."

I gave her my solemn word. "But tell me, Lydia, do you think the *Sentinel-Ar*—"

"It's okay if Father Benny Wombat helps to dig my grave, but don't you *dare* let him speak. I *hate* religion."

"*De acuerdo*, ma'am. But listen to what just happened over at the newspaper. Edna—"

"No tombstone, either." Lydia yawned. "If they don't know where I'm interred they can't declare a Scenic Right-of-Way and run the highway by twenty feet to the west of me."

I said yes. I reassured her on everything. I vowed to carry out her final esoteric wishes. Then I shook my fist at the firmament, calling down the wrath of God upon Edna Poddub—

Lydia fell asleep—*plop!*—and her face landed in a plate full of half-eaten marzipan tofu.

Kelly blew on her fingernails, then held them up to the light, assessing the effect. At the same time she asked, "Whattayou think of this, Chuck?" and read aloud to me a new Voice of the Butterfly blast from her notebook:

"Jack Bannerman has walked those idiots at the Planning Commission around all the pitfalls that could sabotage airport expansion. He has taught Sam Clendennon and the Town Council how to install a lodger's tax and how to float obligation bonds to pay the town's share of expansion. First State Savings and Loan also drafted all the necessary changes in zoning regulations and stole seven one-hundred K muni-zips at a rate two points below market value for the city to fund the industrial park. Jack forced Sam C. to wheedle for the Electric Co-op's low startup fees on all FAGERBAN industries, and he got the village tied into the State Investment Council's venture fund. In short, our municipality is being run by a plutocratic werewolf crazed for the smell of blood."

"Sounds logical to me, Kelly," I said.

"It *is* logical, love bunny," she replied. "So let's wake up Methuselah and record her."

I CAUGHT Randy Featherstone midway through a homage to Jello Biafra, Patti Smith, and Ziggy Pop. As soon as he spotted me, the lad jumped up, ripping off his headphones, and yanked open a desk drawer, removing a large silver Ukrainian cross that he feverishly jabbed at me, all the time barking, "Get back in your coffin, Charley! I already gave at the blood bank! Your Mom wants you to call home in Transylvania!"

"Very funny, Randy." I ignored his puerile littleboy theatrics. "Take a deep breath, exhale slowly." And I reached into my knapsack for our latest tape.

"I'm not kidding, dude," he persisted. "You're a flake, I hate you. Now make tracks, catch a wave, boogie on before you destroy my life, wreck my marriage, and alienate my kids from me."

"Yo, get a *grip*," I ordered, dropping the tape onto his desk and parking myself in a dilapidated canvas director's chair across from that gangly redheaded ranter, who had on a garish polyester shirt, highwater chino pants, and S.K.-style Doc Martens.

"No, no," Randy continued, waving the cross as he paced angrily back and forth. "You're poison in this town, Charley Mac. Because of you lousy monkey wrenchers, everybody hates my guts. They're blaming *me* for those billboards."

"We're not monkey wrenchers," I said. "We're liberation ecologists."

"Fuck you. At school the principal actually called Tiffany a 'communist.' One of Jack and Lu Ann Bannerman's kids called Jamie a 'gothic nerd' in the cyber lounge and almost put out his eye with a paper clip fired by a rubber band. Johnny Batrus has stopped me ten times for non-existent traffic violations even though he knows I'm only a puppet of that flaming rich idiot and if I wanna earn my dimes I gotta do the crimes. It's all because of you, smartass, and your incendiary political diatribes on 'The Voice of the Butterfly.' So hurry up and get scarce, bud, before somebody sees us together and thinks we're skinning babies alive in here and eating their private parts!"

He backed up against a poster of Mookie Dirigible in his skin-tight Styroflex codpiece-condom outfit (the one that, coincidentally, had caught fire during a freebasing gangbang on Jello Biaffra's yacht in Bolinas), and continued to wiggle his cross at me in a threatening manner.

Right before my eyes he was turning into a Trans-Neptunian Object. I said, "Randy, you are *seriously* overreacting."

"No way, dude. We had to destroy all the pot plants in our greenhouse because the SWAT copter hovered over it three days hand running playing John Philip Sousa tunes from loudspeakers."

I reminded him, "But Mr. Griffith said it was okay. We both heard him with our own ears."

"Sure he said it was okay, but he hadn't *listened* to that crazy dame."

"You tried, but he cut you off."

"One privilege of being the boss," according to Randy, "is you get to be temperamental, indecisive, and unfair and nobody can hassle you for *any* of it."

"They didn't ax Tiffany, did they?"

"No, but Jesus. There were veiled threats and hostile innuendos. We're scared."

"If they fire Tiffany, Farragut Wallaby will take her case for free."

"*That* geriatric bumblefuck?"

I said, "What are we all becoming in this country, people or mice?"

"Is that a serious question?"

"You better believe it."

He squeaked. Then he said, "Gimme some cheese."

"Not funny."

"Wasn't meant to be."

"We can't give in," I said. "How could we live with ourselves if we did?"

"Whattayou mean 'we,' white man?"

"Did he fire *you?*" I asked.

"Not yet," Randy said tightly. "But there's a menacing tone in his voice whenever we talk."

"Did he tell you not to run our ads?"

"No," Randy admitted glumly. "In fact, he said if I *didn't* play the ads I'd be fired. But I'm petrified. Tiffany is freaked O-U-fuckin-T. The kids are all on Zanex. It's a Catch-22 situation."

"It'll never happen," I said. "Have a little faith, man. This is an autumn of miracles. The underdogs shall rise and smite their ruthless masters. Bo Hrbyk will classify half the loans at First State and topple FAGERBAN. You and me both, we'll be heroes, I promise. It's a lock."

"A 'lock'?" he muttered cantankerously. "Oh goody. You mean like when you promised to shut down the Suicide Canyon Ski Resort for good eleven years ago by invoking the infamous Development Congestion Act? Or like when you organized a boycott and picketing of Wal-Mart for unfair labor practices and only four people showed up—you, Kelly, Father Benny, and Farragut Wallaby? Or like when you passed around that recall petition for Sam Clendennon three years ago that amassed the incredible total of eleven signatures, six of which were disqualified by Thelma Weed at the county clerk's office because they were deceased? But this time it's a 'lock'?"

Randy stopped. He took the deep breath I had suggested earlier. Then he exhaled slowly. And after that he said:

"Hey, Charley, you know what? *Your mother wears combat boots.*"

A CTUALLY, THE WAY that a pro gets real ink is not through flashy pyrotechnics, radio blurbs, or big spender payoffs. It's by working The People, the true electorate, the backbone of the nation, one-on-one on their home turf, down in the trenches of Democracy.

Yes, you go door-to-door, you pound the shoe leather, you ring the chimes, you talk to *everybody* in person about the real issues they care about. You press the flesh in the white-collar neighborhoods; you press it in the ghetto. Nobody is unimportant; you leave no stone unturned, and that's where the game is won or lost. Three yards and a cloud of dust, again and again and again. It's not glamorous, it's not fun, it doesn't make the six-o'clock news. In fact, it's tedius and it's boring, but it gets the job done right.

That's how John Elway finally won a Super Bowl, it's how Nelson Mandela freed South Africa, and it would be how the Butterfly Coalition defeated Prop X, by God. Because the truth is, in this day and age: *There are no shortcuts to glory.*

So on Thursday, October nineteenth, I took a sick day off, Xeroxed a bunch of Vote "NO!" flyers, and hit Willow Road like a one-man canvassing army determined to win the heart and mind of every registered voter on my street.

I started with Tom Florissant, the real estate agent who lived next door to my shabby trailer in a three-story late-Scarsdale pre-fab

Tudor-style monstrosity surrounded by four acres of Kentucky blue grass, apple trees, a frog pond, a massive weeping willow, three Shetland ponies, a croquet court, and flower beds that seemed to have been nuked by enough chemicals to make "an entire desert bloom."

Get a load of this bucolic scene:

While Pachelbel's *Canon* issued from the open living room window, Mildred Olney-Florissant, on her knees in a batch of peonies, was working peat moss and organic plant food into the ground. Tom, astride his noisy Lawnboy, and dressed in a lavender Patagonia shirt, beige Dockers, and white Air Jordans, waved. One of their kids, Melanie, reclined on yellow cushions in a pink rowboat in mid frog pond, making folded paper origami peace doves for her class project on avoiding nuclear war. The other brat, Melissa, sat cross-legged in their sandbox typing a French theme on a laptop for her Montessori kindergarten independent study.

What was missing from this idyll? How about two exploding hand grenades, a clip of AK-47 bullets going off, or a lunch bag for me to barf in?

I gave Mildred a flyer. She was wearing a wide-brimmed straw sun hat, a plastic Happy apron, and tight little gardening gloves covered by stippled rubber goosebumps (for better trowel gripping).

Tom drove over, killed the engine, and perused my flyer like a high-school shop teacher inspecting a badly made wooden teacup display holder. At length he said, "Charley, you can't stop progress."

"But it's your *home*." I gestured at the suave landscaping, at their child in a rowboat, at the countless store-bought bird feeders whereon starlings, grosbeaks, Lewis's woodpeckers, magpies, siskins, and a few chittering juncos disported.

Mildred said, "With the state settlement we can buy a place in Nob Hill twice this size. The tax breaks alone would be phenomenal."

"But that's not country living," I protested vehemently. "It's like a phony AstroTurf world of hot tubs, swimming pools, burglar alarms, and restrictive covenants prohibiting ponies and bird feeders, where everyone is insulated from everybody else, and they all get cancer from the radiation off burglar alarm systems, and nobody can sleep at night because of the high-end electrical Bug Zappers frying insects by the billions."

They stared at me with an exaggerated puzzled mien.

My next foray involved the herbal proctologist, Ethan Chambers, who lived in a rambling old adobe (converted to passive solar) with his wife, Linda, and two boys, Amos and Andrew, who were shooting baskets when I arrived. They had identical blond cowlicks, blue eyes, ski-jump noses, freckles, and recessed Peter Gammons chins. Their dog, Camus, a snotty little terrier type, went apoplectic at my arrival, and a peacock on the lawn started shrieking.

"Hi," I said to the boys. "Are your folks around?"

"You mean like a donut?" sneered Amos, whom I took to be about thirteen, going on four. His younger brother, Andrew, snickered. "Mom used to be round, but the spa and Sen Sen took care of that."

Clever fellows. Tweedle-dimwit and Tweedle-fuckface. I rang the doorbell. After a long wait, Ethan opened up wearing a Cinzano bicycling jersey, black Lycra padded cycle shorts with appropriate crotch bulge, and well-worn, comfy, alligator slip-ons. Before I could even say "Howdy," he twisted his head, calling back to Linda:

"Guess what, dear? *It's Chicken Little!*"

One hour later I knocked on the gorgeous oaken baronial door of the Abe and Charity Gingivitis House Beautiful. It took them a while to answer, so I had time to case the joint: well-manicured lawn, of course; a sprinkler system quietly burbling; numerous ornamental shade trees flaunting fantastically radiant autumn plumage; two well-groomed Appaloosas in the corral; a concrete birdbath that would've looked swell on an angel-bedecked mausoleum; a white iron flagpole atop which flapped a mint-condition Old Glory; and five cars in the driveway (including a Blazer, a Scout, a Karmen Ghia, and a Tracker) whose bumper stickers ran a typical gamut: FREE TIBET . . . NO NUKES . . . PRO CHOICE . . . GIVE PEACE A CHANCE. . . .

When Charity opened the door her face fell into one of those *Oh dear there's dog doodoo on the stoop* looks, then she smiled politely.

"Hiya, Charley. Come on in. Abe!—guess what dropped by? A THREE-POUND SPIDER MONKEY!"

We reclined on the back patio surrounded by empty humming-bird feeders Charity had not yet put away for winter. Several enthusiastic Corgis kept bouncing around stupidly, a real nuisance. Their names were Gerald, Damian, and Lilith. An odd-looking frazzled bird was wading in the goldfish pond, nibbling at invisible insects. Their ten-year-old, Lars, sat on a large plastic Indian motorcycle replica, pretending to drive it. "*Brrrm!*" he said. "*Brrrm! Brrrm! Brrrm!*" The kid had on a Shalom Mozzerella soccer uniform and some kind of Pokémon helmet sporting silver wings and a wee erect penis. He seemed troglodytically pale and his nose was running. Charity chain-smoked Virginia Slims as we talked.

"It won't happen," Charity said. "You can't mess around with private property—"

As I headed north on foot, an incredible thing happened. Lu Ann Bannerman's emerald green Lexus convertible drew even, then braked, and Jack's youthful trophy wife herself motioned me over. Lu Ann had honey blond hair, a golfing tan to die for, and perfectly aligned radiant white teeth. Politely, this paean to health, wealth, and pedigree tipped down her expensive sunglasses: Wow, what provocative azure eyes! Her accent was solid Princess Di:

"Hello, Charley. Keep up the good work."

Good-bye.

Our beloved transvestite stockbroker and owner of WPNX, Tristan Griffith, was wearing a Dolly wig, a double string of pearls, a silk flapper dress, and blue and white pumps while hosing down his enormous sheepdog, Beowulf, with a cannister of Canine Flea Demise attached to the nozzle of an ordinary garden hose. Welder's goggles protected Beowulf's eyes. In the background, Tristan's elegant modern ranch dwelling simmered confidently in the shadow of large yet carefully pruned peachleaf willows, aspens, and silvertip poplar trees, some of whose yellow October leaves were sprinkled across the rich green lawn with celestial equanimity. When I showed up,

Mr. G. twisted off the water spigot and strode manfully over across his springy Kentucky blue rug. His cheeks were lightly rouged, his eyebrows plucked and painted on—very Japanese—and his lipstick hue might've been called Cherries Jubilee.

"It's like this, Charles," Tristan explained. "Contrary to the message of your 'Voice of the Butterfly' philippics, we live in a system with built-in checks and balances. There are building codes and extraterritorial rules and neighborhood zoning regulations. All this land is governed by unencroachable covenants and usage permits and historical precedents—"

Stupidity personified in those dumb goggles, Beowulf sloshed over and sat beside his master. Tristan patted him—*patty-pat-pat*—on the top of his massive head. The spoiled beast whimpered lovingly, and the broker squeaked intimately in return.

"What will you do if they condemn *your* house?" I asked.

"Invest my winnings in industrial park companies like Genetevil, Bioguard, and Ghetto Guns."

"Suppose the Butterfly Coalition comes out on top?"

"I win a hundred-dollar bet with Manjo."

I wisely counted to five, then gently complained, "You're not taking any of this seriously."

He leaned forward, eyes shining mischievously. "It's all a big cosmic game, cowboy: stocks, bonds, international commerce, Bo Hrbyk, S & L defalcations, Peter Lithgow. It's silly, stupid, and wonderful. It really doesn't matter what happens, who wins, who loses, we all die anyway. History is a big farce related by a befuddled clown involving a bunch of human ants no more intelligent than aphids and parameciums. Clarence Fagerquist threatened to destroy my radio station? I begged him to go ahead, so he backed off. You see, it takes a specific lack of revenue to generate more lack of revenue if you wish to turn a profit by deducting the loss. I depend on lousy ratings, but if they're too bad I'll have to fire Randy, and—"

Gobbledegook . . . it's why those people always win . . . because nobody but *nobody* understands what they are saying. You *think* you understand, because of the rational way they speak, or because you're too timid to admit you're so retarded that you don't exactly understand (but feel you'll lose your competitive edge if they know this). But they know that what they are saying is gibberish and so you can't possibly understand, and if you don't admit that, then you are playing right into their hands. Weighed against Obfuscating Language, the Hydrogen Bomb *pales* as a weapon.

OKAY, ON TO the ghetto.

Where, weighed against hydrogen bombs *and* obfuscating language, poverty came out on top, hands down, every time.

For twenty-five bucks, Miranda Satan, bless her apolitical heart, was willing to go with me in the Buick on a sullen overcast Friday afternoon with a touch of panic in the smoggy air. Luther's bald moll had eyes that were lime colored and drear. The rings in her nose had become infected. She wore a lowcut dishwater gray minidress (with spaghetti straps) and black engineer boots. This delicate waif had discarded her pacifier and was chain-smoking Camel cigarettes as we entered Suicide City's Kurdistan, a ten-square-block area dedicated to misery and shattered dreams.

Imagine the aftermath of Hurricane Mitch in Honduras, but change the name to Hurricane Class Warfare. Every town (big or small) in America has one, the oil that lubricates the empire, the Red Hook, the Strawberry Mansion, the South Chicago, or Watts. Dumping grounds for the uneducated hoi polloi, the jobless peasants, the Asians, the blacks, the Dominicans, the fodder that keeps our opulent society humming, the little people who kill the chickens and disembowel the cattle and pick the cotton and work in the sweatshops and wash the dishes, scrub the toilets, mop floors, and buy all the cigarettes. The devastated landscape they inhabit is NOT an accident of history, nor an act of God, nor the careless ruin caused by an inferior people. Rather it is the deliberate creation of an economic system that depends on a disenfranchised proletariat to provide the cheap labor upon which all profit is generated.

Everything in our picturesque minighetto had been burned: the grass, the wooden fences, the old porches on the row houses that cost eight hundred a month to rent despite a leaky roof, monoxide fumes from the faulty heaters, asbestos ceilings, and backyards turned to swamp from the overflowing septic systems. Steel bars against all windows kept out the riffraff, though most of the window-panes were broken. Boarded-up squatter's tenements and crack houses faced the street like Halloween horror masks of witches, were-wolves, and brides of Chuckie. Torched autos sank onto their rims against the curbs like tanks and other military vehicles populating desert terrain after a lopsided war. Weeds, broken glass, and toxic noxious detritus littered most "yards" where ravenous pit bulls, scarred German shepherds, and Doberman pinschers with muti-lated ears tugged against their chains. Bullet holes pockmarked the walls, and trees along the streets had long ago been hacked apart for firewood. Filthy mattresses oozing garbles of bloody ticking lay about at random, and every surface, gutted auto, and tree trunk had been garishly tagged by gang enthusiasts. To boot, rancid garbage clogged the gutters because city trash haulers feared entering the cesspool on collection days without police protection, which our town "could not afford."

"Buy me a tank and four fifty-caliber machine guns," Johnny Batrus had once shouted at a council meeting, "and I'll *guarantee* you can collect their garbage."

Somebody fired a MAC-10: *Brrrraaap!* Somebody answered with an assault rifle: *tchak-a-tchak-a-tchak!* I asked Miranda, "Are you packing any heat?" She answered, "It's not about weapons, dude, it's about karma. If they fuck with us it's our own fault. If you screwed up in a past life shit will eat you alive in this one. Kosovo is getting what it deserves."

Thank *you*, Miranda, you chipper little chipmunk.

In Tijerina Park, in the middle of our petite slum, heroin addicts were scattered around in the twisted attitudes of shrapnel victims. Directly before us small ganja fanatics sat in a circle in a kiddie chatter pod passing a pipe while numbly thumbpunching Gameboys. Strung-out mommas reclined on park benches breast-feeding their cute little AIDS babies while off to the side some really fly druggies did deals with a bunch of fourth graders wearing Shaq jackets and Michael paraphernalia. Mexican flags dangled off car aerials and shattered tree branches like white flags of surrender. Peppy music featured mariachis, rancheras, and Tex Mex, including—most notably— cumbias by the late great Selena.

I steered to the curb at the park. Who knows why, but the ghetto always made me a trifle glum. Nevertheless, I was born to attack, so I hefted a batch of leaflets and tiptoed forth while Miranda remained seated in the Buick.

"Are you coming with me or what?" I asked, alertly casting about like a nervous sparrow on a bird feeder for predatory animals assessing my vulnerability.

"I don't think so," Miranda answered quickly. "I am so *not* into this kind of anxiety issue. Frankly, this also looks like a low return on my investment opportunity. I can't process. My emotional NASDAQ just cratered."

A '52 Olds lowrider with no suspension, a sunscreen on the windshield, and an elaborate Virgin of Guadalupe decorating the trunk inched past us at .000175 miles per hour. The wasted tecato inside clutching the chain steering wheel was smoking a Kansas City bomber. A strangled Beanie Baby hung from the rearview mirror on a red rosary. The ruca beside him was so good-looking she made you want to commit suicide.

I entered the park and casually glanced toward pigeons pecking at a discarded fetus half-wrapped in a soiled Pamper. Beyond some blasted-apart elm trees I could actually see to the distant smoky summit of Nob Hill where gaudy pennants flapped gaily from the pre-fab turrets, parapets, and camouflaged guard towers of the Fagerquist's polyester chateau.

I said, "Um, hello . . . can anybody hear me?"

On that cue, a consummate cholo, Eddie "The Ferret" Ulibarri, pushed aside a manhole cover and climbed up into The World about twenty feet in front of me. He plucked a strand of kelp off his shoulder and lit a Kool Filter King. Then he coughed his guts up, spitting clots of brackish blood onto the ground.

"Hey ese, what's happening, bro'? What are you mutha fuckers doin' in my hood?"

"I brought leaflets," I said. "We're organizing against the highway bypass. We need everyone to vote 'No!' on Prop X."

"Well why didn't you *say* so?" Eddie remarked sensitively. He dropped his cigarette and crushed it out. "Thanks so much for stopping by." Then he shoved the needle on *his* gobbledegook meter over to the Jackpot category:

"I bet I can deliver every eligible vote in the barrio for you guys. In fact, me and the homeboys were just sitting around last night rapping about it, man. We *love* that mariposa. We're tired of the systematic suppression of our rightful heritage to a decent life, good education, health care, and honest jobs that would allow us to earn an honest dollar at fair and equitable exchange rates. And your butterfly is the *answer*, cuate, the Big Kahuna, *El Lobo Grande*. You're not going to believe this, but already I've set up an electoral organization with block committees and drivers to ferry the elderly to the polls and—"

A ND SO TO HELL with door-to-door. We *needed* a shortcut to glory! That's why I organized another crucial Butterfly Coalition meeting toot sweet on the Plaza at the Snort N' Fodder. But I arrived late, much to my chagrin, because during the interim Kelly had been sitting on a stool yakking with Luther and watching game four of the World Series on a TV over the bar while she had annihilated about a dozen Kahlúas and cream. Where did she get the money?—who knows. Where does *anybody* in America get the money? (Drugs . . . day trading . . . grave robbery.) By the time Susan Delgado and I arrived pushing Lydia in her wheelchair, my estranged helpmeet was so many sheets to the wind that a tobacco-colored anaerobic froth had gathered on her lips like grasshopper vomit on a pair of slugs.

I halted inches from her titubantic nose. What was I supposed to do: Kvetch? Threaten her? Find another scriptwriter at this late date? The inevitability of dysfunction in alcoholics and their enablers is a law Newtonian in its predictability. By rote I said, "I told you, Kelly, no drinking at meetings. This is a serious campaign. You're screwing up worse than Hillary Clinton with health care."

While I prattled, Kelly monitored my lips like an illiterate deaf person trying to read them. Then, to make the interaction between all of us more interesting, Luther fed an electric charge to the neon chip balanced precariously on his shoulder:

"Pop, I thought the mark of a true revolutionary was to have patience with the less advanced members of the proletariat."

Oops, am I *hearing* correctly?

Yes, that was a bit of a flip-flop for the lad, so I ignored him: Obviously, Luther had imbibed his fair share, also. But I'll admit, I did congratulate myself: *A brilliant idea, Charles, to have a meeting in a bar with these gonzo retards.*

Enunciating clearly as if for foreign children, I said, "C'mon, gang, let's all go sit at that table."

We went there. Naturally, Kelly missed her chair, crashing as noisily to the floor as a fat tapir breaking through the rattan mat over a large punjii pit. Luther and Susan scrambled to her aid, grabbing arms, hands, and ankles (while two of the cameras around Susan's neck bashed Kelly in the face). They lurched her erect and lodged her properly on the seat puffing noisily and with a major nosebleed.

"You okay?" Luther asked solicitously, yanking thirty napkins from the dispenser to stem the flow of blood. "You're not hurt?"

I said, "She's too drunk to be hurt. It's like Jell-O landing in a vat of talcum powder. Let's call this meeting to order. Our main problem is: What's the next step? Frankly, we need to do something *radical*. We keep attacking them, but they're too smart to fight back. They ignore the radio program. Edna won't print a thing about us that Susan writes or photographs. The Man on the Street is a putz. We've got to grab headlines immediately by pulling another outrageous stunt that's sensational but nonviolent, of course."

They stared at me.

I said, "Kelly, do you think you could hack into FAGERBAN's Internet Web sites and plant a Butterfly virus to derail their entire cyber network?"

Kelly said, "No."

"Waitress," Lydia clucked obnoxiously at Ripple Mongiello, who ignored her: "I want a Dewar's on the rocks."

"Hey, pipe down," said a fellow patron at a nearby table: Luther's boss, Moe Pelletier, the manager at Burger Boy and a real bubonic fruitcake. Imagine Nick Nolte in a flattop haircut with biceps the size of ostrich eggs and the attitude problem of Teddy Roosevelt charging up San Juan Hill. According to Susan Delgado, Moe's deaf wife, Swoozie, was another of Jack Bannerman's extracurricular tidbits.

Moe's cell phone rang and he answered it.

Kelly wiggled her eyebrows sideways, saying fawningly, "Don't look now, but guess who just swaggered in?"

All our heads turned as state representative candidate William Watrous and three of his frisky Topless Au Go Go girls falling out of peek-a-boo Spandex bodysuits—Christie LaRue, Rusti Husky, and Sally VaVoom—leaned their brand new butterfly nets against the wall and pulled up chairs at a table across the smoky room.

Each bimbo displayed a William Watrous "Right to Work" sash slanted across her chest like an ammo bandolier. They all had tangled Farah Fawcett hair and deliciously prominent breasts. W.W. himself could have been the late great Sonny Bono doing a Wayne Newton impression.

Lydia perked up, raised her voice, and shook a fist at Billy. "Look what the cat dragged in, people: the Smut King of Suicide City."

"Yeah," Luther said, desultorily waggling his right fist in the air: "*Smut King. Smut King.*"

The dapper slimeball smiled at us, tipped his head politely, then called over, "You better stifle it, dipshits, before you choke on your own invective. Those Butterfly radio spots give me a hernia from laughing."

For some reason that irritated Kelly, and after casting a servile petition for approval at me, she said, "Hey, Billy boy, I understand that Topless Au Go Go is in receivership and your wife just filed for divorce on the grounds of mental vacuity."

"Yeah," Luther echoed, "*mental vacuity.*"

The lighthearted Smut King cupped an ear: "Come again, you cirrhotic lush puppies?"

"Write this down for our next VOB," Kelly ordered me, reeking of a desperate need for my esteem. Then she addressed that bilious rodent across the room in a brazen voice: "The way I heard it, W2, she got tired of changing your incontinence diapers and fed up with heating your Pablum."

Though you could tell he was miffed, William Watrous feigned mirthful disbelief to his obsequious concubines. "What the heck is that loopy boozehound talking about?"

Not even hiding his face from Moe Pelletier, Luther said, "She's talkin' about *you*, pond scum."

Then Kelly fired another excellent salvo:

"My lawyer, Rollie Cathcart, says her lawyer, Helen O'Shea, said the last time you got it up for conjugal relations Herbert Hoover was Secretary of Commerce under Coolidge."

The candidate laughed: "Ha ha ha. Kelly, I hate to say it, but your dementia has become life threatening. It's time for a brain-marrow transplant."

Kelly's face reddened. "*I* read in *Newsweek* last week, W.W., that somebody said when the price of ignorance goes up to forty dollars a barrel they wanted drilling rights on your head."

Luther croaked, "Yeah, *forty dollars a barrel.*"

Moe Pelletier said, "Hey, button it you wild turkey before I button it for you!"

My wife leaned toward me and came up with another of her awesome proposals. "We need ink, Charles? I'll get you ink. Suppose I suddenly jumped up, unleashed a bloodcurdling scream, and hurled myself across the room at those four extraterrestials, tipping over the table into their laps, then grabbed the butterfly nets and scrammed— *then* would you love me again? Could I come home for good?"

I gave her a hard, mystified once-over. "Get real, Kelly. We don't want to engender publicity by committing either murder or suicide. This is a pacifist operation."

She pouted. "But you ordered Luther to cut down those billboards."

"Billboards, sweetie. Paltry pieces of wood and paper, not human flesh and blood."

"But he'd probably sue me," Kelly insisted, still eager to please. "Can't you see the headlines? PURVEYOR OF PORN SUES HOME-LESS DRUNK."

Implacable Lydia cried, *"I want my goddam Dewar's!"*

Ripple Mongiello said, "Hold your horses, you old bag, I only got two hands."

Susan begged, "Oh please, *do it, Kelly*. God, what a scoop that would make. I'll give you ten dollars."

Kelly glared at her: "Oh sure, why not? I get killed, then you wind up in bed with my hubby."

Susan twitched her kooky features in my direction, appalled and blushing guiltily. "That's not even remotely true," she protested.

Kelly said, "Yes it is. You're always hitting on Charley. The minute I drop dead the two of you will be all over each other like a pair of garden slugs on a squash plant."

"Kelly," I said, "give it a rest. You're overstepping my boundaries."

"*You* give it a rest, butt monkey. I'm tired of always being the bad guy."

"Yeah," Luther said, "she's tired of being the bad guy."

Lydia hollered, "I WANT MY GODDAM DEWAR'S!"

At that Kelly suddenly kicked back her chair, screamed, "EEEEEYYYYYAAAAAHHH!" and took off like a professional full-back, bulldozing tables aside, stiff-arming chairs and patrons this way and that, sweeping setups and ashtrays right and left with her pinwheeling arms. She landed upon the astonished candidate and his T & A retinue before they could react, gripped their table and explosively inverted it atop all four scrambling victims, then she snatched the butterfly nets, and, pulling an ostentatious exit, she caprioled, entrechated, and jetéd gracefully across all the wreck-age, then leapfrogged out the door . . . right into the path of Moe Pelletier, ex-Marine DI, karate black belt, and a right-winger more intransigent than Jesse Helms.

When Moe tackled Kelly, they tumbled end-over-end down a flight of stairs (with Susan in hot pursuit clicking pictures), banged through the Entrance door, and wound up spread-eagled in the gutter. Kelly tried to rise, but Moe—no chivalrous cavalier he—punched out her lights, then whistled at a passing cruiser. Johnny Batrus slammed on his power brakes and was out the door, manacles flapping, before you could say José Perovich. Kelly tried to get up, lost her balance . . . and the law won.

"Charley, help!" she cried.

Yeah, sure—*when the Cubs win a pennant.*

YOU CAN BET THAT Edna just laughed at Susan's graphic pictures of the William Watrous bimbo meltdown and flipped them into the photo morgue.

Meanwhile, elsewhere in a smoke-filled boardroom, William Watrous (and Clarence Fagerquist and Manjo Poddubny and Jack Bannerman) was growling, "*Enough!* Stop them butterflies before they kill again. Ax that asshole—*now.*"

Two days later, I'm seated at a library conference table with Pamela Avery and her ex-husband, Gary, talking about their dyslexic child, Lorrie, whose progress in our literacy program leaves much to be desired, when John Spoffard pokes his sorry *cabeza* into the room . . . and my life collapsed.

I said, "Don't tell me, Mr. Spoffard, lemme guess. We're running a little over here and nobody's at the front desk?"

"Actually, Charles, Mary is holding down the fort. Nevertheless, something is going on in the rest room which I feel requires your immediate attention."

"Oh no—*Kelly again?*" I cried, already in motion scooting past that well-groomed geek. "She's supposed to be in jail for assault and battery." I clocked my knee on a table leg and yelped.

First, I pressed my ear against the door: It sounded as if dolphins were playing water polo in there.

Then I banged my knuckles against the oak wood. A voice called out, *"Adelante, cabrón!"* Gingerly, I twisted the handle and vast green fumes of marijuana smoke boiled forth, almost making me giddy. I pushed the door ajar just wide enough to slip in sideways, then shut it quickly and punched the lock.

Groan.

Kelly was naked, all wrinkled and blubbery, taking a sponge-bath. Her heavy horribly out-of-shape body was puffy and saggy and pimpled and bruised all over: She stunk. A joint the size of a small pickerel hung off her lower lip and she had one foot up on the toilet seat while rubbing her thigh with a loofah. Two inches of water eddied across the floor; the towel dispenser was empty; the waste-basket overflowed with crumpled paper.

That did it; I hit bottom, no bounce. She looked like a plane wreck in a bucket of circus clowns.

I said, "God. Damn you. Kelly."

"Hola, Chuck. Long time no see." She puckered her lips and had the sheer effrontery to blow me a kiss.

"How much did they pay you, Kelly?" I asked wearily. "Fifty bucks? A hundred dollars? At what price do you sell your soul these days? Who went your bail, Clarence Fagerquist? Cover yourself up, for God's sake."

Her beautiful green-gray eyes awoke for a moment, gazing upon me with such naked Irish melancholy that they actually caused a crack in my hardened shell . . . but only a minor crack, easily ignored, like a tiny flaw in a melting ice sheet atop a bottomless lake.

I said, "Kelly, the Snort attack was stupid, but this is worse . . . I'm sorry, I give up . . . good-bye."

Urgently, she said, "I heard last night that Peter Lithgow is under investigation for taking kickbacks to quash our endangered species application."

"Big deal, Lucille." I stepped into the hall.

A frantic note entered her grating voice: "Wait. I also heard that Clarence set up an REIT to control the shopping center leases, but

Manjo forced him and Sam to sell most of their stock to Jack to meet loan payments at Eagle S & L when the Fed complained Manjo had insufficient reserves five months ago. Bo Hrbyk is *on* the trail."

"Drunken twaddle, sugar. All you sordid losers deserve each other."

And feeling nauseous—or do I mean nauseated?—I slogged back to the front desk to wait dumbly for the shadow of God to fall across my green blotter and the Friends of the Library Rolodex. It wouldn't be the first time Kelly had destroyed my life. Frankly, I didn't care anymore. Sooner or later fatigue *has* to become a factor. I mean, your arm can get so tired from beating a dead dog that it finally just plain falls off, qué no?

Mary said, "I hate to say this—"

"Then don't say it."

But it happened soon enough.

John Spoffard cleared his throat, and then cleared his throat again. Evidently, the creep had decided no more shilly-shallying.

"Charley, I don't know how to say this, but we can't go on any longer together. There's some real work-related decorum issues that need to be addressed here."

I closed my eyes and bit my lip. He paused, swallowing loudly four times, and shuffled his feet, cowering.

"You know it's got to be done," he whimpered sadly. "This is a public institution and we must have the rule of law at all times and at all costs."

He actually had the brass balls to add, "This hurts me more than it's going to hurt you."

Next, in his most wussified, apologetic, and puling voice, my boss said, "Please understand, Charley, I've worked hard to get to where I am today. I've sacrificed, I have travailed long hours, and I've made this library a first-class institution we can all be proud of, right?"

Mary had put on her dark glasses and was pretending to read a report while Rome burned. Pusillanimous was too civilized a word for cowards of her ilk.

"I have a pension plan, Charley." The fraudulent, cozening bastard. "I have health care and a really good retirement. Nobody in their right mind would jeopardize those things, not even you and your damn monkey wrenchers, am I correct?"

"We're not monkey wrenchers, we're liberation ecologists."

Mary kept reading her report, pretending to be At Work.

"Charley," Spoffard moaned, clicking into his memorized speech, "you're the best librarian I ever had. You're intelligent, conscientious, imaginative, diligent, creative. Without you, I believe the library would collapse. Without you, I'm afraid *I* will collapse. I'll never find another person as adept at running the literacy program and our books for the blind recordings and at doing the payroll when it's due. And . . . and . . ."

"And *what?*" I finally interrupted, starting to seethe.

"And you're fired," he blurted in an appallingly squeaky voice. Then he actually revolved sideways in anguish as if a belligerent phantom had discharged a pistol into *his* gut.

I said, "Oh, come on, sir: Fart, and ease the pain." I checked out Mary, presuming at least now she would leap to my defense. But Mary was still on planet Mars, engrossed in her reading material . . . or maybe asleep behind those opaque shades.

Calm as the sea at dawn, I asked, "Who told you to do it—Jack Bannerman? Clarence? Manjo?"

He realized maybe I wasn't going to take it gracefully, and promptly summoned up all the cold-blooded reserves at his command:

"Charley, I'd appreciate it if you'd gather up your things and be out of here in fifteen minutes. I intuit that if you remain any longer something awful will happen to my library."

I suppose I could have stood up, pulled out the middle drawer of my desk, turned it upside down, and let it clatter to the floor in a noisy jumble of paper clips, Elmer's glue, pencils, pens, pencil sharpeners, rubber bands, notepaper, postage stamps, coins, paper dollars, and two million other sundry geegaws, gimcracks, and doodads crucial to my job.

Then it would have been fun to knock every last book off the reshelving cart—*Wham! Whack! Splat!*—watching them bounce at Spoffard's feet making him dance like a hapless cowpoke in one of those western movies where the guy with a six-gun is calling all the shots.

After that I could have tipped over my computer console (good-bye e-Butterfly@WinBIG.org) and yanked out all the rarely used card file drawers one by one, dumping them into my mess—*wheee!*

Then I could have toppled our eight video racks, punched my fist through a Styrofoam bulletin board (balanced on an aluminum easel) cluttered with announcements of library events, and kicked my metal wastebasket into Spoffard's shins—

But I am a pacifist, right? The sober one, the leader of the Butterfly Coalition: Commander McFarland. The Voice of Reason for a better life through democratic electoral politics. And, like, what *good* could I accomplish in jail from being sodomized around the clock by crazy biker chicks? I mean, I had *responsibilities*. And in his book on guerrilla warfare, Che says—

Mary never even looked up as I split.

B UT ELEANOR PODDUBNY sure did. In fact, she must have had a fucking intercom in her Plaza office connected directly to the library's front desk area two blocks away. Because the second fresh air struck my burning cheeks on Ledoux Street, Eleanor fell in step beside me positively radiant from gloating. Today's outfit included a maroon beret, an ecru jersey that grotesquely advertised her large-nippled nontits, a bizarre box-pleated miniskirt, black lace pantyhose, and elevated green clogs: the erotic cheerleader look from Bloodsucker U. It actually scared me stiff.

"I understand you've been cashiered," she crowed. "Pity. Is there anything I can do to help?"

Ignore her, Charles—she'll drown in her own venom.

"What will you do now without money to put food on the table—sell pencils on the Plaza? Donate blood? Give some poor bastard a kidney?"

At the Buick I opened the door and got in. Eleanor rested her elongated raptor fingers on her nonhips. The nails, painted silver, reminded me of my old pal Freddy Kruger, the scarfaced dream assassin in those Grade-B Elm Street gorathons, who just kept coming at you.

"I really enjoyed your pathetic attempt to destroy my billboards, Charley. And I love catching those Hans Christian Babcock economic fairy tales on Whip-Nix. I hear your wino wife writes the scripts. How do you two have sex these days—by parthenogenesis?"

To make matters even worse, when I turned the key I was *not* rewarded by the guttural roar of a healthy engine. Instead, I was greeted by a sickeningly stifled *click*.

"Oh, tut tut," Eleanor commiserated, backing away from the car. "I wonder how much a Wal-Mart battery will cost you today? It couldn't've happened to a nicer chump. See you later, alligator."

But as the bitch sauntered off toward the Plaza, I reached into my glove compartment and removed a .357 magnum loaded with steel-jacketed armor piercing slugs. My first shot spun her around like a top, the second bullet knocked her sideways into a telephone pole, the third lump of lead caught her in the groin and she doubled over, taking my fourth blast square in the center of her minuscule pea-sized brain. Eleanor went down hard, landing in garish explosions of blood, and my fifth projectile flipped her over into the gutter. A last shot made her body jump, lurch, and shiver in agonizing death throes. After that she lay very still, thoroughly deceased.

Then four salivating jackals, recent escapees from the local zoo, leaped upon Eleanor's body and tore it all to pieces in five minutes and twenty-one seconds, flat.

A misogynist fantasy by a pacifist saint? So what? I *came.*

THIS TIME I located Kelly in the parish hall of the First Baptist Church eating a cheese and peanut butter sandwich at a long picnic table surrounded by homeless derelicts participating in the Free Grub From Christ program sponsored by the church and its effervescent minister, Dagoberto Wapner, a thirty-two-year-old hellfire and damnation advocate who figured the shortest distance to a man's soul was through his stomach. A banner stretched across the north archway above this cheerful congregation said GOD WILL KILL YOU IF YOU DON'T REPENT. I had asked Luther to come along, but "I am so not into the homeless," he said, hungover and bleary eyed. "What *are* you into," I asked, "skinhead dorks like yourself who murder black people waiting at bus stops in Denver just for the racist hell of it?" Luther gave me one of those looks Kurt Cobain probably fired at Courtney Love after one of their happy nights of cocaine speedballs and heroin doobies . . . but he got in the car, yes he did.

We had convinced Miranda to tag along on the pretext that sometimes women can communicate better with other women than men can. Her bizarre outfit included condom earrings, cork wedgies, and a T-shirt with realistically painted big naked breasts on the front.

Kelly seemed totally anesthetized. You think when alcoholics you love hit bottom that it can't get any worse, but then you discover that every bottom is really a false bottom and there's another false bottom beneath it. The possibilities for entropy are unlimited. It's called the *other* 12 Step Program, where the only Higher Being is more booze. You start with a Desert Storm in Iraq, descend to a Chernobyl blowup, raise the ante to an Ebola plague across Africa, proceed to a Bhopal, India, chemical disaster, then Bosnia-Hercegovina and a Rwanda genocide. After a Kosovo slaughter comes the Greenhouse Effect, an Ozone Hole, a worldwide AIDS epidemic, then both polar ice caps melt, leading to . . . The Flood. Kelly looked as if she'd just passed Bosnia and was heading toward Rwanda. Her familiar features were melting from that misshapen face, and her once voluptuous body had become literally amorphous. One of her eyes was swollen shut, the one in the *middle*.

My wife was seated between two sorrowful inebriates, Sweeny Dancebow and Nicolai Aragón. All three of them seemed to have just survived a head-on collision with a Greyhound bus. Nicolai had a cleft palette, cauliflower ears, and a Dallas Cowboys cap on backward. You could tell by Sweeny's eyes that he was so hammered his liver had swollen to the size of a halibut. Both men were ex-ligtonite miners dying of fibroid lung disease.

Other winos, bums, losers, and luckless lumpen at the tables would've made a good crew of extras in a sadistic vagabond movie. Talk about rags, space cadet headgear, and numerous broken noses: *Last Exit to Suicide City*. With that much misery in America squashed beneath so many tons of wealth, you *know* the answer is revolution.

I squeezed onto the wooden bench between Nicolai and Kelly, who had cut her peanut butter and cheese sandwich into small chunks that she was fastidiously dunking into her cola before eating. Luther and Miranda gingerly positioned themselves on either side of Kelly. This may sound a trifle far-fetched, but my son, the heavy metal punk rock alienated thrasher child, felt *uncomfortable* among these tramps and deadbeats. Miranda glanced around like a precocious slothlike critter dazed by an acid flashback. On seeing us, Kelly shrank into an ashamed ball the size of a Chihuahua.

I said, "You fucked me good this time. You went too far. I'm pissed." Understand, this was just rote, this was meaningless. This was like Albanians buttfucking Serbs and vice versa simply because they were there: knee-jerk reactions. Pavlov in a box.

Kelly gurgled inaudibly and drooled.

"I ought to have you committed," I said. "I could probably do it. They'd lock you up in the state hospital for life. You'd die surrounded by lunatics."

She gurgled inaudibly and farted. Luther squirmed. Miranda lit a cigarette, wrong end, the filter, but so what?

"I can press charges," I threatened. "You're a menace. You drive your van loaded all the time. I don't know what is the matter with Johnny Batrus that he doesn't bag you for three DWIs a day. It's crazy that you get away with it while sober people like me are stopped repeatedly for totally bogus reasons."

Kelly gurgled inaudibly and sniffled. A burnt-out swabbie across the table in knitted cap and old Navy pea jacket wearing fingerless hunting mittens grinned at Luther minus all his teeth and winked: *Hiyuh, Froggie, pluck your magic twanger.* My son visibly flinched.

"You got me fired, Kelly, you fucker, you lame excuse for a piece of human meat. Why don't you drink yourself to death for once and for all and get it *over* with? Nobody cares. Nobody will miss you. Not even Mangus and the cats."

My wife gurgled inaudibly and decided to have another bite of peanut butter and cheese. She smelled awful. Luther actually reached up and . . . yes he did . . . he *pinched* his nostrils shut.

"You don't deserve to be in the Butterfly Coalition," I continued, sickened by her condition . . . and by my own. "You're a meaningless wart on the buttocks of humanity. You don't count anymore. You're a coward. You don't have any principles. You're weak and craven and slovenly. You're finished, Kelly. You're gonna die in the gutter and nobody will give a damn. Not even me."

She gurgled inaudibly. Luther had shut his eyes and balled up his hands into fists. The back of his neck was flushed in embarrassment and confusion.

Miranda said, "You shouldn't wail on her, dude. It's not righteous."

Yeah, yeah. "Look at you, Kelly," I droned unmercifully. "You could've had it all. You were talented, beautiful, brilliant, you had a husband and a stepson who loved you and you threw it all away— for what? For this, to become a mindless pig at the trough of humiliation at the bottom of hell in a huge pit of baboon excrement."

Nicolai shifted uncomfortably, coughed, and lit a cigarette. Sweeny finished his cola and began to tremble. Luther started to speak, then thought better of it. His cheeks were flaming red.

I couldn't help myself, I said, "Don't you have *any* pride, Kelly? Don't you have any human *feeling?* Don't you even *care* what happens to the people who *love* you? Or what happens to this town? Or what happens to the *universe?* I gave you a chance to redeem yourself, and you've written some brilliant Voice of the Butterfly scripts, I'll admit. And you could've made a difference. We even could've gotten together again as a family. It wasn't too late to pull yourself up by the bootstraps and stop this grotesque slide toward oblivion. But oh no, not Kelly McFarland, you're not strong enough, you don't give a damn, you have no loyalties, you sell your soul to the highest bidder and for a price that not even a destitute peddler in Calcutta would stoop to. I can't write those scripts, Luther can't either, nor can Susan Delgado, but do you even give a rat's ass? Oh no, not you, not Ms. *Under the Volcano* who used to be as riotously alive and sexy and funny as a dancing golden monkey in the top of a royal palm tree. Fuck. Look at you now. Working for the enemy. What did you spend it on, their bribe—a case of Mickey's? A gallon bottle of Wild Turkey? A twelve-pack of premixed whiskey sours in Michelob tulip bottles?"

Kelly gurgled inaudibly. All the homeless kept on eating in silence, gumming down their bland food, picking their noses with plastic fork tines, licking their paper plates voraciously.

Miranda said, "I don't mean to be, like, *obvious*, man, but you might catch more flies with money than with vinegar."

I said, "It's now only ten days until the election. We may be small, yet everybody in the Butterfly Coalition except you, Kelly, is working their fingers to the bone on behalf of a 'No!' to Prop X. We care about the future. But not you. You promised, you reneged, you copped out, you betrayed all of us, you betrayed our trust, you betrayed the environment, you betrayed every single principle that gives meaning to human life and sacrifice and that separates us from barbarians. And you can sit here in an alcoholic stupor and not even react like some kind of conscious, warm-blooded, thinking mammal with a conscience? I pity you, Kelly. I pity your broken heart." And then I couldn't help myself, I lost control and moaned, *"We haven't made love in two years and I'm lonely as a rock."*

That finally stirred a reaction. Crawling out of her trance like a white parasitic insect eating free of its host's dying body, Kelly twisted her head vaguely sideways and assessed me, her eyelids three quarters closed, her chapped lips puffy and bleeding under a herpes blister the size and shape of Africa. A large red scab glowed on her nose. Think of a mountain climber fresh off the higher slopes of Everest suffering from frostbite and oxygen deprivation.

"When do you need it by?" she croaked.

"ASAP. Tonight at the latest."

"You got a pen and anything edible to write on?"

I unzipped my knapsack, removing a notebook and a ballpoint. Opening the notebook in front of her, I placed the Bic between her palsied fingers.

"Will you love me again if I do this?" Kelly rasped without oomph or expectation. Lifting one crumpled puffy hand she brushed aside a greasy strand of hair with a jerky uncoordinated motion. Then she leaned over the notebook, clutching her pen like a studious six-year-old about to embark on a painful orthography lesson in the cursive mode. She hesitated a few seconds, studying the blank page. And then—haltingly—my terminally damaged wife began to write:

Because of the FAGERBAN project, Jack Bannerman is terribly overextended. Half his purchased liquidity is about to go sour. His past-due list is a mile long. Bo Hrbyk from the comptroller's office is starting an investigation of Jack's preferential loan policies. Jack has been putting up collateral on his own loans for the planned industrial park on the highway bypass. His pricing assumptions are way too high, compliments of T. Garth Radesovich and Casper Pilkington, sweetheart "yes" men if ever there were ones. Apparently, First State S & L is only a few weeks removed from a purchase and assumption if Prop X takes a flyer on November eighth. Half the paper in that jug resides in phony credit files—all the documentation exists in a total twilight zone. Most time deposits are set off against loans, making those loans virtually worthless. And not only that . . .

WHY *hello* there, upChuck," Randy Featherstone simpered quietly. "It's nice to see you in my neck of the woods again."

Yeah, yeah, yeah. Unzipping my knapsack, I handed him our latest Voice of the Butterfly tape: Lydia Babcock high on methamphetamines and Noni juice, doing the nasties to FAGERBAN. Randy accepted it graciously and turned it over back and forth a couple of times, jutting his lower lip in a pensive manner, frowning as if deep in thought. His face was painted orange and black. Eventually, he tapped the cassette against his left wrist and murmured, "Vell, vell, vhat haff we here?"

"You know what," I said routinely, taking out my checkbook. "Just gimme the damage report, skipper, and bag the lecture, okay?"

"Is it a Britney Spears concert?" he asked, pursing his lips in an odd sarcastic manner. "A L'il Kim hip-hopathon? Or maybe that wonderful *Frank Sinatra Sings Slayer Hits* album?"

"Cut the clowning, Randy. I'm in a hurry. What do we owe?"

He cued in a Megadeath song, punched a half dozen buttons, and leaned back in his padded leather swivel chair held together with duct tape and removed his earphones. He patted the cassette lightly against his mouth, then protruded his tongue and slobbered on the tape the way kids on a playground will lick their Tootsie Roll fore and aft if you ask them for a little bite.

"Hey—!"

Ignoring me, Randy stood up and slouched over to a hot plate located underneath a shelf that held instant coffee and four tins of Campbell's Liquid Sodium. After twisting a nob on the hot plate, he went to the nearby sink and half-filled a dented aluminum saucepan with water, then set the pot on the by-now red-hot burner.

"What the hell are you *doing,* Randy?"

His eyes festered in a most peculiar way, and his smile glowed with a kind of self-deprecating humorously rueful chagrin.

"Charley Mac, you guys have destroyed my life," he stated quietly. "I'm really irked at you."

"It's not my fault, man. If Tristan Griffith did not want our message aired he wouldn't have forced you to play it."

"Tell that to the IRS." Randy sprinkled green chile powder into the simmering water and added a can of that Campbell's stuff, stirring the concoction with his finger. To test, he poked the finger in his mouth and sucked it clean with limited gusto prior to leaning against a CD shelf, folding his arms, and gazing at me with what I would probably have to characterize as "barely concealed loathing."

"They fucking audited me, Chaz. I owe twenty-one thousand dollars in back taxes. Although Mr. Griffith has ordered me to run your so-called 'political advertisements,' he has also cut my salary in half for doing so because Sam Clendennon, Clarence Fagerquist, and Manjo Poddubny, those fucking Nob Hill Mobsters, finally pulled all their advertising. When I offered to bag your rap altogether he threatened to fire me. When I told him he was being unfair, he said, 'Isn't it great to be young and a Kennedy?' The Pro-Death Jesus Freak Nativity Biker Girls burned a cross on our lawn last week and threw a brick with a note tied to it through the window. You know what that note said?"

Hard to believe, but his eyes had become red rimmed and crazy, his nose had started running, and sharp fangs were poking through his floppy russet-colored mustache. Talk about anger-management issues.

I guessed, "'We love you, Randy—keep it up?'"

"No, it said, '*Your mother should have used a coat hanger.*'"

"I'm sorry, dude, but you can't give in to the forces of reaction. They just fired me at the library, but am *I* crying? Not in a million years. If the radical right had its way we'd all be church-going polyester heterosexuals driving around in white Cadillacs eating meatloaf and wax beans while mammoth bulldozers leveled all our forests and even hummingbirds were extinct."

Randy harrumphed, nodding wisely. "You know what you make me want to do, Charley?"

"No, what?"

He dropped our latest Voice of the Butterfly tape into his boiling soup.

NOTHING STOPPED us in the pursuit of publicity, however; *nothing*.

Shortly after dark, my Buick stealthily circled the Cruz Alta Subdivision and climbed Gaviota Drive, a looping artery that rose quickly up to those outtasight mansions so promiscuously dimpling the elegant slopes of Nob Hill, where the elite of our town lived their opulent and decadent lives of not-so-quiet desperation.

Even at the very end of October, Nob Hill was green, how they loved their green, the wide green lawns as thick as alpaca fur in winter, the tall green Chinese elms and flagrant weeping willows and delicate aspen trees half hiding all that wealth in a dappled mass of luxuriant foliage that seemed almost musical in its symphonic profusion. When you entered the hallowed landscaping of Nob Hill, life slowed down and became mellow, mosquitoes disappeared, temperatures in summertime were reduced by at least ten degrees, the sidewalks had no cracks, the streets were freshly paved, all lawns sported a uniform cut according to the covenants, and not a single dandelion marred the greensward thanks to the massive applications of Life Erase , the latest domestic herbicide to toxify our exhausted planet. Nothing scruffy or tacky intruded upon the manicured lanes and cul-de-sacs and silky avenues. Our own little Beverly Hills. Not a gated community yet, but the eyes from Neighborhood Watch peeked out everywhere at the casual intruder, and a private, inconspicuous army from High Mountain Security quietly patrolled the perimeters, ever alert for the occasional bad apple or Willow Road *arriviste* who might stray off course from down below into this private wonderland.

In the beginning, at each house Susan Delgado approached (as I watched from the car) the adults (Jerry and Ben Copernicus, Wayne and Melody Kinderfink) went into a frenzy of cloying adulation over her butterfly ensemble. The gauzy blue wings were constructed of screening and coat hangers; the boinging antennae bounced off a propeller beanie on her head; eight black legs stuffed full of rags dangled from her chest. Candies, bananas, and caramel popcorn rained upon the gangly enormous "child." Hilltoppers also graciously accepted a Butterfly Coalition flyer from the precious darling, accompanied by an innocent, "Don't forget to vote against the bypass." Then Susan curtsied and teeter-tottered back to me in her klutzy enthusiastic fashion and we dashed out of there: *"Beep! Beep!"*

But at the Bannerman's elegant adobe mansion we collided head-on against the distaff side of Halloween. Jack's wife Lu Ann had chauffered their kids off to gather garbage, so Jack himself, humorously disguised in a green loot suit, was ladling out the dental disasters. Routinely, he dropped some Tootsie Rolls and two full-sized Hershey bars into the reporter's sack. But when Susan offered a flyer and a "Don't forget to vote against the bypass," Jack's debonair facade crumbled.

"What? Who the hell are *you?"* Jack grabbed her bag, reached in and reclaimed his donations, then ordered, "You get off my property, bitch, before I call the cops!"

Susan lost her balance, careening backward. She tripped over her own big feet and bashed the gravel, splayed out like a cartoon flying squirrel hitting a jumbo swatch of marbles. Scrambling up, she somehow got tangled in her wings, then stepped on one of her own bug antennae, almost breaking her neck.

Floodlamps among the ornamental maples and Japanese cherry trees clicked on in a burst of horrendous illumination as Jack yelled, "I'm turning loose the dogs!"

I ran over, grabbing Susan, and hauled her like a duffel bag to the car—I pitched her in. We left two six-inch-deep side-by-side trenches in the gravel during our departure as a fleet of tubby dachshunds chased after us baying mournfully.

At the Manjo Poddubny palacio, where imitation yew trees (topiaried into smugly malignant cones) flanked imitation marble Greco-Roman pillars (which framed an imitation oak portcullis and engraved baronial door), my tough newshound buddy fared better. A maid, Lillian Tafoya, answered the ring wearing a Monica beret, gave Susan a popcorn ball packaged in Saran Wrap, and signed off— *k-blam!*—before she could deliver her rap. Susan banged angrily on the door and, when Lillian reopened, shoved a flyer into the maid's hand. "Read it," she ordered, "then give it to your *patrón*. And gimme another popcorn ball, okay?"

"Okay..."

At the Fagerquist's architectural fanfaronade two white-turban'd Sikh guards in jodhpurs, puttees, and pleated dhotis, wielding Uzi submachine guns and enormous Eveready lanterns, politely handed the gigantic butterfly some chocolate-coated Tater Tots and a candied pickle, accepting her handbill in return. Susan trundled unmolested back to my car, but at the gatekeeper's command post another turbaned East Indian shined his blinding torch into the driverside window and asked to see my license.

I bristled. "For what reason, pray tell?"

"It is not acceptable Halloween practice to be handing out political circulars," the man said briskly in clipped British tones.

Susan roared, "JUMP IN A LAKE, DIAPER HEAD!"

Boy, did *he* ever eat our dust.

When the Mayor's wife, Tammy Sue Clendennon, got a load of my pixilated journalist pal, her entire face wrinkled into a happy grin. "Honey, c'mere," I heard her call back to Hizzoner. "Look at this absolutely darlin' enormous butterfly."

In three-inch-high pompom slippers and a lowcut silk nightie Tammy Sue cut quite a figure herself in that doorway as Sam shuffled into the hallway behind her, newspaper in his left hand, cigar in his right, already dressed in flannel pajamas, wool bathrobe, and sheep-lined alligator slip-ons. Sam's head was so big it seemed hydro-cephalic. On a background television set Morton Downey Jr. was screaming epithets at a three-hundred pound weirdo in a Beefeater costume and cloth mache toe shoes. *Reruns.*

"Don't this outfit take the cake?" Tammy Sue crooned to Susan. "Did you make it yourself?" Her false eyelashes were the size of grackle tails.

Susan nodded. "Yes I did." And pried wide the mouth of her weighty sack.

Tammy Sue gushed, "Golly day, you really don't want candy, do you? Sweets are so dang bad for chirren. They give you cavities. I read the other day that sixty percent of Americans are prediabetic because of all the sugar in their—"

"Give her the crap and shut the door," Sam said. "What—you wanna irritate the oversized brat? She'll slash our tires, poison the cat, put dog shit in the mailbox." He swiped a salad bowl full of junk off the nearby Shaker workstand and encouraged Susan to gorge. "Go ahead, sugar, live it up. It ain't crank, but it'll give you a buzz."

My accomplice's eyes boggled at the cornucopia: tiny Baby Ruths, miniature Almond Joys, and bite-sized Reese's peanut butter cups. Susan grabbed up a fistload, cocked her antennae'd head in gratification, and dumped the loot into her heavy bag.

Then she disbursed a flyer, curtsied . . . and reached for more grub.

Tammy Sue had barely frowned at our boisterous flyer when Sam rudely appropriated from her that insidious call to arms. He screwed up his features perplexedly, then demanded of the butterfly standing obediently on his stoop scooping extra stuff from the salad bowl, "What kind of nonsense is this?" He cupped a mammoth hand over his eyes, shielding out the light from Japanese paper jack-o'-lanterns hanging along the drive, peering toward me as he demanded of my pal, "Who put you up to this?"

Susan about-faced, and, dragging her overloaded candy sack on the ground, she walked directly into the pole supporting an imitation gas lamp: *clang!* Oh fuck. I raced over again, grabbing her under the armpits, and backpeddled to the Buick.

"Who's there?" Sam called.

We laid down a furious line of scratch as I shouted loudly in reply: "Communists! Monorchidists! *Lepidopterists!*"

"*It's over, rover!*" he bellowed after us. "YOU'RE EIGHTY POINTS BEHIND IN THE POLLS!"

O**H YEAH?**

Fuck the polls.

Our ship was about to dock.

On Wednesday, November first, I ferried Lydia to Burger Boy at noon for her favorite lunch—a Bunyon Burger, fried onion rings, a mocha-cherry malt, two pineapple Pop-Tarts, black coffee, and a side of marshmallow-coated peanut brittle sautéed in green chiles. Luther rang up the order, then helped carry our tray to an adjacent table, where my querulous buddy, who was having a bad coordination day, promptly squirted watered-down ketchup on everything, including her wrists, forearms, lap, and the floor.

Luther said, "Pop, you gotta get her out of here quick. Moe is *this close* to giving me the ax." For work, his Mohawk was waxed flat and parted to both sides, and he wore a clean T-shirt, faded dungarees, and a bronze Burger Boy service medal on a miniature blue-satin retainer ascot.

"Lydia," I sighed, "get a grip, okay?"

She jammed half the hamburger into her mouth, turned purple, and started choking. I whacked her back, then performed a modest Heimlich maneuver until she regurgitated the bun, the meat, the lettuce, the tomato, the onion, and the green chiles.

It was like babysitting an immature chimpanzee. I said, "Jeez,

Lydia, you're more of a slob than Kelly."

As I swiped at her with a napkin, she croaked, "That's why I adore Kelly. She's a pig, and she's contentious, just like me."

She pawed at the onion rings, washing them down with coffee, then licked her fingers and asked me to stick a cigarette into her shriveled lips. I complied and she snapped her fingers impishly: "Gimme fire."

I held a match to her weed, and Lydia politely exhaled into my face tough-guy style. Phlegm rattled behind the wattles of her throat, then she reached for her coffee and I had to jump real nimble to avoid the splatter.

Lydia grinned disingenuously. "Oh dearie me, aren't I a clumsy little martinet?" She barked, "Luther, bring your pappy a rag." And clapped her hands twice: "Chop chop."

At exactly that moment I happened to raise my head, casting a glance out the front plate glass window, and my eye caught an odd movement far down the street.

"Oh no."

Normally, an old blue van headed slowly toward the Burger Boy fast food emporium would have caused little concern in any of us. But this vehicle happened to be the Anti–Prop X Butterfly Coalition Propaganda Sound Truck, AKA Kelly's dilapidated van. And even though it was still a goodly distance away, something about that trashed jalopy's tedious forward progress sounded an alarm bell in my noggin: BONG! It was like watching Hitler marching toward the Polish border. Through the open Burger Boy door I could hear Dolly Parton singing "Love is Like a Butterfly," and over her precious falsetto voice Kelly was giving our standard rap:

> Citizens of this fair town: On November
> eighth you can choose to vote for salvation or
> for Armageddon. If you support Proposition X,
> you will destroy the last natural land of our
> heritage and kill off one of the rarest creatures

on earth, the Phistic Copper Butterfly. Before
you enter that voting booth, let us tell you the
facts. . . .

I caught Luther's eye as he punched open a cash register,
deposited some bread without glancing down, and shut the drawer.
I couldn't speak, though; I simply pointed outside jabbing my finger
hysterically as Kelly continued approaching. Luther blinked, then
blanched. Believe me, we both understood immediately that a special
aura surrounded the Butterfly Coalition wreck and a tragic inevitability
was driving it toward us.

We were in for a bit of postmodern deconstruction by an atavistic
bellicosity paradigm.

"Hit the brakes," I ordered under my breath as the heap bounced
over a curb slightly left of the Burger Boy entranceway, then plowed
through four wooden picnic tables scattering chairs and green-and-
pink Burger Boy umbrellas on its way to the enormous front window
(which proudly displayed a Promise Keepers sticker, an NRA patch,
and a BURN TIMOTHY MCVEIGH decal). The plate glass disintegrated
in dramatic slow motion as our colorful kamikaze entered Burger Boy
like Moby Dick hitting a balsa rowboat full of Chinese teacups. There
was a vast seismic explosion of plaster, glass, particleboard, cheesy tin
I-beams and cheap pine studs, soda pop, Sweet'n Low packets, salt-
cellars, Styrofoam coffee cups, oil smoke, hamburger patties, children's
sneakers, and empty ketchup bottles. The van stopped between tables
15 and 16, about eight feet shy of yours truly and Lydia, scalding
steam spewing in all directions from underneath the hood.

Yes, patrons must have been screaming as they dived for
safety among the splintering chairs and clattering tables, but I heard
nothing. All I could think, as the k-fuffle erupted about us, was that
our Butterfly Coalition was doomed. The woman whom once I had
loved had become a liability impossible to overcome. I spied Luther
leaping over the counter, more graceful then ever I would have pre-
dicted, and he arrived at the driverside door just as Kelly's forward

progress ended. Incredibly, Dolly Parton's chipper voice continued to sing the second chorus, and my wife even managed to bawl "VOTE 'NO!' WHEN YOU GO!" seconds before she passed out. Lydia jumped, startled, her lips covered with Pop-Tart crumbs, and she shrieked "What was *that*?" as Luther yanked open the van door like a man:

"Yo, dude, are you *okay?*"

I showed up at my son's elbow, too bug-eyed and bowled over to speak. Kelly's ravaged face, which had clunked against the steering wheel, wore a beatific smile as its only sign of life. Her *Hey, Vern!* sweat-shirt was on upside down and my first impression was: *She's dead.* My second thought was: *Thank god!* But then the guilt commenced: *Oh no!*

Moe Pelletier clenched in his left fist a large firearm: Picture your typical gung ho balls-to-the-wall Camp Lejeune jarhead. He clapped Luther on one shoulder, and, in a voice dripping with hysterical calm, said, "You're fired. Now get this meshuga and your commie dad and that old bag lady out of here before I lose my temper."

Yes *sir.* Moe's pager burped and he checked it as Luther shoved Kelly over to the passenger side, climbed into the cab, started the engine, and backed out of Burger Boy spouting vapor clouds like an old choo-choo. I pushed Lydia's perambulator through swirling dust and Mount St. Helens—type destruction to fresh air and freedom outside the caved-in west wall. Already, Susan Delgado was quartering the patio, frantically snapping pictures. Dressed in a blue T-shirt, green pedal pushers, and red cowboy boots, all elbows and knobby knees, no hips, and legs longer than an ostrich's, Susan cut an exotic yet maladroit figure as she plied her paparazzi trade, sort of like Shelly Duval with MS.

"Geniuses!" she cried, infatuated by the newsworthy dolor Kelly had wrought. "I *love* you guys!"

And she blew me a torrid kiss.

In the middle of all this, Lydia asked, "What happened to my onion rings?"

On that cue three cop cars slammed to a halt in a V-shaped wedge blocking Luther's retreat and the poor lad sighed, clicked off the ignition, rubbed his eyes. I reached in and pressed the button to quash Dolly, but it was jammed and her cheerful voice continued to blare out just exactly whose pitch wagon it was, and why.

Abruptly, Kelly woke up, stiffened, and all her rooster-red hair frizzed in ecstasy as she gasped, "Suck on this, Moe: *Vengeance is mine!*"

Flanked by a quartet of county storm troopers—Rod Stepanovich, Herkie Pacheco, Shirley Scavcyzk and Jim Caley—Johnny Batrus sauntered over cracking his knuckles, and, dripping a most polite venom, he greeted us all: "Hello, Luther; hello, Charley; hello, Kelly; hi there, Missus Babcock. Now what seems to be the problem here?"

I saw Kelly flare at him, but I couldn't stop it, and I must admit that in the abstract it was almost "beautiful." On television I have seen modified stock cars disintegrate as they bounced end-over-end, flying apart at the seams . . . and on the History Channel on more than a few occasions I have raptly observed the Hindenburg melting in a swift hellish pogrom of helium flames. As to the individual human trajectories of bodies suddenly gone awry, I have witnessed many of them also: Eval Knieval crashing violently at the end of a daring motorcycle leap; graceful skiers suddenly buried and suffocated under surprise avalanches; clotheslined football players landing upside down and breaking their necks. It used to be that such abrupt and diverting images open to public view were rare as hen's teeth and quite traumatic to observe, but we are used to them now. On any evening we can tune into cop-chase automobile crashes, horses breaking their legs and squashing jockeys, or babies falling out of fiery hotel windows onto pavement six floors below. Casual Thursday night news programming almost always features a deranged psychopath waving a sword in downtown Seattle being knocked silly by water cannons and beanbag bullets, or grubby trailer park neighbors carelessly recalling the shotgun blast that drove Bobby into the propane grill that caught his Elvis hairdo on fire as he expired. We have become inured to the tragic consequences of human personality on a rampage, and our disinterest is casually destroying The Meaning Of Life On Earth.

A veritable tsunami of inappropriate epithets directed at Johnny Batrus and his buds issued from the mouth of my soon-to-be ex who had an absolutely *total* lack of instinct for self-preservation:

"Fuck you, you filthy bag of green dinosaur slime, you wretched scum-sucking afterbirth of syphilitic hippopotamus miscarriage, you heaping disgusting pile of fetid elephant dung, you no-good obnoxious—"

Yup, you bet. She went directly to jail without passing go, without collecting her two hundred smackers, and without even the slightest prayer that I could save her. They manhandled Kelly out of the van like a bunch of enraged yearling bear cubs batting around an unlucky woodchuck. Luther cried, "Hey, *what are you bastards doing?*" and he started forward, but Herkie Pacheco jumped in front of my boy and snarled: "Don't even *think* about it, chrome dome." Naturally, Kelly threw her elbows about wildly, kicked their shins, screamed, and tried to bite; consequently she was dropped, kicked, grappled, punched, shoved, and thumped on her way to the paddy wagon, everyone cursing en route. Perhaps I could have jumped in, but what was the use? The primal charade between The Law and Kelly was as preordained as wolves stalking a decrepit elk or piranhas devouring an unfortunate rabbit.

So that little ball of riotous violence tumbled through rubble over to the meat wagon and, after she croaked *"Butterflies rule!"* Kelly disappeared in back. Johnny Batrus reappeared with all the buttons off his shirt and one sleeve missing, sunglasses on backward, and his gunbelt at his ankles. Toward me he exclaimed, *"You Butterfly fuckers are toast!"* Then they careened away, Kelly no doubt being subdued by rough hands, pinioning knees, booted feet, and jabbing elbows. It must have taken the whole lot of them to hook on her handcuffs, it usually did. But in the end Kelly always lay there gasping, coughing, shitting in her pants, yet somehow defiant despite the humiliation. You have to figure that human self-destructive energy parallels that of stars.

And there we were in the aftermath, me and Lydia and Luther and Susan, the fearsome, indefatigable, indestructible stalwarts of the pathetic Butterfly Coalition, standing shellshocked in the Burger Boy rubble, watching Kelly—our genius and our nemesis—heading off to incarceration, abnegation, mortification: the possibilities were infinite.

Luther turned to me, real honest-to-goodness concern tormenting his pimpled callow features. He asked, "What are they gonna do to her, Pop?"

"Beat her up," I guessed, feeling sick and helpless. "Call her dirty names. Throw her in the drunk tank naked. Probably fondle her tits."

L ATER, SUSAN DELGADO told me, "Roly Poly almost refused to print it. When I started to motor out of there I thought for sure she had decided once again not to give us any ink."

More specifically, Edna Poddubny said, "Susan, if I ran it we'd be playing right into their hands. They knew you would take those pictures. It was a deliberate act of grandstanding for the camera, hoping for a publicity coup that would heighten their profile, thus giving them credibility before the election. They duped you again, poor baby, just like at the Snort N' Fodder."

"No, no, it makes the Butterflies look *horrendous*," Susan pleaded, willing to try any gambit to get us in print. "It's worth its weight in gold in *favorable* publicity for FAGERBAN."

"Don't be like my daddy's execrable missus," Edna chided gently. "The story would backfire on us badly." She plunged her puffy fist into a salad bowl full of peanut M&M's, cramming about six of the colorful candies into her mouth all at once.

"But it's an awesome story," Susan insisted. Then my pal flinched as the boss momentarily transformed herself into a large cow chewing on a small tricycle. But the hallucination quickly dissipated, allowing Susan to continue her daring assault:

"It has human interest, violence, democratic politics. I'd think you would want to publish my photographs of those clods just to nail down the FAGERBAN victory."

Edna hesitated, weighing her response: *Hmmn, should I smash this upstart's teeth down her throat?* Nah, she'd long cultivated a tolerant, big-sister attitude toward her simpleminded yet gifted reporter, so it would be better to gently remonstrate, giving a wise lesson in democratic pluralism in the process:

"No, you never can tell the mood of the American public, Suzy dear. It has voted for Bill Clinton twice and once worshiped Jesse James."

But Susan desperately tiptoed out farther onto the limb, dangerously tickling the Poddubny dragon's tail. "I bet one of my photos could win the State Women's Press Association AP News Photography Award in the Human Interest Category."

Whoa, *enough* already! Damned if Edna would be pushed around by an odiously ambitious underling. She grabbed up a Toledo steel letter opener from her desk, inserting it slowly through her neck—from right to left—then calmly withdrew the blade and laid it carefully on her blotter. No blood gushed from the lack of holes, but the gesture had its desired effect. On the verge of fainting, Susan collapsed in a chair.

"In case you forgot, *I* run this newspaper," Edna growled good-naturedly. "*I* make the decisions. *I* decide what pictures to run and which articles to publish. *You* work for *me*, not vice versa."

The editor reached for a donut but picked up her computer mouse by mistake, and, when she bit into it, a thing dribbled out of her monitor, landing on the floor with a subtle plop. It lay still for a moment, gathering its wits, then scampered off into hiding among the dust bunnies beneath a nearby radiator where its two tiny eyes glittered, peeping out.

Susan jumped up and scurried for the exit, squeaking like a gerbil. She almost collided against Manjo Poddubny, who was lumbering through the door dressed in one of his sleaziest polyester lounge lizard leisure suits, a gray satin ascot, and canary suede brothel creepers. His dark hair seemed painted onto his head, and that pencil-thin moustache reeked of funereal insincerity and old-fashioned masher obnoxiousness.

"Hello, Daddy," Edna said, always glad to see her pop.

But the first words out of Manjo's mouth sealed his doom: *"I don't care how many people saw that asshole crash into Burger Boy, you can't print a word about it!"*

Edna crossed herself. "We don't say the A-word in my presence, remember? I don't like blasphemy."

"Sorry, kid, I wasn't thinking. But Edna, honey, just don't get any wild hairs. You've been great until now, yet I know the temptation on this one must be huge. Doesn't matter, though, we've all agreed they can't have *any* publicity—be it good, bad, or indifferent. So you'll ignore it as usual, agreed?"

Edna folded her arms, dropped her eyebrows, squinched her nostrils up tightly, and stared at Manjo, her lower lip quivering while steam hissed out her ears: badabing badaboom. Who the heck was *he* to be telling *her* what to do?

"How *can* I ignore it, Daddy?" she said. "It happened *downtown* in broad *daylight* during lunch hour, and there were a *hundred* witnesses. Ultimately, we're a newspaper, we have an obligation to the public. We'll be laughingstocks if we don't print the story. Right, Susan?"

Susan, who'd been cowering in the doorway, nodded in disbelief at this abrupt reversal of fortune.

Manjo waved his right hand whose fingers boasted a gold pinky ring and a Masonic bauble the size of a walnut: "Yeah, sure, honey, I know. But we all decided that even negative articles could work against us by playing into the Bonnie and Clyde mentality of our constituents. No ink, no stink."

Edna said, "Excuse me, but aren't I the editor of this paper?"

Unwittingly stupid, Manjo cranked his bluster up a notch. He said, "If you print that hysterical story how will it make *us* look?"

"It'd make *them* look ridiculous."

"Nonsense. Half this town will consider them heroes. You know everyone hates Moe Pelletier."

Then Manjo puffed up like a big, self-important tom turkey and stuck his own foot so far down his own throat he could have kicked himself in his own ass from the inside out:

"You simply will *not* give them publicity," he ordered, selecting a green M&M from the bowl. "It's irresponsible journalism. I won't allow it."

"Wait a minute, Daddy. Are *you* telling *me* how to run *my* paper?"

"Actually, it's technically still *my* paper," Manjo reminded her, grinning affably to show off his gold teeth: "I own all the stock."

"Then are you saying that because you own it you can dictate the policies of your editor-in-chief, even if she happens to be your own daughter?"

Manjo laughed, clapping his hands at the growing wisdom of this charming neophyte, the apple of his patriarchal eye: "Exactly."

Edna stood up, straightened her shoulders in a dignified manner, and informed her pop, "All right, I quit."

"You *what?*"

"You heard me."

She dumped all the remaining M&M's into her purse and swung around the desk storming past him. Sissy got up and followed, holding her nose in the air as she pattered by the astonished aging gigolo.

Manjo went flabby and stammered, "Wait . . . what are you doing? . . . Edna . . . lamb pie . . . hold on a second here. . . ."

At the door she paused, reeking of magisterial disdain. "This country is still a democracy, Daddy, in case you hadn't noticed. We still have the Bill of Rights and First Amendment freedom of speech. Hundreds of thousands of American boys did not give up their lives on foreign soil just so an arthritic old cuckold like you could come in here on some sort of inebriated pretext and start pushing me around. C'mon, Sissy—*heel.*"

Manjo wailed, "Edna! . . . honey, baby doll . . . I take it all back! *I'm sorry!*"

Brushing Susan Delgado aside, he scampered after his daughter, catching up to her in the parking lot at the Chrysler just as Edna's butterball body was sliding behind the wheel.

"Sweetheart," the chastened tycoon choked out breathlessly, "don't do it. Everything's okay. I made a mistake. I apologize."

Edna quorked her face into a plump polyp of disdain and milked the twitting for all it was worth: "I'm thirty-six years old, I'll have you know. I'm not a little girl anymore and won't be treated as such."

The humiliated dad sank to his knees. "Okay, okay, I'm sorry, I'm sorry. I promise, *none* of this will ever happen again."

Mollified, Edna squeezed out of the car. "All right," she said. "But in the future I really don't wish to have my authority impugned by the likes of you."

She kissed his cheek. From close by, Susan snapped the picture. Manjo would have liked to knee Edna in the groin, but instead he kissed her back, *mwah,* gave her a fatherly squeeze, and muttered, "All's well that ends well" as he produced a florid handkerchief and mopped his sopping brow.

"Yes, it certainly is," Edna agreed contemptuously, heading back to work . . . from whence she would stick it to all parties concerned, in spades.

One of Manjo's eyeballs hopped clear of its socket and bounced over to Susan's feet like a ripe seedless grape from a genetically altered vineyard in the Napa Valley. My friend bent down and picked up the fruit, popped it in her mouth, then fled while Manjo, in hot pursuit, clacked his yellow beak, rattled his condor wings, and cried, *"Ulupalakua! Pukalani! Makawao!"*

H*oly Toledo!*"

No, I could not believe my eyes. No way, not in a million years. What's too good to be true never happens to people like us. *Never.* Shaking my head, I blinked, rubbed my knuckles in the sockets, and opened wide again. But incredibly, nothing had changed. Same photographs, same newspaper, same enormous black headline:

BUTTERFLY BOZOS BUG BURGER BOY!

Yet for a few more seconds I tried not to gloat because there *had* to be a catch somewhere. There's *always* a catch somewhere, *qué no*? But *where*? The article laid it all out: Kelly . . . the Butterfly Coalition Sound Truck . . . the Burger Boy Demolition Derby . . . Lydia Arlington Babcock. In Susan's photographs Moe Pelletier waved his blunderbus; Johnny Batrus and company assaulted my wife; and shocked onlookers—Kismet Witherspoon, Paul Sweetwater, Winona Stapleton—pointed at the damage. It was the sort of spread reserved for Columbine High School or Michael's final shot against the Jazz in game six, all out, all the way, no holds barred. At last they—the horrible, racist, money-grubbing, eco-destroying Powers That Be—had broken down, admitting a legitimate contest existed. They had? Really? *Yesss!* And for the seventh time I turned to the editorial page where no less than a dozen Letters To The Editor praised

FAGERBAN, castigated FAGERBAN, blamed the Butterfly Coalition . . . or thanked our feckless band of malcontents for daring to confront the corporate golem. A box said you could also log onto ePropX@Sentinel.com to state an opinion. Whatever the message was, pro or con, didn't matter, however, so long as the PEOPLE were in on the play. With the PEOPLE awake and informed, maybe, just *maybe* the Phistic Copper had a chance, the momentum was changing, Edna Poddubny had been forced to *crack*. Love it or hate it, mash it or bash it, hug it or mug it, our Butterfly Coalition existed . . . it had a public persona . . . it had a pair of . . . *wings*.

Listen to this juicy editorial:

> The time has come to acknowledge that in our valley a band of malcontents, known as The Butterfly Coalition, has been performing untold criminal acts all in the name of Democratic electoral politics. They have assaulted FAGERBAN candidates, they have cut down Pro—Prop X billboards, they have demolished respectable fast food enterprises, they have broadcast pernicious lies and libelous accusations over the radio, and, in general, they have behaved like thugs on a rampage. Yet of late we have heard a few misguided citizens speak of this ignoble wild bunch in less than derogatory terms, a habit that must be nipped in the bud. The *Sentinel-Argus* abhors this group of outlaw clowns and hopes *nobody* will be persuaded to vote for their puerile and anti-American point of view on November 8.

Yowsa, yowsa. Shouting, "God bless the *Sentinel-Argus!*" I hopped on my bike and pedaled over to Susan Delgado's house, a tiny square box in the Cruz Alta Subdivision filled to the brim with lopsided macramé hangings and an amazing old-fashioned Japanese toy collection. Her bizarre little schipperke—Roderick—bounced all over the place when I banged through the door catching Susan barefoot eating a tuna fish and honey sandwich for lunch. "You did it!" I cried, grabbing her impetuously into my arms. *"Thank you from the bottom of my heart, you gorgeous slut puppy!"* Susan looked up at me, flabbergasted, her face half hidden behind the sandwich I'd inadvertently mooshed it in, then suddenly she recovered and kissed me avidly until I recoiled, barking "THANK YOU!" again as I fled.

Ink, I thought next day as I pedaled joyfully toward the county calaboose in bumper-to-bumper traffic inching along like high-priced turds in a sewage lagoon. Oh my god, Edna Poddubny had given us *Ink*. I zoomed right past Tammy Sue Clendennon, who was wearing a lowcut blue sundress beneath which her rambunctious bosom was bouncing like happy puppies in a pet store window. You give somebody INK in America today and it's all over, it's like opening Pandora's box, it's like taking the lid off a petri dish with a culture of smallpox inside, it's like passing Wayne Gretzky a hockey puck—you *know* he's gonna score. Billy Watrous in his amped-out Chevy S10 had a boombox with such serious noise management issues that even the clouds high above us were shuddering, but who cared? Edna Poddubny had caved in, she had broken the code of Omerta, she had defied the Mob. So what if it was negative Ink? Ink is Ink. Ink is like *God*. Ink has a life of its own, it flows in every direction at once like poison water from a collapsing tailings dam. Ink controls the universe. Ink compares to the primal ooze in which an amoeba-sized brachiopodal nongilled plankton-ingesting invertebrate arthropod can evolve into a Gargantuan air-breathing meat-munching *Tyrannosaurus rex* overnight. Ink is a foot in the door. Ink is an inch that can be parlayed into a mile. Ink can instantly become enough rope to hang an entire *city!* Ink is a fertile soup in which *anything* can flourish. Ink is like the Internet in cyberspace—infinite. Ink can revivify the deadest doornail, it can destroy the most potent potentate, it can make Madonna a glamour girl . . . or annihilate Richard Nixon. Ink is ubiquitous, all-knowing, ever-present, woeful, devastating, MIRACULOUS. Ink is a will with a way. Ink is like loaves and fishes in the hands of Jesus, it can go forth, be incredibly fruitful, and multiply . . . *multiply* . . . MULTIPLY!

I SECURED MY BIKE in the rack outside the crumbling county clerk's building, then gave brief interviews to Kim Sweetwater of Channel 7 and Johnny Fabiola of Cable 11. That's right, you heard correctly, at last the professional pudsuckers had invaded our town. *Glory, Hallelujah!* Spurred on by the *Sentinel-Argus*, a bevy of them from the Capital had landed in Suicide City the previous night, belatedly onto our story, ink slingers hungry for their usual blatantly concocted and extrapolated-out-of-context inches, eager to catch somebody in a verbal miscue or to blow the slightest kinky angle way out of proportion. Of course, *my* job was to accommodate those puffy raptors the way any American talking head devoid of all taste or principle would humor *Larry King Live, Inside Edition, The New York Times,* or Jerry Springer's atavistic hijinks. Once you get their attention, you *never* let it go.

Kim Sweetwater, thirty-four, a blond ex–New Yorker exiled during her twilight years to the affiliate boonies out West, was made up to appear twenty-eight. She wore a sexy double-breasted Polo jacket with shoulder pads, a very short skirt, and had remarkably shapely gams in opaque green pantyhose. Her scruffy, cigarette-smoking assistant (and field producer) Chris Ledyard, thirty-one, a Dallas Texan and SMU graduate who'd risen to an evening anchor position in Knoxville before being toppled by the usual blow scandal, fed her the questions and gave orders to their cameraman, the aging, over-weight hepcat Barney Lumpen, forty-three, who could do all that stuff in his sleep and never listened to the interviews.

Johnny Fabiola (Cable 11) had an orange toupee. Nearby stood a tall, horsey, abrasive klutz in a houndstooth suit, Richard So-and-So (from Channel 4). By contrast, Sandra Whosamadig of Channel 5, a slim, dark-haired predator in a rose-colored jersey and sheeny emerald slacks, was considered to be The Franchise, an elegant barbarian too big for her own little market . . . but doomed to remain there because she had once openly declared herself gay.

They all gathered around me like magpies around a jackrabbit carcass on Route 10. When Kim Sweetwater asked, "Charley, are you here to spring your wife?" I replied, "We're broke, I can't, but I love her dearly." When Johnny Fabiola asked, "Are you really getting divorced?" I said, "Not in a thousand years: We're a closeknit religious family." When Richard So-and-So stated, "I heard your son is a fascist skinhead," I called forth appropriate indignation: "You heard wrong. Luther may look bizarre, but he's an Eagle Scout, a Christian athlete, a Big Brother volunteer, and the first violin in a chamber quartet noted for playing Chopin."

Then I ducked into our windowless postmodern concrete penal building, and seconds later Orlando Pfieffer, the brutal screw from Hell, roughly shoved Kelly into the bulletproof visitor's cubicle and left us seemingly alone, stomping back off to some remote cavern in the dankest recesses of his punitive castle where he would no doubt continue butchering newts and star-nosed moles for the prisoners' broth.

Surprise, surprise, my beleaguered boozehound wife looked like a girl with her foot in the grave and scarcely the strength of a louse. Picture Ray Milland (*Lost Weekend*) meets Jack Lemmon (*Days of Wine and Roses*) and Tony Curtis (*The Outsider*) in *Under the Volcano* (as interpreted by Albert Finney). She'd apparently evolved through her Kosovo Slaughter, Greenhouse Effect, and Ozone Hole stages, and was now wallowing in her Worldwide AIDS Epidemic phase.

Kelly croaked, "Hello, lollipop, did you bring my heroin?"

"Not funny, babe. How is life in gaol?"

"Not bad. They feed us once a day whether we're hungry or not. Of course, I *do* miss my tofu aspic, carrot juice, and vitamin C tablets. And I wish I had my reading glasses, I want to knock off *Jean Christophe* while I'm killing time."

"Are you comfortable?" I asked. Her nose seemed at once both inflated and deflated, like a miniature colostomy bag nailed to the center of her grubby face.

"Oh I'm incredibly comfortable," she replied. "Thank you for asking. There's only ten of us in a three-by-eight cell. I sleep standing up with my beak stuck in a giraffe's asshole and blood clots dribbling down my thighs. I'm fresh out of Tampax but not quite yet into toxic shock syndrome, thanks God."

Unhappy as I knew it would make her, I figured we better come to an understanding right from the git-go, so I confessed: "I'm not here to bail you out, Kelly. We can't take a chance this close to D-Day, you're too dangerous."

"*What?*"

"You heard me."

She went through a few changes, all of them phony, insincere play-acting: surprise, puzzlement, neutrality, frustration, naked anger, impudent disdainfulness, and, ultimately, a nonchalantly false bravado: "Hey, I never asked you for a rose garden, Charles."

"Good. 'Cause if you walk it would ruin everything. It would be like unleashing King Kong in New York. You have unresolved control issues. Despite my aversion to violence, however, I'll admit you did a good job in Burger Boy, and the tide is finally turning in our favor. They gave us ink. Believe it or not, I'm here to thank you."

"I understand." She poured on the caustic smarm. "Believe me, we're all better off if I remain in a low-profile situation. But *gracias* for your sympathy and consideration."

"It's nothing personal." I was trying to keep it civil. "You just go berserk from all the drinking. I'm afraid that next time you might do something really counterproductive like failing to signal for a left turn and getting a fifteen-dollar traffic ticket."

"Yes, yes, you're absolutely correct, my darling spouse. No problem." Talk about snide undertones. "I *deserve* to be in here. I'm not worthy. In fact, I should be locked in solitary in a concrete hole full of cockroaches and silverfish, then maybe I'd be scared straight and would fly right."

Uneasily, I vowed, "As soon as the election is history I'll raise the money to spring you. Meantime, in jail you're sober," I reasoned. "It's actually *healthy* in here. They give you odd edible plants and pieces of meat called 'food' instead of Sterno, Jack Daniels, and Baby Ruth candy bars. There's central heating in your cell. And chances are the water you drink doesn't have mosquito larvae, blowfly maggots, or dog pee in it. You're required by law to take a shower daily, and they'll even introduce you to a synthetic lye product called 'soap.' So you should look on the bright side, sweetheart; don't be a nattering nabob of negativity."

With not a wrinkle compromising her scornful facade, my wife said, "I *accept* your decision, oh wise one. It's best for *every*body. *Thank* you for dropping by."

Pause. . . .

She reminded me of homeless Korean beggars from long-ago newsreels (on the History Channel) dressed in filthy quilted jackets picking maize kernels out of donkeyshit: The background was *always* rubble.

Well, I'd fed her The Long Slow Curve; now it was time for The Fast Break. "While you're indisposed, Kelly, we could use a final Voice of the Butterfly—okay?"

"Sure thing. Just spring me first."

"Actually, I can't."

"When pigs fly, *entonces*."

"No, listen," I said, "I'm serious, *please*. They're on the ropes. Suddenly Prop X and the Phistic Copper is a *story*. The press is agitated. Tristan Griffith is pumped. We need a killer conclusion to the

VOB series for Monday before the election. I'm sure if it's done right it would grab even Bo Hrbyk's attention. But you're the only one who can invent that gibberish convincingly."

Kelly said, "Drop dead, twice."

We stared at each other like two angry tomcats in a turf war. Kelly's face was so battered and misshapen it seemed almost as deformed and sad as the Elephant Man's phizzog, or, say, the mug of that poor kid in the Cher movie, *Mask*. Usually I could delineate, within her hurt, remnants of the golden girl who used to be, that vivacious and sexy harlequin who'd made me laugh like a hyena, fucked my brains out daily, goosed me into a social conscience again, and seemed gloriously indestructible. Well, I had news for myself: I couldn't see any of that old sweet ebullience anymore.

I admitted, "I really hate you, babe."

"The feeling is mutual, Chuck."

Face to face like two punch-drunk street fighters, we were stymied, at a loss for further words.

So I got up and jammed.

But some felonious desperado had cracked the Kryptonite lock on my bike and stolen it (the bike), lock, stock, and water bottle right in front of the fourth estate.

I stood there, the way we all do when these things happen, bewildered, hurt, stammering my shock and outrage, uncomprehending, staring at the spot where my Rock Hopper had been, trying to make it reappear.

Richard So-and-So shoved a mike in my face: "How's the little woman?" he asked.

"We're all worried about her," said Kim Sweetwater from Channel 7.

"Give us the straight poop," inquired Channel 5's Sandra Whosamadig.

"Where were you when they stole my bike?" I wailed.

Y OU NEVER GET TO savor the good times for very long, though, before God slams you down on the mat again and kicks you in the head. That's a cardinal rule in life, *bet* on it.

So when I arrived home after that jolly jail Chautauqua, Bob Maelstorm, Abe Gingivitis, and Tom Florissant were camped on my portal all bloated up like bullfrogs in mating season because a few moments ago they had formed The Committee to Save Willow Road. Hello? *Earth to Uranus?* Surprised (to say the least), I settled gingerly into my weathered rocking chair and ventured this opinion: "It's a little late to be waking up." Mangus was chewing on a Teletubby in the driveway, while Oopboop and Carlos perched atop the woodpile peering into its depths at something which no doubt carried either the plague or the hanta virus.

"We didn't know how things really were," Abe (the pizza baron) said, nervously clicking the remote car gismo in his hand. "William Watrous is a chauvinist thug who exploits women."

"Nobody warned us," Bob (the New Age lawyer) said, adjusting the collar of his blue and gold Polartec pullover. "Clarence Fagerquist is a Superfund polluter."

"I thought we could trust Jack Bannerman," Tom (the Realtor) appended. "His children are so polite."

He wore a mint green Patagonia shirt and was puffing on his meerschaum.

"What made you change your minds?" I asked in a genial manner, tapping my fingertips together thoughtfully and smiling officiously.

"All the papers are talking about Prop X," Abe said. "Even the *Sentinel-Argus*. We didn't know it was so important." His cell phone rang, but he ignored it: *ring, ring.*

Bob declared, "People are now saying that FAGERBAN is a fifty-fifty shot to go bankrupt whether or not Prop X passes."

Ring, ring.

Tom, a paragon of genteel bourgeois angst, frowned: "We have three money market accounts through First State. If it collapses everything we have worked for all our lives goes down the toilet." His pager beeped and he checked it, making a quick mental note.

I mentioned the obvious: "I've been warning you guys for months, but nobody twigged."

Ring, ring.

"You undermined your own message by being a total flake," Abe said.

Ring, ring.

"If I'd shaved my beard and worn beige Dockers would you have listened?"

"See, you're so *aggressive*," Tom complained.

Ring, ring.

"Not half as aggressive as FAGERBAN, I'm afraid."

Ring, ring.

"Well, it wasn't in the papers before," Bob explained, getting edgy. *"Shut that fucking thing off, Abe."*

Abe shut it off.

"Neither was the Holocaust for eight years," I said.

"Hold your horses, man." Tom reared up, his well-groomed thirty-something hackles quivering. "I'd hardly call this the Holocaust. That's the problem, you exaggerate with reckless abandon. You destroy your own credibility by willy-nilly tossing around unsubstantiated rumors. You never communicate in measured discourse."

"Translated, you mean I look funny, I'm poor, and despite the moniker you suspect I'm Jewish?"

My neighbor, a real Plimptonian WASP with pale skin, erect bearing, and a Harvard accent, blushed but held his temper, which he had *never* in his whole life lost even when seething underneath. In the driveway Mangus nervously abandoned his Teletubby when it began talking, and Carlos swooped in, grabbed it, then trotted off carrying the stuffed toy like a dead baby prairie dog.

Bob was resplendent in a baggy sweater, green golf slacks, Gucci loafers. "We didn't come here for you to put us down," he said evenly. "We came prepared to offer help."

Fair enough. "We need five thousand dollars for TV ads tomorrow, ten people to make phone calls to Democrats, Independents, and undecided voters, and at least a dozen volunteers with automobiles to drive folks to the polls on Tuesday."

Oh for a photograph of their reaction. I would've blown it up, had it framed, and hung it on my wall with an inscribed plaque underneath:

BABY BOOMERS IN SHOCK!

Bob: "Sorry, tomorrow's a bad day for me. Butchie has the Subaru and the Mazda's in the garage. But otherwise—"

Abe: "Tomorrow sucks for me, too. Charity is at the pizzeria all day so I have to take Gerald, Damian, and Lilith to their morning sessions with Patty Gusdorf and then Lars to play soccer in the afternoon, followed by a flute lesson and cyber-counseling. And I promised Babette Quicksilver I'd help her trim the topiary of sedge bushes around their wading piscine."

Tom: "Damn. Tomorrow I'm supposed to go up in a glider, have lunch with Bill Snipes, and take Zack and Jeffry to Sharon Ludlow for their monthly brushup and tick check while Mildred has her hair done by Margo Snead at the Coiffe Shoppe and then undergoes aromatherapy with Cathie Bayless for an hour."

I said, "Okay . . . what about Tuesday?"

Bob had scheduled a morning tennis match with Lu Ann Bannerman at the Nob Hill Country Club, lunch with the proctologist Ethan Chambers, and a rendezvous with Butchie at three P.M. at the architect's office to discuss the plans for their new walk-in hypoallergenic parakeet aviary.

Abe was fasting with Charity that day for World Hunger and would not be able to leave the house except for an herbal colonic enema from Leroy Schnaable at the Southside Health Annex toward sundown.

Tom was slated to help build booths at the CTA for the Gourmet Delight raffle on Sunday. Then he had plans to help Mildred make oatmeal cookies for Melanie's scout troop's bake sale. And if any time remained, he'd promised to go with Ethan Chambers (after lunch) when the proctologist took Amos and Andrew to be gelded.

"Bob," I said. "Our lawyer needs help filing for an EIS, getting injunctions, requesting impact fees."

"Who's your lawyer?"

"Farragut Wallaby."

"*That* geriatric bumblefuck?"

"Well . . . what about cash donations?"

"We're pretty broke," Bob said alertly. "I yelled at Butchie last night because she was eight thousand dollars over budget. We're also financing Peter's orthodontist's kid at Yale, and we just reloaded all the Gateways with Windows 2000—"

"This is a bad month," Abe admitted. "I had to ask the IRS for an extension and the Dow fell three hundred points last week—"

Tom confessed, "Mildred's liposuction set me back a fortune. And do you know the insurance rates on our timeshare in Cabo tripled over the past six—"

Sorry, but in my mind I came out of my chair like an alien bursting from a human stomach, karate-chopped Tom's aristocratic throat and kicked him in the ribs as he dropped, grabbed Bob's shirt at the throat yanking him toward me and skull-bopping him between the eyes with my own forehead before slugging him in the belly for good measure as he headed toward the deck, caught Abe with the heel of my left fist in a blindside haymaker that sent half the teeth in his fat mouth clattering like bloody Chiclets against my screen door, then I grabbed all three of the preppy Nazis by their stylishly pierced ears and dragged them off the portal, into the driveway, and over to my woodpile, where Oopboop and Carlos scrammed as I dumped my cargo on top of the logs, struck a match, and watched those wealthy educated pus bombs BURN!

BUT HEY, despite a few niggling setbacks, the Butterfly Coalition was on a roll. Like shake, rattle, *and*. FAGERBAN was suddenly *threatened*. And a visiting press corps, sensing an upset of epic proportions, was scurrying about our ville shoving a camera lens, a microphone, or a ballpont pen into every darkened orifice looking for news, scandal, gossip . . . *chlamydia*!

On Monday, the day before Election Day, I raced over to attend a FAGERBAN damage-control press conference at 10:25 in front of First State S & L, where at least two hundred citizens had gathered in the parking lot, buzzing about the election tomorrow. Edna Poddubny, who overnight had become the beleaguered pariah editor of the *Bolshevik Daily Sentinel-Argus* (trashed by her dad, by all the other FAGERBAN principals, and by every religious zealot in town for giving us commies ink)—Edna was mingling with the hoi polloi, covering the hysterical event herself although she looked horrible: Tears streamed down her hefty cheeks and she seemed flustered, disoriented, and confused. On the other hand, afire with excitement and devil-may-care attitude (and dreams of a Pulitzer, too), Susan Delgado appeared everywhere at once, snapping photographs, bumping into people, amassing quotes as fast as she could scribble them upside down on her pad.

The downstate media cavorted in droves, recording each minute seismic tremor as zero hour approached. O. J. Simpson, Ted Kyszinski,

Monica Lewinsky, and now. . . REVENGE OF THE BUTTERFLIES!
Check it out, homies. Click into *this* Web site all you Dot Commies.
There was Sandra Whosamadig and Richard So-and-So directing
cover shots of the madding crowd for their Second Unit. Kim Sweetwater and Chris Ledyard from Channel 7 were interviewing Tammy
Sue Clendennon, who stuck out like a sore Dolly Parton in her mini-
jumper and knee-high musketeer boots. Johnny Fabiola and Lenny
Brightmaster, pilot and co-pilot of Cable 11's Eye-In-The-Sky, were
setting up for a stint with Eleanor Poddubny, who looked psychotic
and feral in a black Lycra body suit. SIN, the Spanish station, was
represented by Ricardo Martínez and Jenny Archuleta: They had
Moe Pelletier up against the wall giving his fortieth interview about
the demise of Burger Boy. Everybody wanted to know: Was Bo
Hrbyk heading north? Who cut down the chauvinist billboards?
How did that alcoholic creature crash into Burger Boy and *survive?*

Voracious piranhas out on a spree, they all wanted a fresh
angle and we had it, lucky us. Lunatic kamikaze drunks! Aged female
curmudgeons! Skinhead billboard hit people! A brilliant plastered
scriptwriter! What was more American than a tiny butterfly with its
finger in the big bad dike of Proposition X? Ladies and Gentlemen,
welcome to the all-new, ever-resourceful, constantly amazing, zany
but never-say-die, once in a lifetime . . . Butterflyyyyyyyyyyy. . .
COALITION!

I'll admit that one Very Special Thought crossed my mind as I
waited among the murmuring proletariat for FAGERBAN to speak.
Yes, indeed, I was incredibly, slavishly, *unctuously* grateful that Kelly
had remained in jail. I can't describe how peaceful I felt, even in such
a stressful ambience, with that hellraising rum sponge safely behind
bars. Not to impute callous insensitivity on my part—God forbid!—
but the operating shibboleth here was, if Mike Tyson needed to stay
caged between bouts, Kelly McFarland kept safe in solitary was a no-
brainer shoo-in.

Then, as always happens when you speak of the devil, sure
enough she turns up. First I smelled the sulfur, then I spotted the

horns. Kelly was actually far away, on the other side of the crowd, almost lost among the faces and caps and overcoats, but I located her immediately as if she'd been a bright red cardinal bird in the middle of a deserted snowfield. If you're connected by love and despair to another person you know instinctively when they're in the general neighborhood. There's a psychic pull between you as scary as the music in a cheap horror movie, or akin to the arthritis that blows up and commences throbbing whenever the barometer falls before a storm. Out the corner of my eye I caught a faraway lurch, a patch of bobbing russet hair, the slope of one of her shoulders—and then she came directly toward me, blind as a bat, I know, and absolutely unaware of my position, driven lemming style simply by her genetic urge to reach the sea, which was me. There was no will or consciousness involved anymore. Kelly had damaged herself far beyond that pale, becoming as impersonal and as effective as a "smart bomb." And I waited like a fatalistic Iraqi peasant soldier huddled in a concrete bunker for her arrival.

As soon as she reached me, Kelly tried to mollify me with a sheepish grin, followed by a casual and breezy salutation, deceptively coherent:

"Good mornin', sunshine—what's up?"

"You bum," I sobbed. *"Who let you out?"*

She reeked of peppermint schnapps and avoided the question. "It's almost Election Day and we have work to do."

Kelly always looked terrible, but now she had an aura of insane decay and instability that defied easy explication. Think of Satan, once an angel, after his rough plunge from a serene firmament down through the turbulent atmosphere to crash against Earth's imaginative crust and continue on through granite veins lining our plates tectonic straight to the portals of Hell. Her booze breath hit me like roadkill fumes. White slime covered her lips. Sharp hooklike grasping tongs had shredded her clothing. Obviously, her polar icecaps had melted and she was heading toward The Flood. I said, "I'll kill whoever went your bail."

Her bloodshot eyes fired up with sardonic loathing: "Are you dissing me, Charles? Am I decoding your vernacular correctly? Are you not happy to see me?"

"Happy?. . . Kelly, I'll give you a hundred bucks right now, cash on the barrelhead, to go back to jail and stay there until tomorrow night."

I even whipped out my wallet and waved the bribe in her face while in the background top-heavy Tammy Sue Clendennon, perky as a June bug in Texas, and her Life Coach, Kismet Witherspoon, the afflicted shadow archetype dental assistant, remained steeped in banal conversation.

Kelly promptly shriveled into a sarcastic three-and-a-half-foot-tall half-baked human being with a withered left leg. "I'm sorry," she snickered, affecting a slightly pathetic lisp, mock groveling to the hilt. "I know I'm a total space cadet, but I wanted to participate in this important election. You see, I'm part of the team, a valued player, an architect of our preordained stunning upset tomorrow. I'm entitled to do one last great thing before I croak, aren't I? Please? *Pretty* please? Pretty please with sugar and honey on top?"

"They're paying you, aren't they? You've been on their payroll since day one."

My wife made her swollen face appear hurt, trying (unsuccessfully) to project an aura of actual sentient awareness. "Gee, you sure picked a great place to start bellyaching," she scolded.

Seldom during our chaotic life together had I experienced such a strong desire to slug her. I know, I've admitted to violence fantasies, aggressive tendencies, even dreams of murderous scenarios against women. Very un-PC, especially for an avowed pacifist like me. But those were fantasies, this was real. So real, the bile bubbled up and made me dizzy from an urge to simply get it over with once and for all. *Stop, already!* Annihilate the turkey! Invade her Normandy! What were we, doomed to be attached forever like a sadistic twisted version of Abelard and Héloïse? Kelly had badgered and butchered, tortured and flummoxed, dissed me and kissed me off and ignored me and destroyed herself despite my loving attempts to salvage her rotting soul: Basta ya! *Off with the charlatan's head!*

All I said, however, was, "Kelly, please get away from me. I don't think I can deal right now. You're giving me a really big anxiety attack."

"Hey, yo, I'm *dyin'*," she scoffed rudely, her voice mincing and satirical. "And all you can do is berate, you jive honky? The lockup was *hell*." She wiped away an imaginary tear. "I have no money, I'm sick, I'm always bombed, my heart never stops flip-flopping, I'm scared shitless all the time, my fingers are numb, I have to gobble fifty Tums a day to soothe my ulcer—"

Thirty thousand feet above Reality and no vomit bags on this flight!

I said, "Sorry, sugar, get real, I left my violin at home."

Theatrically she groaned, "Oh what a heartless prick you are."

For one tick of eternity I nearly lost it again in front of all those journalists. For the slightest quiver in time I almost hauled off before at least twenty Nikon motordrives (and a dozen video Minicams) and punched that inebriated crumb-bum, a gesture which probably would have undermined everything we had all worked for during the past two months, endangering the future of the Phistic Copper butterfly, and, of course, obliterating my credibility as a sensitive pacifistic political firebrand dedicated to the rational politics so desperately needed to salvage the blundering planet. You think John Rocker got a bad press by shitting on Jews, blacks, and immigrants? Blowing my cool in the age of PC and decking Kelly in front of all those people would have been an act as woefully nihilistic as a spark hitting the middle fuel tank of TWA 800. And so guess what, folks—?

Heroically, once more with feeling, I resisted the temptation.

Stifling it (for the Sake of The Cause), I even let a tenuous smile blossom. Unfortunately, at the same time a vengeful sadist took me over, proving—once again—that you always attack the ones you love:

"Kelly," my super-modulated derisorily compassionate voice replied, "I'm truly sorry for you, you poor widdle tumkins. Does my pretty fuzzy-wuzzy teddy bear have a boo-boo? Aw, that's tewwible. Where does it hurt? Why don't you let Daddy kiss it?..."

The mask dropped, the curtain went up, the clouds parted, and her blob face actually changed, becoming nakedly open and wrathful. Shakespeare explained this transition in *Macbeth* and *King Lear*; Francis Bacon caught it on canvas; Hitchcock gave it a whirl in *Psycho;* and Fat Man elucidated it competently at Hiroshima. We dance the light fantastic alongside Winnie the Pooh and Kermit the Frog until all of a sudden the trapdoor falls open, dumping us down the rabbit hole into a scatalogical darkness where babies are raped by priests, tobacco companies manufacture cigarettes, and sheep are cloned by amoral alchemists plotting Aryan revenge.

In short, Kelly quit being crazy and spat these words at me— venomously, fiendishly, brutishly cynical:

"You know why I drink, Charley? I'll tell you why I drink. Because the fucking world is doomed. There is no hope. You're an asshole to even try. A hundred species daily go extinct. A forest the size of New York State is eradicated each year. We're gonna kill off all the ozone by 2040, when the world population will be ten billion souls. The atmosphere is dying. Most wild animals and birds will be gone in three decades. Human beings will exist in a perpetual state of famine, warfare, and revolution. Everybody will have AIDS. Murder over tiny tidbits of food and water will soon be the leading cause of death on all continents. *There is no hope.* Every battle you ever fought was useless. The planet laughs at your crackpot idealism. Only a brain-damaged ignorant lunch bucket would think that by stopping an irrelevant highway bypass he could—"

It felt as if both my index finger and pinkie had fractured instantly upon contact as I drove my right fist directly into the middle of her obnoxious, bloated face:

POW!—right in the kisser!

I screamed, "OWWWWWWWCH!"

Caught by surprise, Kelly dropped like a ton of rocks wrapped in a wire-mesh bag—poleaxed—hitting the concrete so hard she bounced.

With my left hand I gripped my right wrist, and it wasn't just pain I experienced, it was as if every bone in my fist had been shattered by a sledgehammer banging at my flesh against an anvil. I saw stars, I saw tweety birds, I saw neon exclamation points the size of ponderosa pine trees dancing across the horizon! My tongue splashed forward two and a half feet, reached the end of its tether, and snap-curled back into my mouth like a heavy-duty rubber band shot against my lips at point-blank range:

WHAP!

And above the consternated murmur of the rabble scuffling toward the point of impact, I could hear the nauseating whir of at least a dozen motor-drives advancing thousands of frames of Tmax film at vertiginous speeds through many cameras, all of whose lenses were focused on me just as Clarence Fagerquist and Jack Bannerman ambled out of the S & L to make their world-shattering pronouncements about FAGERBAN and tomorrow's electoral imperatives.

On TV that night I saw a clip of my Hulk Hogan KOs Gorilla Monsoon act. Barney Lumpen had actually been taping our argument when I put the hammer to Kelly. It was the damnedest thing. My back was to the camera. You saw Kelly's mouth moving. She could have been one of those slow, bug-eyed, fat-lipped deep-sea fish called groupers, a kind of mournful, soporific tub of sludge trying to digest a rotten sea urchin. Then lightning struck as my tunderhook rearranged all the marbles in her brainpan. I didn't even step into it or cock my arm before launching the punch. My fist simply snapped forward like the slim steel shaft of a big switchblade knife. Channel 7 first showed it in live-action time, then ran it again in Super Slowmo magnified radically on their Jumbotron. Kelly never saw it coming. Upon contact, my fist started rolling at her upper lip, cruised through the nose, and ended up in the middle of her left eye. My shoulder was jolted as if from the recoil of a high-powered rifle or maybe a bazooka. Kelly's face went through a series of changes I can only describe as indecent. If you likened my fist to a hippopotamus dropped from a helicopter hovering one hundred feet above a giant three-ton lemon meringue pie floating in the center of a shallow African water hole, Kelly's face would have resembled what happened to that pie when the hippo hit.

Instantly, she dropped out of sight. Instinctively, I whirled around to confront the camera with a look of surprise on my mug I bet not even a professional nubile empty-headed teeny bopper in one of those *Friday the Thirteenth* ax carnivals could have imitated. And I yelled so loudly the videotape went haywire, showing herky-jerky blips of sky and feet and tipsy automobiles and frenetic bits and pieces of people—

Perhaps at some other nadir of my existence I had experienced a comparably excruciating pain, but I doubt it. Not when a mounted cop's horse ran over me during an anti-war demonstration on Fifth Avenue over thirty years ago, not when a fellow Little League teammate accidentally banged my front teeth out with a baseball bat, not when I slammed my right hand in a car door, not ever, not like *this*.

This was special.

The Mother of all Sudden Painfulness.

Dimly, I remember Luther exclaiming in horror, "What did you do that for?" as he leaped to Kelly's assistance.

Susan Delgado saved my life, she grabbed me before I hit the pavement, braced an arm around my waist, and started guiding me through the legions of journalists feasting upon my newsworthy dolor.

I worked my mandibles up and down, back and forth, opening and shutting my mouth, from which no coherent sound issued:

"*Hamma, hamma, hamma . . .*"

Amazingly, despite having a raphe nucleus on serotonin overload, Miranda Satan had stationed herself at my other elbow, muttering repeatedly in her vastly empathetic way: "That was gnarly, dude, like really bodacious."

My eyes must have revolved ludicrously backward into their deep-set sockets as I continued stammering, "*Hamma, hamma, hamma . . .*"

Then my *nose* began to bleed. Paul Sweetwater dodged out of the way. Ripple Mongiello made the HOOK 'EM, HORNS sign, wiggling the index finger and pinkie to ward off my evil vibes.

At the microphone, Clarence and Jack lifted on tiptoes, peering over the heads of the agitated populace to ascertain what, exactly, had caused the feeding frenzy:

"Ahem"—Jack tapped the mike.

Yet probably half the crowd pursued yours truly as Susan and Miranda guided me through the paparazzi: Barney Lumpen, Sandra Whosamadig, Lenny Brightmaster, Ricardo Martínez—

"Stand back, give him breathing room," Susan ordered.

"Are you two getting divorced?" Ricardo asked.

"We're not married yet," Susan explained.

At the mike, Jack Bannerman cleared his golden tonsils: "We called this conference here today to inform you all that—"

Through the bustling riffraff my amazons continued to propel me. Yeah, I recognized some faces, but they were all elliptical and jerky as in photographs and newsreels of D-Day landings. Christie LaRue, in a *Trollops For FAGERBAN* T-shirt, twirled expertly out of our slipstream; Eleanor Poddubny took a swing at me, but missed; and Tristan Griffith, tony in a double-breasted Versace smoking jacket, gave me a conspiratorial wink.

"Hey," a testy Clarence Fagerquist barked into the microphone. *"Hey, you people—"*

"What did she say to you?" Cable 11's Johnny Fabiola asked.

Susan Delgado let go my arm, surged ahead of me, turned, and fired her camera—*rat-a-tat-tat!* Then she elbowed her way back and grabbed my wrist: "Oh sweetie, are you okay?" Before I could answer, a tiny green krait dropped out of Tristan's nostril and slithered swiftly toward Susan's sandaled feet: She eeped, dropped my arm, and fled for her life. Miranda said, "Who spiked *her* axons?"

I pushed ahead with my good arm while using the other arm to ward off flashbulbs.

"Yo, Charley McFarland!" cried that gorgeous over-the-hill bombshell from Channel 7, Kim Sweetwater, "did you hit her out of love, or is it because she embezzled from the Butterfly Coalition and spent it on Las Vegas Chippendales?"

"Hamma, hamma, hamma . . ."

At the microphone, Clarence tried again: *"Hey you people, this is Clarence Fagerquist and I'm talking to you about the biggest outrage to hit this town since—"*

Then: Oh no, who was that apparition bobbing and weaving in front of me, that knobby awkward beanpole with Coke-bottle eyeglasses, a mustache like a moulting Irish goat, and his scrawny fists in an old-fashioned John L. Sullivan boxing stance? Not Randy Featherstone, ex-DJ, former husband of Tiffany and onetime father of three, the Captain Dreyfus of our own bucolic Suicide City, falsely accused, unscrupulously beleaguered, unfairly terminated (just today!), unconscionably ruined, a man with a king-sized chip on his shoulder and a Twisted Sister cassette in his front shirt pocket looking for a pressure relief valve in all the wrong places—?

POW!

Nope, *I* never knew what hit me, either.

Then it got a trifle Byzantine as Miranda stepped forward, firing her own left hand without thinking, and Randy never knew what had bashed *him* flat on his non-existent buns, he simply went down like an erector set, striking the earth in sections.

Before I could rise to one knee, Edna Poddubny hurtled clear of the confusion like an enraged beachball and knocked Luther's *outré* significant O for a righteous loop with a blow of sensational accuracy. Miranda went airborne in a kind of thrasher Tinker Bell moment, then landed on her scalped noodle—SPLAT!

Yet 'ere Edna had a second to gloat, the clenched skeletal fingers of her stepmother, Eleanor, rearranged her cookie-dough features in a decidedly emphatic way, and Edna stumbled from whence she had vaulted bellowing, *"You are all Satan! God will punish you! Jesus abhors a vacuum—"* BLONG!

Then Tammy Sue Clendennon blindsided her rival for Jack's illicit attentions, grabbing Eleanor's sticky hair and wrenching her head sideways while kicking her in the groin. But on her way turfward, Eleanor latched onto the front of Tammy Sue's sunset yellow Barbie jumper—*riiiiip!*—and at last those fantastic, rosy, darling, and voluminous BREASTS popped free for all the world to ogle!

But those were only the preliminaries. That was the under card. The warm-up act. The preface to What Happened Next. Did you forget about Kelly McFarland during the ensuing hubbub? Tch tch. Shame on you. Because here she came now, eager to be on center stage again. What her entrance lacked in coordination it made up for in belligerence. It seemed almost as if Luther was pushing her forward, though actually Kelly was dragging *him* along as he tried to restrain her. She slipped, tottered sideways, and bellyflopped on top of me even as Luther finally ensnared one of her wrists. "Don't hurt my dad, Kelly!" *"Fuck your dad, Luther!"* They began to wrestle beside me, Kelly blindly kicking, jabbing, and squirming as Luther worked to pin down her thrashing appendages, more on Kelly's behalf, I suspect, than out of genuine concern for his poppa.

I rolled away from them just as Johnny Batrus squirted through the crush of bodies and landed with a loud grunt on top of Kelly and Luther. Herkie Pacheco and Shirley Scavcyzk joined the free-for-all, tackling flailing arms and ankles while Johnny fought to free the handcuffs on his belt. In rodeos they call it steer wrestling; in rugby it's just a scrum. The Discovery Channel plugs these shows as "Crocodiles Eating Zebras."

But I'm a pacifist and I had an election to win on the morrow, hence I kept rolling away from the fray until I could regain my shaky feet. All around me the carnage sizzled. Flashbulbs popped while Tammy Sue giggled, demurely cupping her love monkeys. Irate citizens were stomping that pinko newspaper editor, Edna Poddubny, who'd tucked herself into a hedgehog ball for protection. Somehow, Miranda Satan's spindly gams had become entangled in Eleanor Poddubny's scrawny drumsticks, and both ladies were twisting and kicking to escape. "I am so definitely *not* having a multiple orgasm here," Miranda griped. And nearby Randy Featherstone lay in a puddle of moustache and broken teeth, groaning vociferously.

The last words cast upon the airwaves behind me as I zigzagged to freedom between jabbing microphones, whirring video cameras, and coked-up hyper-journalists, were Kelly's desperate exclamations: "Let go of me, you dirty rats! *I want to kill my husband!*"

You gotta get up,
you gotta get up,
you gotta get up in the morning!
You gotta get up,
you gotta get up,
you gotta get up today!

Y ES YOU DO, and I did. Early on Election Day I flung aside the pillows, the cats, and the blankets, jumped out of bed, admonished my bruised face in the mirror—"Yo, get a grip!"—then let out a shout, *"Banzai!"* and headed for the kitchen where a half dozen mouse gallbladders were strewn across the linoleum: barf. Carlos had shredded a roll of toilet paper in the bathroom: Good for him! *Go, Carlos!* A dead junco lay on its back with its feet sticking up in the sink. I fed everybody their Science Diet, then gobbled a bowl of cornflakes and brown sugar. My right-hand fingers were swollen double and throbbed, but nothing was broken. At the conclusion of the hurried repast, I wrestled with Mangus for a minute, then brushed my teeth, dressed in patriotic red, white, and green, and, as always in my illustrious career as a protean political gadfly, I dashed outside with my heart on my sleeve (and my poor brain reeling) to kick ass on Election Day.

A blissed-out Susan Delgado was seated on the portal in my old rocking chair sound asleep with Tommy on her lap. When I shut the kitchen door behind me she woke up, immediately alert and involved.

"Good morning, Chuck, I worried about you all night."

"I'm okay. Not to worry. It's time to flail, quail." And off the portal I hopped, down the walk, into the driveway, toward the car, in a big hurry: no time for idle badinage. Susan jumped up, tagging along right behind me like Dennis Rodman guarding Muggsy Bogues.

"Did you hear what happened last night?" Her lips danced about six millimeters from my left ear.

No, I hadn't heard, nor did I particularly wish to hear, thanks anyway: My frequencies were already pretty jammed with thoughts of upcoming obligations. Or, to be more specific, I was overdetermined and in no mood for her style transduction of affect. Hence, I tried to ignore the reporter on my way to the Buick, but Susan would not easily be deterred. As I reached for the door handle she dropped a hand on my shoulder, yanked the rip cord on her gossip cornucopia, and an amazing abundance of stuff came tumbling out:

"Somebody shot down the FAGERBAN pro–Prop X banner plane with a surface-to-air missile. Johnny Batrus threw Luther and your wife in jail for that fracas at the news conference. *The New York Times* reprinted my picture of Kelly's van in Burger Boy and said it had Pulitzer potential. Down in the Capital, when ATF men tried to arrest Peter Lithgow for taking kickbacks to squelch our endangered species petition, he committed suicide by diving headfirst without a snorkle into his own empty swimming pool. There's a six-column photo of you pasting Kelly on the *Sentinel-Argus* front page: BUTTERFLY SLUGS DRUNKEN THUG! Supposedly Inside Edition, Geraldo, and ET are flying into town on Lear jets. Somebody tried to rape that reporter, Kim Sweetwater, in the Hot Rod Motel last night, but she had a can of Mace in her bra and zapped him. Tristan Griffith and

Manjo Poddubny rammed each other's shopping carts in Smith's ten minutes before closing time, and Mary, from the library, had a miscarriage. Channel 11's bubble copter Eye-In-The-Sky smashed into one of the surviving Tammy Sue Clendennon billboards, but, miraculously, nobody died. In real life, Tammy Sue won a right-to-work benefit wet-T-shirt contest sponsored by William Watrous at Topless Au Go Go and Lu Ann Bannerman caught Jack in the ladies' rest room again with Marbella Tremaine. Unfortunately, Mookie Dirigible croaked onstage later on when he had an orgasm into his Stratocaster strings and was electrocuted. Bo Hrbyk is heading up from the Capital with a cease and desist for First State S & L. A tailings spill at the mine killed eight thousand trout and a Shriner from Tulsa. And half the voting machines are jammed even before the polls have opened. I love you for a hundred thousand reasons, Charley: *When are you going to respond?*"

With a lot on my mind I had tuned her out, settled behind the wheel, applied the ignition key . . . and zilch occurred. "OH GOD DAMMIT!" I hollered, "I'M SO GRATEFUL THIS HAPPENED ON A DAY WHEN I DON'T NEED THE CAR! THANK YOU GOD FOR ALL THE CONSIDERATION YOU NIHILISTIC UPTIGHT TRUCULENT STUD-MUFFIN!"

Jeez.

Susan unlatched the hood, flung it up, scrutinized the large V-8 engine for a minute, then reached in and tweaked something.

"Now try it, Chazz-ma-tazz."

I tried: *Roaaar!*

"Oh *thank* you, Susan, you saved my life, I owe you forever, just name it, I'll always be in your debt—"

Susan nonchalantly slammed the hood down . . . on her own left hand . . . but she didn't scream. Instead, she calmly unlatched the hood with her free hand, lifted it (the hood) a bit, removed her fingers, and blew on them. Soon enough a look of saintly adoration entered her eyes . . . and she sneezed.

A *miracle!*

Lydia was alive, dressed, and waiting among a chorus of hungrily meowing cats when I arrived. Her Sunday finest consisted of an uncombed wig clotted by dabs of stale peanut butter, a one-piece button-up blue-checkered dress radically enhanced by splashes of ketchup, soy sauce, and mayonnaise, and boat-sized Nikes on her feet. Completing the outfit was her old tweed jacket (with a faded FREE HUEY button on the lapel) and a pair of moth-eaten brown leather driving gloves. In her ears?—a set of tiny Biswa pearl earrings. And on her mouth?—Holy Toadstools, mergatroid!— *a dash of lipstick.*

"Wow, Lydia, you look fabulous."

"Where were you?" she grumbled. "I've been waiting over an hour. You should be shot."

I noticed that the vulgar old suffragette had been rewriting her will again. Pages of it were half buried in a cat box, scattered beneath the kitchen table, spread across the stove (partially burned), and lodged in branches of a large dead geranium plant. Hastily, I collected all the sheaves, trying to arrange them in a semblance of order, berating Lydia as I did so: "What are you trying to do, babe, sabotage your own posterity, destroying everything we've worked for?"

"Shuttup," she replied. "I was just clarifying some stuff."

Yeah, right. I couldn't see anywhere in her atrociously messy dump where the will would not get lost in the detritus or be chewed, shat upon, or pissed at by cats, so I thrust the document into the refrigerator's freezer compartment among a great buildup of frost humps and about a dozen aluminum-foiled trout caught by Father Benny Wombat and Dr. Lorenzo Jackson years ago.

Then I rapidly poured eight pounds of Chef's Blend into a feeding trough for the cats, and from a closet I grabbed an overcoat, two scarves, her blue knitted cap. I yanked a blanket off the bed. Lydia grimaced as I snatched away her cigarette and stubbed it out. When I pulled her erect her bones "snapped, crackled, and popped." Twice, the old woman gave an oddly embarrassed peep and threatened to call her lawyer, suing me for every cent I owned. While she was stabilized at her walker, I worked on the overcoat, tugged down the knitted cap, and pulled colorful Scandinavian mittens over the driving gloves.

"I can set up the wheelchair, you know."

"Like hell," she groused. "Today I *will* stand to be counted."

We were in a real hurry, but Lydia pushed her walker ahead a foot and then ventured one birdlike step, and then another. Six inches at a wallop the feeble nonagenarian progressed past the kitchen table to the portal doorway where I helped ease her over the jamb, urging, "C'mon, Lydia, get the lead out, we got a lot to do today."

That certainly speeded her up. The aged fingers in my grip seemed lighter than air, mere wisps of flesh, icy to touch. Scrooch, scrooch, scrooch—Lydia's feet scraped daintily down her wooden steps into the driveway. Like a tiny glacier she needed fifteen minutes to travel ten feet. The passenger door waited, already open. It required a deft touch to maneuver her into the car without too much pain, but we accomplished that all right. Lydia breathed hard, however. And as I tucked the blanket and adjusted pillows, I asked, "Are you okay?"

"None of your damn beeswax." She folded her arms defiantly underneath the blankets. "Now, get this show on the road."

"Yes ma'am." I leaped behind the wheel and fired that sucker up.

As we crawled along at ten miles per hour I couldn't help noticing that it was a golden autumn morning to take your breath away, the air clean and brisk and tainted with a refreshing hint of evergreen off the nearby looming mountains. For a moment the dust and the drought had dissipated. Enormous fluffy bouquets of bright yellow cottonwood foliage arched over the road in a dazzling profusion that stimulated our senses. A bright blue sky hovered above Suicide City, unblemished and sensational, the blue so vividly blue it seemed to have derived from ancient Chinese porcelain dyes or indigo cloth manufactured in Pakistan. A day so ostensibly pure perpetuated one of the great illusions of our times: That nothing was rotten in Denmark. However, invisible poisons by the score—extracted from malathion, tebuthiuron, DDT, toxaphene—tickled the billion tiny alveoli in every lung with each eager inhalation. Yet blithely the denizens of Suicide City gazed skyward at the blueness blessing them and thanked their lucky stars.

Lydia sucked in her hollow cheeks and made a malevolent pouty face. "Did you bring any liquor?"

"On Election Day? Heavens to Betsy, dear soul, what's got into your frivolous head?"

Lydia sulked as I steered into the grade-school parking lot beside a gymnasium where many other cars had already gathered. Naturally, the Fourth Estate's swelling ranks of jackals were out in force on The Babcock Watch, as eager to glimpse the derelict behind the myth as America had once been stoked to learn secrets about the reclusive billionaire Howard Hughes. Dozens of grubby electioneering maggots were on hand also, jabbering and waving placards for incoming voters to be influenced by. Tamara Pez de Balmaric and Melanie Ann Margaret Fagerquist held up their BOMB THE BUTTERFLY slogans. Randall Mobley waved his WIN WITH WATROUS banner. Douthit Hawthorne (no doubt on Buddy's payroll) held up a "YES" ON X IS BETTER THAN SEX. Other arrested life-forms in the FAGERBAN camp posturing their irritating propaganda in our faces were Cranston Pelletier (the clodhopping scion of Swoozie and Moe); Sherman and Sherlock Kinderfink (under the watchful eye of Melody, their mom); and Marcia Stonebutter Crawford, mother of little Alex and Gwyneth (who were at Grandma's house today).

Lydia tilted her head back, attempting to focus her one eye through the lower focal screen of her glasses. "I *hate* the media."

Yet a dash of crimson colored her sunken cheeks, and her beady little eye sparkled in anticipation.

"You ready?" I asked.

"Absolutely."

I clambered out, retrieved the walker, and opened Lydia's door. By then the cattle had arrived and were lowing impatiently.

"Hey Charley! Is this Lydia Arlington Babcock, the infamous 'Voice of the Butterfly'?"

"You better believe it," Lydia replied.

"Okay, tell us, then—is it true you used to be Father Benny Wombat's secret cooze?"

Lydia did not even hesitate: "FAGERBAN is a bunch of yellow-bellied old blowhards trying to 'save' our town by destroying it."

As I helped my old pal out of the Buick onto her feet, Susan Whosamadig asked, "Is Father Benny also a switch-hitter with his longtime companion Farragut Wallaby?"

Lydia gave a painful cry, but then her bony fingers tightly gripped the side bars of her walker and her voice rasped loudly and strong:

"FAGERBAN will pollute our town, further destabilize the economy, and double an already-atrocious crime rate!"

"What about Tammy Sue Clendennon?" said Johnny Fabiola. "Did you target her billboards because she's one of Jack Bannerman's jellybeans?"

"Make way, please, give us room." My hand was poised near the old bird's elbow, but Lydia ignored me. She was pumped up and determined to show the world her tough and independent spirit. Let their photographs prove she had her boots on.

Catherine Savage, a young reporter on one of the downstate dailies, said, "Did you hit Kelly yesterday, Charley, because you just learned that she's the lesbian lover of Swoozie Pelletier?"

"He hit her because Kelly's nuts!" Lydia clarified, irritated at their truly retarded dirt fixations.

Lenny Brightmaster said, "Are you implying that FAGERBAN will collapse because Jack Bannerman is also shtupping Eleanor Poddubny?"

"No we are not," I responded emphatically. "The Butterfly Coalition *always* occupies the high moral ground."

Chris Ledyard wanted to know, "Is it true, Charley, that you and Susan Delgado have become a bouncy-bouncy item despite your marital status with Kelly?"

Lydia countered, "No, you must never confuse capitalism with democracy: They don't even live on the same planet!"

Unfortunately, lichens eat rocks faster than we approached that gymnasium. Flashbulbs popped, motor drives churned and clanked, and a handful of well-dressed youthful TV sharks spoke into hand-held mikes, backs to Lydia, facing their respective cameras, obtaining exclusive footage of this memorable occasion as the venerable old lady tottered across the background:

"Bob," I heard Channel 7's nubile Kim Sweetwater say, "I'm standing right near the door of the Garcia Middle School here, which is the polling place for all members of Precinct 18, and behind me, as you can see, is the hundred-year-old leader of the Butterfly Coalition, Ms. Sylvia Darlington Crabcock, credited with being the mastermind behind a number of sexually explicit, violent incidents during this election season, including the felling of sado-erotic FAGERBAN billboards, a fast-food eatery car crash engineered by a jilted lover, and, just recently, a free-for-all at a FAGERBAN press conference because of improprieties between the lefty biased newspaper editor, Edna Poddubny, and her dog groomer named Sharon Ludlow—"

M EANWHILE, DOWN AT the county jail Luther awoke with one of those headaches you read about in a *World Weekly News* article describing how a thalidomide dwarf, shot from a cannon, whose parachute fails to open, hits a brick wall going ninety, but is saved by a teflon motorcycle helmet with a good luck copy of the Kamasutra stitched into its cranial webbing.

And it was all coming back to the poor kid now. My blow that had keelhauled Kelly, the ruckus that ensued—a tag-team free-for-all—the cops, the guns, the threats, the cufflinks, the paddy wagon, the jailers, the strip search (even up his asshole!), the keys jangling, the metal doors clanging shut, the echoing footsteps retreating down the Lysol'd cement of empty corridors, the camera angles tilting dizzily as his eyes scrutinized every inch of the dank and dismal tank searching for an exit . . . but to no avail. He was trapped, his reputation ruined, his life destroyed, and him but a wee broth of a lad, hardly grown—

Luther rolled over, searching for Kelly. Because their cell measured only eight by ten, he located his stepmom pretty quick, captured in a slanting early-morning sunbeam that had penetrated the tiny barred porthole miles above their heads. Don't ask how she had procured yet another half-pint bottle of peppermint schnapps, but she had.

Drunks are like that. Ludicrous things metamorphose out of thin air around heavy boozers. Unexpected stuff happens. Suddenly all their teeth fall out or a confused rabbit ricochets off one ankle. I remember when Kelly opened the driverside door of my Buick and fell straight down an embankment thirty feet to a half-frozen river into which an enormous female moose was pissing. Another time she struck a sulfur match on her zipper to light a joint and all her hair went up in smoke without an inch of scalp being singed.

Prisoner number 55697143 stared at Luther as the gooey booze sluiced warmly down her ragged pipe. Her face looked as if it had been mangled in a sickle-bar. Normally, they did not sequester females among the male jail inmates, but there's a chance that nobody had realized Kelly was a female. You couldn't tell by the shredded clothing, nor either by the hair, the red hair splattered all over Kelly's swollen noodle like a chicken used for a target in a marathon paintball game. During open heart surgery they almost freeze your body and you bloat up and turn blue and lose your facial definition, which had happened to Kelly also. The fingers that gripped her bottle were Nutty Professor digits. The black hightop sneakers on her feet lacked laces. Kelly was a genderless bum.

Luther ran fingers through his caked and filthy Mohawk, rubbed his eyes, yawned and scratched an itch at his chalky throat, then dug wax from both ears, rubbing it off on his crotch—*his crotch.* Oh my God, "Why aren't I wearing any clothes?"

Matter-of-factly, Kelly said, "You went nuts when they arrrested us, so they requisitioned them as a precaution against suicide."

"Who smuggled you that bottle, dude?" Luther asked irately.

"Nobody. They stole all my belongings, too."

Luther sat up, scrooching his knees in tight and folding his arms around them, making himself as compact as possible in order to hide his nakedness.

"So how did you get that liquor, Kelly?" Suddenly, the skinhead became a self-righteous inquisitor.

"I conjured it."

"What does that mean?" Luther was beginning to feel really pissed off at the so-called "adult" world.

Kelly said, "I woke up thirsty, hallucinating, DTs. I thought 'Girlfriend, if you don't get a hit right now you're worm food.' So I closed my eyes real tight and conjured up a bottle. It ain't easy, but I've got an aptitude for it."

Luther stared at her for thirty seconds. Then he said, "You really fucked up this time, Kelly. In fact, you're a first-class jerk. Pop will never speak to me again. You know what I'm *supposed* to be doing? I'm supposed to be driving people to the *polls*, but what am I doing instead?—I'm in a *jail* cell naked with a *moron*."

Kelly fitfully raised upward the baggy lid of one bloodshot eye and muttered, "What do you care?"

"No, I'm serious," Luther said bitterly. "What am I gonna do now? If Prop X passes and FAGERBAN becomes a reality, my ass is grass. My dad will blame it all on me. The goddam environment will self-destruct, the Fascists will control the government, acid rain will kill every lake in AmeriKKKa, cholera will maim and eradicate most of the kids in Latin America, Haiti will explode and vanish and only the pig oligarchy will escape safely to Miami, the ozone will disappear, the Greenhouse Effect will fry all our brains, and, worst of all, the Phistic Copper butterfly will be rubbed out. How does *that* make you feel, you lowdown cheap . . . drunk?"

A shadow fell across Kelly's features. She knitted her brow in consternation. Finally, she said, "It makes me feel good."

"Why, for God's sake?"

Kelly said, "Because I'm still in love with your dad."

What? Luther stared at her, uncomprehending. Maybe he saw, for the very first time, how truly terrified and fragile and fallen apart Kelly was. It clobbered him hard and all the organs inside his body cavity lurched uncomfortably. "Love?" What sort of demented human equation could she possibly be talking about? Luther questioned hoarsely, "Why are you killing yourself, Kelly?"

She said, "Because I'm afraid of dying."

Luther could not compute that answer, either. "Why don't you go back to AA?" he croaked unhappily.

"You don't understand," Kelly said gently.

"It's never too late to try again," he moaned.

"I don't want to try again," Kelly said. "Been there, done that, kiddo."

Luther gathered himself and said, "You have to quit drinking." And after taking a deep breath, he added, "You could live with me if you want. I could take care of you during the worst part of withdrawal. I start a new job next week at Tastee Freez. My place has running water, a toilet, a refrigerator. I'll clean it up, if you want. It would be a castle compared to that van—"

Kelly shrugged, hugging herself, and shivered, shaking her head. She was crying for the first time he could ever remember. "I'm sorry, but it doesn't work like that," Kelly explained in a whisper. *"It isn't logical."*

Well . . . Luther was tough. Luther was gangsta and skinhead and drug hardened and bruised by a hard life already. Luther had lost his real momma in a car accident, and had lived with a dad who never quit raging about the dire nightmares on earth. Luther had been formed by the Sex Pistols, Slayer, the Dayglo Abortions, Tupac Shakur. Luther had always worked at minimum wage for bosses who called him a maggot. His girlfriend, Miranda, had been sexually abused when kidnapped by aliens. His Generation X/Y buddies thought the answer to life was a shotgun and Kurt Cobain: "Oh well, whatever." Despite the harsh facade, however, deep down my boy had hope. But Kelly . . . Kelly was something again that Luther did not understand. Kelly was a new kind of monster in his life because in the beginning he had loved her, just as I had, and that love symbolized hope. To Luther, Kelly had been everything you might call a life force out of control, the very chaotic act of creation itself. Kelly was the volcanic Angel of Life and Death, the Dervish of Humor and Laughter and Sex. Kelly had promised to Luther everything *They* tried to squelch in school, or on TV, or in Boy Scouts.

Kelly was unfettered, crazy, *alive,* the stepmom of any kid's dreams. Kelly was sheer beautiful vitality . . . and hope.

But now look what had happened to the patron saint of that carnival. Something had killed all her buffalo, strip-mined her Mesabi Range, and polluted her Mississippi River. Yes, you bet, it sure wasn't "logical." Luther had to avert his eyes. The lad slumped . . . his body ached . . . he hadn't the energy to persevere. He was kind of maxed out on trauma issues for one day. Plus, anyway, he didn't know what else to say, what was he, a headshrinker? He had nothing to barter with for this woman's life beyond his pad . . . and his anger . . . and his clumsy budding compassion . . . where had *that* come from? And, at this late date, what good was it against what's hopeless?

Like a recently captured mountain gorilla, Luther swung himself in a painful half-waddle across his cage into the corner farthest from Kelly, conglobated in surrender, furrowed his brow, and brooded for a spell on the hazards and vicissitudes of this perilous existence. His stepmother regarded him sadly as her eyelids drooped . . . then Kelly began snoring loudly. Outside their cell, in the Real World of Liberty and Justice For All, Election Day, in all its variegated pomp and circumstances, continued unabashedly to unfurl.

An ambulance siren, blaring jarringly, headed south on the highway past the prison, aiming toward Holy Cross Hospital. Luther almost thought: *There but for the grace of God—*

Then he gave it the finger, growling, "Screw you, God."

BUT NO GOD (and very little grace) plied the highway, only Lydia Arlington Babcock flat on her back on a stretcher hooked up to a three-lead cardiac monitor with a trache tube down her throat, a D5W IV in her arm, and a paramedic (Dakota Namath) on one side ventilating the patient, and an EMT (Mimi Spitz) on the other side keeping one eye glued to the monitor screen while performing CPR chest compressions. Susan Delgado crouched in a far corner capturing the moment for the ages with her trusty Nikon, and yours truly was squatting at Lydia's feet holding tightly to one of her ankles, asking her not to die, not yet. "You're gonna screw up Election Day! Wake up! Can she hear me?"

"Hard to tell," said Mimi. "She's not conscious, but nobody really knows what they can hear. Go ahead and talk if you want."

"Lydia, dammit—don't go yet. Do you hear me, you nasty old crone? *Yo!*"

It was tough to make myself heard above the siren as pell-mell down the highway we raced, swinging right and left, jouncing high over bumps, clattering through potholes—I had to hang on tight.

Dakota said, "Hey, Mimi, hit her again, she just went asystole."

"Three hundred joules?"

"Christ no, you almost killed her last time. Better make it two."

Susan cried, "Stop! *I'm allergic to electricity!*"

Mimi placed the two defibrillator paddles against Lydia, handed me the FREE HUEY button, told me, "Don't look," snapped "Clear the patient!" and, soon as Dakota took her hand off the rubber vent bag, released a jolt: *whomp!* Lydia shuddered and her pitiful thin frame went up in the air like a flapjack out of a frying pan, then her face turned redder than a traffic light saying STOP and a sinus rhythm reappeared on the monitor screen.

"What do you think?" I asked Dakota.

"I'm not paid to think, Charley Mac. I just bang 'em, shoot 'em full of adrenaline, and dump 'em in the mail slot at Holy Cross."

Rubber squealed as we careened into a hospital emergency space, the siren died, and a frantic scrambling ensued. Larry Boggs, the driver, jerked open both doors from outside and I hopped out as he reached in for the hind rail bar of Lydia's rolling stretcher. *Squawk, rumble, thud, bump!* Seconds later we were trotting in a group toward emergency doors held open by a nurse, Judy Rimbert, who'd been notified ahead by cell phone. Susan, limping, had put in a new role of film and was punching the shutter button, shooting blanks. Behind us, a flotilla of media vehicles poured into the parking lot, including ones with ABC, Fox, and CNN logos. The Channel 4 news crew scrambled from a mobile unit van and charged toward the hospital like GIs leaping from a helicopter onto a hot LZ. Susan pointed her infernal camera at them: "Stop, or I'll shoot!" But they kept advancing as we trundled into a hallway, turned right, entered the Emergency Room, and merciful doors slammed shut behind us.

Doctors, interns, nurses—it was all a blur to me. Lydia disappeared into an antiseptic cacophony of flapping white wings and calm professional voices: "What's her pulse?. . ." "How many cc's?. . ." "Oops! Asystole again." Bewildered, I chose a spot on a bench in the corner, thoroughly ignored for a moment as half a dozen human beings brandishing wires, hoses, meters, instruments, tubes, monitors, bags, and bottles labored over that seventy-nine-pound yenta in her ninety-second year. All emergency workers were very calm. Their role in life was to keep her alive at all costs. And I do mean "costs." The minute Lydia had gone through those doors the meter was up and running on the most expensive ride in town. Already the ambulance had cost eight hundred bucks. The first pair of surgical gloves that the lowest troll in the medical food chain tugged onto her hands set back Lydia (her insurance company, Medicare, her 401-K, her pension fund, and any living relative) forty dollars. Blood pressure was $120. Her temperature taken by one of those newfangled press-a-button gismos?—$89.95 . . . plus tax. The stethoscope against her chest?—$48.50 and counting. The epinephrine injection totaled $78.30. And the glucose IV bag they started automatically?—seventy-nine dollars even. The rhythm strip they ran off cost two hundred and forty smackers. I looked at my watch, four minutes had passed, and the bill was already three thousand dollars. Medicine in America is like a train wreck . . . a Las Vegas casino . . . the muscle that collects on gangland usury. When they wheel you through the door of any hospital on the mainland a bell rings in the vault of Morgan Guarantee Trust in New York so that the doors will open in time for a representative of your local HMO to cart in another canvas duffel bag full of "blood money," I believe it's called.

Susan snaked an arm around me solicitously. "Don't worry, Chas, it'll be okay, they're not going to hurt her." I thought she added, "I'll take care of you," but maybe she only said, "I saw a dozen crayfish." Susan raised her hand and tentatively massaged the back of my neck. When I checked out her eyes they seemed oddly whimsical. Curiously, the green hair spikes on her head had wilted.

Oh no, here came Dr. Roderick "The Zipper" Nuzum, tall and businesslike, shedding tatty wisps of superiority off his Bill Bradley cowlick as he broke away from the scrum at Lydia's body and approached us. Yes, it's true, doctors cruise through the world like prey fish quartering the flats, dominating their environment, secure in the impenetrable mystique of their sacred mumbo jumbo. And this one, The Zipper, had more superior airs than Britain's royal family.

"Well well, Charley—" He held out a large, clean, hairy-knuckled and paternalistic hand, which I could not figure how to avoid, so I shook it. I like a gentle, non-macho, non-threatening handshake, but this bastard squashed my fingers together with cruel Anglo-Saxon vigor until I almost kicked him in the shins.

Susan clicked a photograph, then ducked as a school of laughing hushpuppies made a low pass over us, veering north.

"It's nice to see you," The Zipper remarked cheerlessly. "How is Mr. Stalin?"

"What is her condition?" I asked, resisting the urge to belt him.

"Offhand I'd say she's a goner."

"Can you do anything?" I asked.

"Sure, if I had a shovel and a fifty-pound bag of lime."

Yuk yuk. That square-jawed handsome putz must have shaved with Gillette Foamy Gel and a three-bladed razor. He vacationed in Maui, windsurfing. His girlfriend, Angela Glamm, pumped up at the spa and also taught Jazzercize.

Baffled, Susan peered down into the optics of her Japanese soul stealer. Then she twisted off the lens, poked in her finger, said "Yipes!" and yanked it out (the finger), because a tiny pit bull half the size of a maraschino cherry had tenaciously attached itself to the tip of her index finger.

The Zipper said, "Just to be legal, Charley, I better gather some info. What kind of pills was she taking?"

I tried to think, but it wasn't easy: "Lanoxin, a diuretic, lasix, K-tabs, I think prednisone, a stool softener, Percocet . . ."

"*Ouch.* That fucking Lorenzo is an animal."

"He kept her alive," I said.

"In a chemical soup," he grumbled.

Occasionally, through the barrage of flapping white wings I caught a glimpse of tiny Lydia sucking oxygen through a tube, an IV needle attached to one arm, colored wire leads trailing off her chest to the heart and oxygen monitors—like a low-budget Japanese Frankenstein thriller. The meter beside her bed registered $11,386.42. When a nurse plucked a Kleenex tissue from a box to wipe Lydia's nose, the amount jumped by another double sawbuck.

The Zipper asked, "Did she have a long history of heart trouble?"

"Not until a year ago."

Susan opened the back of her camera, allowing twisted ribbons of the film strip to bulge out writhing like little flattened space snakes, a debacle she contemplated in paralyzed yet tranquil imbecility. The reporter was starting to make me nervous.

"Any allergies to medicine?" the good doctor queried.

"I don't think so."

"Okay, that's fine and dandy. Now why don't you tell me *exactly* what transpired at the voting booth."

I said, "It happened after she voted."

"You were with her?"

"Not in the booth. An election official went in—Sadie Puerifoy."

He nodded. "We used to bowl together in the Frito League. Nice ta ta's."

"When they came out, Sadie gave me Lydia's arm and I asked, 'How'd it go?' Lydia said, 'Fine. If we win by a single vote I'm the one to blame.'"

"Then it hit her like Two Ton Tony Galento?"

"Exactly."

"Better give me the gory details."

". . . I had her arm . . . I reached for her walker . . . and suddenly she stiffened."

"And?"

"And she ripped her arm out of my grasp, both her hands shot straight up in the air, and her face turned bright red. So I ran to the car, grabbed her oxygen, raced back inside, and clapped the mask over her face. Then I offered her a cigarette."

"You WHAT?"

"I offered a cigarette."

"A CIGARETTE?" His hair literally bristled—*twang!*

"Sure. Nicotine always perks her up."

"NICOTINE? Christ al*mighty*."

"I know. But this time it didn't work."

A nurse came over, Joanie Galveston. She was petite, blond haired, pert, and lively. "Dr. Nuzum, the heart's not responding well. Shall we put her on the respirator? Do you want a catheter?"

"No, just give her a cigarette, Joanie."

The nurse turned pale: "WHAT?"

"She likes nicotine," he said.

"Nicotine *kills* people, Dr. Nuzum."

"Tell me something I didn't learn in kindergarten," The Zipper guffawed, nudging me conspiratorially with his elbow.

Joanie said, "Well, I never . . ." and walked away.

An intern broke off from the scrum around Lydia and hurried over: Michael Snead (Margo's nephew), a disheveled sporty young fellow who drove a Vespa. To me he said:

"I'm afraid your friend just passed away."

I said, "Excuse me?"

"Gone."

"It's over?"

"She passed away."

"Don't say 'passed away,'" I corrected. "I hate that expression. Lydia did too."

Michael said, "I . . . don't understand . . ."

"She *croaked*," I explained. "She *kicked the bucket*, she *bought the farm*, she *ate the daisies*, she *caught a taxi*, she *died*, okay?"

Michael looked to Dr. Nuzum for help, but already The Zipper had evaporated. At Lydia's gurney the meter kept ticking away, however, mounting up the expenses as, with vertiginous speed, the Emergency Room emptied out of everybody except a janitor, Bainbridge Clews, who was pushing a long-handled broom, sweeping up the Band-Aid wrappers, tourniquet rubbers, discarded sterile gloves, hairnets, pill bottles, and used syringes. He pushed a pile of stuff over to a wastebasket, hoisted it up in a disposable dustpan, dropped the whole shebang into the garbage, then whapped down Lydia's meter flag as he split.

The charges stopped at $16,873.46.

Susan and I were alone with Lydia's body . . . her corpse . . . her carcass . . . her cadaver . . . her . . . *worm food*. Lydia's mouth was so wide open you could have driven a Peterbilt eighteen-wheeler right into it.

And all of about eighteen seconds had elapsed since they'd pronounced her.

Wow. I thought to myself: This is an interesting development likely to really bollix up my Election Day. That might sound a tad harsh, but we weren't talking about an unforseen calamity here, right?, only the timing involved. Legally, of course, I needed to confer immediately with Farragut Wallaby, which meant he'd be nowhere to be found. Decisions (re Lydia's burial) had to be made quickly, however, before the press went crazy. And then I'd have to spring Luther—

Tiptoeing over to Lydia I took a good "last" look, fully expecting one of her eyes to open and wink at me, but it didn't. They always say a corpse seems smaller than the real person and I guess that's true enough. Lydia, dead and shriveled, had about as much bulk as a thirty-cent box of farts. But for just a beat I was overwhelmed by the panorama of her long existence with its social commitments, and all the rallies against racism and marches to halt the war and demonstrations of solidarity with the wretched and the oppressed and the reeling environment that Lydia had attended, that she had helped to organize, that she had written about and been devoted to body and soul. And that's a life, in these harsh times, I thought to myself during a very brief moment of reprieve, that a person should make an effort to honor. No, I didn't cross myself, I'm not that hypocritical, but I pinned the FREE HUEY button back on her lapel, and then laid my hand against her wrist with gratitude and love. *Good-bye, old Shep . . . you were a better man than I am, Gunga Din.*

But soon Lydia's wide-open mouth became a trifle disconcerting. Then curiosity got the better of me and I peeped in anyway to see what I could see . . . expecting, perhaps, one of those cat hairball moppet things with tiny bright eyes peering out—?

"Lean in a little closer," Susan commanded, aiming and focusing from six feet away. "Put your whole fist in her mouth."

GOOD NEWS travels fast, they say, and it was reported to me later that by eleven A.M. the Nob Hill Mobsters Clarence Fagerquist, Jack Bannerman, Manjo Poddubny, and Sam Clendennon were drinking champagne over Lydia's death at the Throne Table in the Quail Creek Dining Salon while the Copernicus brothers (Jerry and Bob), Tony Stryzpk, Wayne Kinderfink, Tamara Pez de Balmaric, Eleanor Poddubny, Pinkie Tattle, Hank Wattle, William Watrous, and other sundry reactionary FAGERBAN investors looked on, boisterously joining the toasts and choruses of "Hear! Hear! The wicked witch is dead!"

While those overconfident fat cats were rejoicing, however, we crippled dysfunctional underdog mousies continued our spastic keystone antics in hopes of snatching a miracle victory from the cruel jaws of inevitable defeat.

Orlando Pfeiffer twisted his rusty iron key in an ancient lock, swung open the cell door, and told Luther and Kelly, "You're free. Beat it. Good riddance."

"I don't *want* the older one," I said.

Up front at the desk Kelly reclaimed her teeth and Luther donned the clothes I'd brought. Kelly had two black eyes, a lopsided nose, and a herpetic lower lip the size of a small (rotting) banana. I cringed. That haymaker yesterday had been the first and only time in my life that I had struck a woman. Her eyes avoided mine and she seemed a bit under the weather, just standing there in a catatonic heap awaiting the next step. Needless to say, baggy shaggy clothes dripped off her body in formless multitudes of rag. One thing about Kelly: I *never* ran out of adjectives to describe her.

My son wasn't too happy, either. He mumbled, "What took you so fuckin' long?" then he began to kvetch because a freaked-out howlie in the neighboring cage had pissed through the bars onto Luther's head causing fuschia dye from the Mohawk to melt all over his skin.

I said, "Muzzle it, Fido, now's not the time to bitch, we've got important work to do."

Kelly drawled, "Oh I just loves important work, massa. Important work makes me feel like a million dol—"

Outside, I grabbed Luther's arm, hustling him toward the parking lot and heard Kelly grunting behind us. Flashbulbs attached to the cameras of at least a dozen reporters on the jail watch went off, banging against us like a barrage of inessential bullets. A pigeon swooping low over the crowd was disoriented by the bright lights and crashed into the jailhouse wall.

Still on her feet and cranking, Edna Poddubny elbowed her way to the paparazzi forefront, rumpled shirttails leaking from under her soiled yellow sweater, eyeglasses held together with safety pins and white adhesive tape, the fly on her slacks unbuttoned, and a pair of dainty Chinese slippers on the wrong feet. An air of beleaguered humiliation had transformed her pudgy features into a freaky psychopathic mask, but, with her pad out, pencil poised, she said, "Charley Mac, you spawn of the—"

Va-ROOM!

They all dived aside, flinging up their arms to ward off a hailstorm of gravel bits spitting backward from under our spinning bald retreads. At the last possible instant Susan Delgado ripped open a rear door and swung inside, legs flailing for a melodramatic beat, then she hauled them in, too, and the door slammed shut behind her. As soon as we were airborne, Luther leaned forward saying nervously, "I can't believe that Lydia passed away."

"Hey Luther, I hate to be a stickler for syntax, but I can't tell you how much I detest the euphemism 'passed'—"

Susan slammed her fist into the dashboard: *"Watch out for that bear in the road!"*

I started to ignore her, then realized, "Christ, *it's Sweeny Dancebow!"* and swung the wheel so violently we lurched over the curb into Gil's Southside Exxon Station, grazed by the Number 6 pump (shearing off the hose), and came to a standstill four inches from an open window in the cashier's booth: *safe!*

Darla Sandoval said, "Hiya, Carlos—fill 'er up?" She was a good-natured bosomy party doll with cholo cross tattoos at the interior bases of both thumbs.

Her question caused me to notice the gas gauge needle pointed at one inch *below* empty. "As a matter of fact, yes," I said, handing Darla my Visa card praying that she wouldn't discover it was $8,437.15 over the limit. I backed up to pump Number 4. Luther slouched out to wrangle the hose while I sucked in a few deep breaths and Susan bemusedly dug a pregnant trilobite out of her ear.

As gas flowed into the Buick, I noted that across the highway a gray stretch limousine had just parked in front of the Inn of the Sun God Restaurant, and a chauffeur in a cap, a stiffly formal overcoat, and kidskin gloves was opening doors to let out his passengers—a tall bespectacled spinster secretary, a handsome young Latin banking type in a three-piece gray silk suit, and a short immaculate thug wearing a fedora, a diamond stickpin, and classic double-breasted threads. Immediately I recognized the latter guy from newspaper photographs and TV interviews: My God, it was true—*Bo Hrbyk and his ruthless samurai had arrived.*

Then Luther made an astute observation:

"Where the hell is Kelly?"

"She's not in the backseat?"

He said, "Duh."

"Oh no." I cringed again. "Didn't we all leave jail together?"

"I know she came out with us," Luther said. "But I never saw her inside the car. We better return, maybe she sprained an ankle."

Hastily, I nixed that proposal. "No, first we need to stop at the Body Shoppe for a cardboard casket. They want Lydia out of the hospital pronto."

"Don't go to Manjo," Susan cautioned prudently. "Termites are eating his insulation."

At the mortuary, Elton Gaverdine leaped to his enormous feet, and, even though he hated our slimy guts, he was officially At Work and on the prod for his percentage of the sarcophagus tab, so he assumed an ingratiating pose: Uriah Heep meets Regis Philbin. His pale features caused goosepimples in us and his blue serge jacket was mottled by clusters of cat hairs that wife Gladys should have dapped off with duct tape before sending him to work. When the subservient toady heard our request he denied it:

"Sorry, we're all out of body cartons. Can I interest you in one of our bronze Eternity Lazyboys?"

"Bag it, Elton. I'm a commie agitator, remember? I've read all the burial laws and I'll tear this lugubrious clipjoint to shreds if you don't comply with what I want."

He folded his arms, jutting his weak receded chin, and courageously barred the door. "You people will not obtain any cheap receptacles from me on my watch."

I reminded Elton, "I also worked here part-time for a week as a janitor ten years ago during the CETA training program, so I know the score. You have to oblige the poor. Now step aside, little man, we're coming through."

I goose-stepped right by that officious twerp down the hallway and through swinging doors into the prep room where only a single corpse, unattended, huge, fresh, and reeking of alcohol lay under a sheet on a slab awaiting disposition. Snatching a gold key off a nail in the side of a bookcase containing bottles of pickled frogs, I gained access to a dimly lit storage area full of packaged caskets and cases of formaldehyde, sodium chloride, glycerine, methyl-engenol and eosin dye, plus other paraphernalia relating to the funeral arts.

Expertly, I zigzagged between pallettes, honing in on exactly what I wanted.

"Here we go, just as I suspected."

I hefted a large, narrow cardboard box onto my shoulder and trotted quickly out of there.

"Lock the door and hang the key back up, Luther."

"When Mr. Poddubny finds out he'll be furious!" Elton trailed after us waving his arms and banging his beavertail-sized brogans loudly against the floor.

"Tell Mr. Poddubny to fuck a rubber corpse and get a bouncing zombie."

Her shutter clicking as we departed the Body Shoppe, Susan bobbed, weaved, and duckwaddled, hitting all the angles, a fanatic at work determined that nothing would stay her from documenting the Butterfly Coalition in action during its Finest Hour. Weegee, Witkin, Weston—she came, she saw, and by gum she *conquered.*

From a quarter mile away—three minutes later—we could see a humid ratsnarl of journalists bubbling in the hospital parking lot. Damn. Sunshine glinted brilliantly off camera lenses, Minicams, walkie-talkies, cellular phones, tape recorders. Mobile-lab Winnebago vans from several TV channels were parked on the outskirts, quivering as they idled. Richard So-and-So, Sandra Whosamadig, Johnny Fabiola, Jenny Archuleta, Kim Sweetwater . . . it was a veritable litany of knee-jerk character assassins glowing with Absence-of-Malice eager for The Scoop at any price. Also, many citizens who'd heard bulletins on the situation helped swell the murmuring throng. Early reports had Lydia felled by a ganster's bullet. Cars were spilling off the highway into the hospital lot, three helicopters hovered overhead, and other onlookers had parked across Tabitha Road in the Furr's shopping center: They hurried toward the flap. The Voice of the Butterfly was dead—Long Live The Voice Of The Butterfly!

Susan said calmly, "Use the back entrance! Turn here and sneak past the crowd!"

But the county clerk, Thelma Weed, spotted us as the Buick tiptoed by—*"There they are!"*—so I floored it, skidding around the corner on two wheels. We one-eightied to a hockey stop in front of the ramp leading up to loading doors which were, fortunately, unlocked. I slung them open wide as Luther thundered up the ramp with our coffin. Behind us Susan Delgado retreated jauntily like Mel Gibson or Kenneth Branaugh at swordplay, fending off the rabble by swinging her camera bag in a wide arc: Sharon Ludlow, Bunny Watrous, Gladys Gaverdine, Melody Kinderfink. . . . Susan stumbled into me backward and we fell inside. I threw the bolt behind us just in the nick of time as Winona Stapleton banged her fist against the metal door . . . and the rest of those rabid biddies crunched up against the door like ten pins striking a bowling ball.

We hurried along the corridor toward a small room where the mortal remains of our venerable Butterfly songbird lay. Luther stopped in the doorway and put down his coffin, terrified at the sight of a corpse. Beside Lydia sat Miranda Satan, smiling sweetly through yet another neuropharmacological intervention, in the right place at the right time again. She looked hot in a suede fishnet tanktop and a necklace of Mardi Gras beads.

Susan crawled G.I. style by Luther lickety-split into the room and lay on her back fussing with the Nikon, hoping for an original angle.

What I did not know was that Luther had suddenly remembered something. He had remembered the stink a moment ago—at the Body Shoppe—of peppermint schnapps. Then a lightning bolt sizzled down from the sky and banged him in the head, splitting it open: *eureka!* Not to me did he reveal this, he hadn't that focused a disposition, but from himself he could not hide the truth:

That blob on a slab at the morgue was Kelly.

THE CARDINAL RULE of revolutionary political action has always been: Make up your mind and do it. Seize the day. Whoever waffles is lost. So I said, "We have to whisk her away in secret. Those reporters mustn't know where Lydia is buried. If the press invaded the Phistic Copper breeding grounds and trampled the fragile cocoons clinging to the stalks of *Calexis trifida* plants, our bug would be extinct in an hour."

Luther asked, "Why can't we just leave her at the Body Shoppe until everything mellows out?"

I should have replied, *Because that makes too much SENSE, Luther, you dodo, it's too fucking LOGICAL, it's too EASY, it's not INTERESTING and CRAZY and DANGEROUS enough, it smacks of INTELLIGENT decision-making and that would DESTROY our reputation.*

Aloud—instead—I said, "Because I promised Lydia no refrigeration, no formaldehyde, no Manjo. She wants to be buried immediately without fanfare in the Phistic Copper feeding grounds. If we get her in before the election is official they can't disinter her on a habeas corpus and the bypass is screwed no matter what because of the cemetery laws. But we have to plant her before the polls close in a gravesite unknown to the press, the public, and our enemies, which will further stymie the bypass if FAGERBAN wins."

Gobbledegook. Luther regarded me with what I can only describe as stupefied amazement. Miranda scratched her nose.

Susan crammed coils of haywire film into the camera, then squashed closed the backing door: Tongues of tattered celluloid protruded through the cracks. She cranked the advance lever oblivious to a ruptured tearing sound inside, and brightened. "I'm back in business, boys."

Dazedly, Luther said, "Okay, so how do we do it, Pop?"

"Simple. We send a decoy out the front door, and, while the reporters are buzzing around the decoy, we sneak the real body out the rear exit to my Buick."

Luther cocked his head: "But we only have one coffin."

"That's the decoy. You will carry it on your shoulders and make it seem heavy. Grunt and puff a lot."

"And Lydia—?"

"We'll sit her in that wheelchair wrapped in a blanket, pull the knitted cap over her wig, and who'd ever guess it was her?"

Luther gave me an oddly incredulous look that seemed to be saying: *It's genetic, I know. From generation to generation American left-wing radicals like my dad have one thing in common: It's called the Suicide Chromosome. It lives right next door to the Self-Destruct Chromosome. Which dwells just down the block from the Nincompoop Chromosome.*

Miranda asked, "'Decoy,' as in 'ducks'?"

But I am a political man of action; I'd done this before. When the chips are down, you act. So I elaborated:

"After you display the empty box at the front door, you'll run it over to Poddubny's Body Shoppe and explain to everyone that's where Lydia is reposing until the funeral. You even check in the imaginary cadaver, do the paperwork, release copies to the press. Meanwhile, me and Susan hustle the real Lydia out the back way into the Buick. We pull this off at the same time you create the diversion by going through the crowd with a coffin on your shoulders. Even if they catch on it'll be too late. Afterwards, you will meet us at the trailer and help dig a grave while the press is on a wild goose chase."

Luther stared at me, a (very) far cry from being stoked.

But not Susan. She blinked in a flirtatious way. "Wait, *I* have a better idea."

We gave her our full attention. The reporter opened her mouth to give us her great pearls of wisdom . . . but nothing came out. She held the pose for a moment, then her features adopted the sort of startled expression you might observe on a hungry monkey's face if it bit into a rubber banana: I could tell that either my hair was on fire or Luther's Mohawk had become a blood-stained ax embedded in his own cranium. Then Susan lifted the camera to snap our collective portrait, but when she pushed down the shutter button the recoil banged into her nose, almost breaking it, causing a bell to ding inside her head as small aluminum coins ejected from each ear, tinkling onto the floor.

"*Bueno*," I said. "Let's rassle Lydia into that damn wheelchair."

I moved into position, though nobody else did. "Help me out here, Luther," I said. And when he hesitated I added: "NOW."

Luther stood up and declared, "But she's *dead*."

My turn to load a single syllable with all the slimy, biting, unfair, scornful sarcasm I could muster: "Duh."

"I don't want to touch her," Luther squawked. "I have some mortality issues!"

Miranda blurted, "In heaven you can get your life back on track again!"

I said, "I can't do it alone, dudes. So snap out of your fucking trance. Grow up and get with the program." I grabbed Lydia's head and one arm. "Latch onto the other arm and her feet, son. They won't bite. Jesus, I thought you crypto ska thrashers had balls."

Luther finally obeyed me, his features wrinkled as if to sneeze.

"Grip tightly," I admonished. "Don't think, just obey. Now yank her in opposition to my levering actions."

For a moment we pushed, tugged, and grunted, loosening Lydia's appendages. Though she hadn't become rigidly stiff yet, the old harpy wasn't all that supple, either. It sounded creepy—*click!*

crunch! sclurp!—as we wrestled with her limbs. At first, Luther handled Lydia as if she were red hot or radioactive; later, he turned green like a frog.

I said, "Watch it . . . careful . . . not too hard . . ."

Deftly, we doubled up the body at every joint and dumped it unceremoniously into the wheelchair. Then we yanked and readjusted dead limbs until Lydia was propped up right comfortably. Luther stepped away confronting his hands in horror fully expecting warts or swamp slime to break the skin while I adjusted her wig and pinched her cheeks to urge forth a bit of a blush. After quickly tying her sneaker shoelaces, I announced proudly: "There. Whattayou think?"

I thought Luther would hurl. He couldn't stop fixating on his hands. Miranda cupped her breasts and nibbled on the Mardi Gras necklaces.

For good measure I strapped Lydia in and arranged the blue-knitted cap tightly over her gruesome wig. Then I wrapped a blanket around the body and stepped back, assessing my handiwork.

Susan said, "Okay, Gomez, Uncle Fester, let's amscray."

Right. I toed off the wheel brake, pushing Lydia into the hall and turned left, heading north, trailed by Susan. My admonition to myself in times like this was: *Don't think, Carlito, just pretend we're invisible.* Truth is, however, I felt as if we'd just jumped out of a plane at 30,000 feet wearing clown outfits and no parachutes while high on LSD and Super Glue. Action is an amazing tonic for the soul . . . *if* you survive.

Where corridors crossed I stopped, calling south in a rational, clearheaded voice to Luther and Miranda: "We'll stay right here so we can see you at the front door. When you're ready to go out, give us a signal and we'll make a break for it."

No longer in command of his senses, Luther hoisted the weightless cardboard coffin onto his shoulders, grunting as per instructions under the "heavy" load, and plodded in a stupor toward the hospital's front doors at the other end of the corridor trailed by his bead-sucking rave slave. He couldn't believe he was doing this. To insure our privacy those doors had been locked and were being guarded by none other than—guess who?

Johnny Batrus and Herkie Pacheco, Suicide City's most testosterized stature-challenged little green peace officers.

"Okay, I'm here!" Luther called inanely when he reached the front entrance, and I went deftly into action pushing Lydia toward the ramp doors, Susan scampering after me.

The operation's snafu began with these words, spoken by a nearly paralyzed Luther to Johnny Batrus: "Open the door, please, sir, *now*."

WRONG.

Johnny had just about had it with the Butterfly Liberation Morons, Lydia Arlington Babcock, and The Voice of the Papillon. Nevertheless, when America voted, Johnny felt obliged to maintain public decorum at all costs so the electoral farce could go down without a hitch.

Therefore, he obeyed the smelly teen dweeb's request, inserting a key in the old-fashioned lock and twisting it. But for some reason the door would not respond.

"What the—?"

Johnny wrenched the key left, then right, then he jiggled it back and forth, but the recalcitrant tumblers balked at every assault.

Luther paled. "What's the matter?"

"Shuttup, you bottom-feeding dork. I guess it's jammed."

"I have to be out there immediately. Otherwise—"

"Yo, John-John," Herkie said. "Lemme try that." And, taking over, he gripped the key and jiggled, rattled, cajoled, then scratched his head, puzzled.

"Damn."

"Let *me* try." Luther set down the coffin and reached for the key. But Johnny Batrus laid a restraining hand on my boy's shoulder:

"Hold your horses, l'il buddy. Does my partner look incompetent?"

On seeing me and Susan making tracks toward the rear exit, Luther suddenly panicked. "Jesus Christ, man: Ineedtogetthrough-thatdoor!"

"Herkimer," Johnny said calmly, "remove this fungus from my presence and explain to it the traditional courtesies involved in addressing a police officer."

Herkie grabbed Luther's arm. "Over here, butthead. Give him room to work, he's a professional."

"If you hurt him," Miranda said, "I'll rip your teeth out with metal tongs."

The last time I glanced back, I couldn't believe my eyes. But it was too late to hesitate, so I wheeled Lydia through the rear unloading doors and into history while Herkie Pacheco asked Luther "What are you, a licensed locksmith?"

"No sir, I was only—"

"Then shut the fuck up."

Luther sagged. It was too late now to avoid calamity. Through the closed front doors he could hear the maelstrom stirring . . . a roar of recognition . . . shouts back and forth . . . then the excited rumble of many feet pounding toward the rear delivery area of the hospital's west wing where myself and Susan Delgado were trying to maneuver Lydia free of her wheelchair and into the Buick.

Day of the Locust meets *Twitch of the Death Nerve.*

We lost our grips and Lydia slithered to the ground.

At the front doors, with nothing else to lose, Luther said, "I can see from here that you jammed the key in upside down. If you tugged it out with pliers, then reinserted it rightside up, I bet the door would open."

Johnny stooped over, assessing the problem. "Hey, the stupid key *is* jammed in upside down." Rolling his eyes—oh brother!— Johnny entered the admissions cubicle beside the ER and demanded some pliers from Xaviera Mayhew, the computer operator. Xaviera located a pair in her bottom desk drawer. Using the pliers, Johnny yanked the key, reinserted it correctly, gave it a twist until the innards clicked, and, with a flourish, flung open the door. "Okay, get scarce you hippy maggot."

Luther grabbed his coffin and sallied forth . . . but of course he had missed the boat.

A last mobile van swung out of sight around the hospital's southwestern corner, heading for the rear delivery ramp, leaving the wide front parking lot devoid of the media personnel Luther had been ordered to lead astray so that Susan and I might escape with our corpse—and a portion of our dignity—intact.

Luther slouched west, ventured a glaum north, and shuddered. Untold members of the ravenous Fourth Estate had my Buick surrounded and it looked like curtains for the Butterfly Coalition. Still, through the fog, Luther thought he caught sight of a way to be constructive. So he spun around, tucked the coffin under one arm, and lumbered off south on the highway in search of his dead stepmother.

Miranda cried, *"Wait!"*

P ROBABLY IF I HAD TO write a scenario depicting the worst nightmare I could possibly imagine happening to me in my life, this would be it," I complained.

From the rear seat Susan Delgado said, "What about being gang-raped by a dozen drunk Hell's Angels on an antarctic iceberg while suffocating to death from pneumonia? Wouldn't that be worse?"

"Not hardly." I added, "Lydia, I never thought I'd say this to you, but I'm sorry."

My dead friend was slumped against the passenger door, mouth still wide open, and she had no audible comment as we progressed north at a relatively demure rate of speed.

Demure, I'm afraid to say, because ahead of us traveled the Channel 7 mobile TV RV from the capital. Balanced on its rear hydraulic-loading platform was a tripodded rolling camera (operated by Barney Lumpen) recording—live!—the "clandestine" journey of Lydia Arlington Babcock's body north to its final resting place, wherever that might be. Kim Sweetwater stood braced beside the camera, giving a running commentary. Behind my Buick trailed the rest of the press corps: three more large vans, eleven trucks and automobiles, and a half dozen motorcycles. And after them came the fucking public, every weirdo, ambulance chaser, gossip monger, and death freak in Suicide City, starting with Ward Potter, Betty Martínez, and Tranky

Ledoux, and moving right through Charity Gingivitis, Misha Quicksilver, and Elvira Schectman to Karl Cronkite, Paul Sweetwater, and Kismet Witherspoon—all the anatomically correct language-compatible citizen drones of the biggest little socio-environmental disaster in the southern Rocky Mountains behind the wheels of their up-to-date Jeep Grand Cherokees, Ford Explorers, Chevy Suburbans, Isuzu Troopers, Mitsubishi Challengers, Dodge Caravans, and Pontiac Crocodiles, on the prod for the latest in impeachable and salacious macro-entertainments at the expense of Dignity, Integrity, and Truth under the venerated American Democratic System created by that great racist hypocrite Thomas Jefferson, who'd fathered a kid out of wedlock with a slave.

Put simply? I was caught in a parade of perhaps fifty rapacious inkslingers, vidiots, and kibitzaholics, all gleefully attached to the local election's biggest story with lots of Absence of Malice, Intent to Capitalize, and a (very) deep-seated Hunger for Blood.

I said, "I swear, if Luther ever dares speak to me again I will not be responsible for what happens. No more Mr. Pacifist nice guy. Kelly thinks I hurt her face yesterday? Hah! Child stuff. Oh no, if my son ever darkens my eyesight again he'll wish he'd been at Nagasaki when the bomb dropped compared to the devastation I'll rain upon his body!"

Susan rested her chin on the seat cushion next to my shoulder, her hair spikes jabbing me softly. "Aw, come on, Chuck, calm down. This is hardly a time to spout invective. Whatever happened, it wasn't his fault." She fingered my head. "He's a good kid."

"You call this 'trying'? He screwed up. I've never been so humiliated. We blew it, we'll never bury her in secret. I've broken my promise to a dying friend and I'll go straight to hell in a handbasket."

Susan tweaked my earlobe. "Hey, we're all trying our best. The important thing is to plan our next move.'"

"What is our next move?" I inquired sarcastically. "Look at me, our hallowed leader. I'm sitting beside a ninety-two-year-old corpse. In my backseat is a hallucinating journalist taking pictures with a broken camera who probably thinks the rattling in my glove compartment is caused by an immature gaggle of Amazonian cassava frogs. Who knows *what* has happened to Luther and Kelly? Despite all my efforts, our entire organization is in hopeless disarray. We're probably about to lose an election by the widest margin ever in the history of American Politics. I don't know if I'm capable of any 'next moves.'"

"Not cassava frogs," Susan corrected, licking my earlobe inquisitively. "Phainopeplas."

Yet even as she spoke we were about to be bailed out by one of the campaign's more thaumaturgical manifestations.

No lightning bolt from heaven would shatter the parasitic caravan, nor would a minor seismic tremor create a midhighway fissure into which all vehicles (except my Buick) would plummet. No, this marvel derived its juice from a more commonplace phenomenon. A woman, blissfully cockeyed, behind the wheel of a heap (which she had commandeered from the County Courthouse parking lot), was approaching the road at right angles to the long line of cars slowly snaking north. By coincidence that junker was traveling at a rate of speed which would propel it onto the asphalt at exactly that moment when the Channel 7 mobile news unit would be in a position to block its entrance onto the autobahn, thereby causing great havoc to the funeral cavalcade.

In short, the Channel 7 mobile news lorry was broadsided by the Butterfly Coalition's kamikaze sound wagon, piloted by none other than the Great Recidivist herself, Kelly McFarland, who but an hour earlier had been officially pronounced deceased.

Uh-huh, okay, *sure.* Yes, it was a convoluted story, the tale of my soon-to-be ex's progress from a jail cell at ten, to a slab in the undertaker's abattoir at ten-twenty, to a major league car accident at noon. No time to elaborate here. Suffice to say that she had indeed traveled (somehow) from Manjo Poddubny's Body Shoppe to the County Jail Complex, and thence to her beloved (quasi-annihilated) wheels that had been stagnating in the county sheriff's impoundment lot ever since the unfortunate (yet blessed!) Burger Boy incident. As a hedge against those numerous occasions when she chanced to lock herself out of the van, Kelly always kept an extra key to the jalopy in her wallet. Thus, without asking permission from her recent incarcerators, the colorful inebriate simply started the Dodge and peeled away, hoping to be gone before anyone commenced slinging hot lead in her direction. In fact, it was because Kelly happened to be studying the sideview mirror for signs of expert markspeople plinking at her rear wheels that she failed to exercise appropriate caution upon entering the traffic flow of a major artery, and promptly smashed into Channel 7.

Thank you, God.

I wrenched my steering wheel left, floored the gas, lurched right after skimming through a narrow gap in oncoming traffic, then jackknifed sharply right again onto a dirt lane 50 yards north of the courthouse, immediately hung a Luigi onto another dusty path, two-wheeled it around a corner, and disappeared from the four hundred millimeter sights of those flabbergasted Fleet Street correspondents.

I acted so abruptly that several media limos immediately behind me crumpled into the Channel 7 van. There followed a remarkable chain reaction, a thirty-two−car pileup. Inside ten seconds the entire blacktop was littered by demolished tin, chrome, glass, and rubber, which effectively blocked all traffic headed both north and south. The motorcade clanged to a grinding halt. Drivers appeared angry as hell, waving their little pink arms, among them Marcia Stonebutter Crawford, Tony Stryzpk, and, of course, Clinton Simpson, a man with an eerie sort of delirious equanimity at the heart of the noisy wreckage.

Kelly flopped onto the macadam, turbinated erratically (getting her bearings straight), then melted into the confusion, heading west, then south . . . then east . . . then north by northeast . . . not at a particularly fast clip, mind you, though she knew *exactly* where she was aiming.

MORE MIRACLES!

Luther and Miranda and Kelly arrived at Lydia's trailer simultaneously about thirty seconds after I had nosed into the drive with my corpse in tow and my faithful albatross in the backseat hugging herself to stay warm. Granted, Kelly appeared a tad worse for wear, and even Luther seemed frazzled underneath his out-of-date shock doc punker exterior. Miranda was projecting weird energy from within a fey air of nervous anticipation. But here's the kicker: For once in our lives together nobody complained. My son did, however, scrutinize Kelly in radical disbelief for about ten seconds. Then he just plain gave up trying to figure it out. Why? Because there are twilight zones in space, girlfriend, that even the starship *Enterprise* would not traverse on a bet.

Contrite from top to bottom, Luther limped up to the Buick and asked, "What's the plan?" Susan Delgado said, "We have to bury this dame right away." Luther danced nimbly aside, explaining, "I don't want to touch her again." So Kelly opened the passenger door and jerked Lydia out as easily as if she'd been a sack of gosling breastfeathers. Then she dropped her like a hot horseshoe, exclaiming, "Holy mackerel, she's *dead!*" But even before the echo of her words had died out Kelly remembered she already knew that because I'd announced it at the jail, and she grabbed Lydia up again, slinging her over one shoulder, and apologized: "Sorry, I had a fantasy there for a moment. Where do you want to plant her?"

Kelly lisped worse than before, having lost two more teeth. My eyes she avoided in an odd, embarrassed way. Her splotchy red hair had turned half-white in the last three hours. Her filthy shirt was torn from stem to collar, her blue jeans hung down below her buttocks, she wore no socks, and her sneaker laces were gamboling off in multiple directions, trying to escape. Kelly McFarland, the human incarnation of the *Exxon Valdez* oil spill: How did she keep coming back? And why? And to what *purpose* in the cosmic order of things?

I said, "We'll put Lydia in the Phistic clearing where the butterflies mate in springtime."

"Careful, she bites," Susan joked, then uncertainly glanced at me for reassurance.

Kelly carried Lydia bent over one shoulder like a limp cat. Luther and I followed single file, arms laden by three shovels, a pickax, a posthole digger, a crowbar, and a galvanized bucket. Miranda tripped along compliantly. Susan brought up the rear, fiddling with her broken camera, jumping over the largest toadstools, kicking at sluggish guajalotes that reared up and flicked their forked tongues at her.

At the clearing's edge we propped Lydia in a sitting position against a juniper trunk and proceeded to stake out her final resting place. Piñon and cedar trees encircled us, plus a handful of cholla cactus. Magpies chattered in the evergreens and I heard a chickadee twitter. The toxic sky was as blue as the china eye in a porcelain baby doll and just as unblemished, too. At moments, when the poisoned earth is radiant despite itself, all you can do is swoon. And for a second I cast my gaze toward the nearby mountaintops with a prisoner's morbid yearning. Then Kelly took a first swing with her pickax and the steel bit clanged against a rock, nearly fracturing her forearms. Her eyes did a 360° roll in their sockets, her teeth clacked loudly while dust briffits puffed from each ear, and Kelly sat down abruptly. . . and *howled*.

As a child I had laughed at the bewildering cruelty of animated cartoons on Saturday-morning TV shows that featured coyotes slamming into brick walls at ninety miles per hour, wabbits falling a thousand feet onto horrible black wocks where they splatted in vivid annihilation, and dynamite exploding in the faces of stupid, gullible ducks.

And this time around I couldn't help myself either. As Kelly— her hair frizzed, her eyes lopsided, her teeth literally inside-out—hit the turf, I guffawed. Me *and* Susan, both of us in unison cracked up nervously over my poor wife's comic dive. Yes, you might just as well laugh at Bergen-Belsen, or at the Amazon on fire, or at the *Titanic* bubbling toward the ocean floor (mercifully killing Leonardo DiCaprio at last!), as find mirth in Kelly's pain. But the roots of tragedy are comic, and in mirth we truly indulged .. until Luther suddenly yelled:

"WHAT THE HELL ARE YOU GUYS LAUGHING AT?"

That stopped us; we were instantly ashamed.

Then, kneeling beside Kelly, my flustered son started brushing her off as she raised onto her hands and knees, rocked into a crouch, and wobbled erect once more. Miranda reached over and delicately tweaked one of Kelly's ears.

"It's not funny," Luther added, his voice cracking with emotion as he solicitously plucked twigs and leaf bits off Kelly's shoulders. "You people are mean and vicious."

Kelly said, "Bag it, Luther." She grappled for her pickax again. "You don't want to go there, dude. It's way too complex for a child."

"We weren't laughing *at* her," I began to explain. "We didn't mean . . . it's just that—"

This time Kelly drove her pick in up to the hilt . . . and Luther also began digging immediately. A minute later, when I snapped awake and bent to the task with them, our labor went real fast. If one of us hit a rock, Luther pried it free with the crowbar. Two feet down our implements struck a shallow vein of caliche, but soon after we reached a softer loam devoid of roots that gave way almost like butter. Quickly we found a rhythm, alternating shovel stabs and pickax blows, a music rich in counterpoint, I suppose.

Definitely a woman possessed, Kelly flung dirt to either side in great fan-shaped sprays. She was shabby and misshapen, yet I do believe outlines of vestigial muscles quivered in her ruined flesh. Sweat droplets popped off her forehead, neck, and shoulders. When she bumped against me or Luther, Kelly recovered quickly and even apologized, civil at last. Her demeanor reeked of Apology, Appeasement, Expiation . . . before it was too late.

It's no fun to dig a grave, but my son worked hard, a tireless machine born to the excavating metier. His bizarre physical appearance notwithstanding, Luther was acting pretty grown up, I thought. Had I been more coherent and less pooped, I might even have started apologizing for all the years that in my head, if not my heart, I had sold him short. Pointedly, he avoided looking at either me or Kelly.

Susan Delgado joined us briefly, but she handled tools the way monkeys perform brain surgery. She scooped loose dirt in the bucket and carried it off . . . for about two minutes. During that short spell she clunked me, Kelly, *and* Luther on our heads, stepped in the empty bucket and almost broke her ankle, tripped three times spilling all the dirt, and sprained her back. After that she lost interest, limped away, sat down beside Lydia, and spent the next half hour interviewing the corpse, scribbling copious notes, happy as a little old corn fritter in a puddle of blackstrap molasses.

Miranda deflated to earth lotus style and closed her eyes, assuming the om position.

As for myself at a time like this?—no welching. I shoveled my aching heart out, kept quiet, and tried not to fling dirt into anyone's face or get hacked by an errant shovel blade.

The work went so quickly that after only forty minutes we were done. Luther handed me a last bucket of sand that I set down at my feet as he pulled himself out. Below him, Kelly reclined, belly up, trying the sepulchre on for size, and I'll admit that sure rent my sternum like the pike of an ice pick. In your heart you know it's a sure thing, but the brain *always* rebels.

"Not funny, Kelly," I protested. "Get out of there this instant. Alley oop."

My wife said, "No. This pit fits me like a glove. Go ahead, throw in Lydia then shovel the dirt on top of us. Two for the price of one."

"Don't be absurd," I said. "Come on, Kelly, time's a wasting."

"No way, Cholly. Sorry."

"What do you mean, 'No'?" I asked.

"What is there about 'No' that you don't understand?" she asked me in return.

Luther interjected nervously, "C'mon, c'mon, this isn't the time or the place—"

"It's a good time for me," she answered cheerfully. "And I feel right at home in this place."

"Listen, Kelly—" I spoke slowly, working real hard to maintain a small facade of composure: "It's Election Day. There's still plenty of work to be done."

She reasoned, "Without me, your work will be a lot easier, I promise."

"That's hardly the point—" I began.

Luther said, "Yo, dude, do us a favor and get *out* of there, *now!*"

Kelly closed her eyes and folded her hands emphatically together over her chest. She smiled. I stared down at her completely buffaloed.

So Luther tossed a shovelful of dirt on top of her, but Kelly did not react. In fact, she seemed to have miraculously fallen asleep.

Desperately, I cajoled, "Kelly, I love you, it's okay, you can come home, again. We'll work it out, I promise."

Nothing. Nada. She wasn't that gullible.

And that's when Luther suddenly went totally postal. Launched like a rocket, he bolted rudely past me and leaped into the grave, his boots landing on either side of Kelly, then he stooped over grabbing one arm and her sweatshirt at the throat and yanked her brutally into a half-sitting position, then shifted to one side and, with all the power at his command, he wrangled Kelly's limp blob of a passively resisting body upright and, like an ant with a piece of pork twenty times its own weight, he literally heaved his stepmom out of the pit into a heap at our feet. Miranda yelped. Kelly rolled alertly out of the way as Luther bounded free of the hole like some kind of super-monkey, and she stuck up a fist, ready to rumble, but my boy steamed directly over to Lydia's corpse seated on the ground with its back against a juniper trunk still giving the interview from hell to Susan Delgado, who by now had filled half her notebook with Lydia's pithy rantings from beyond the mortal fringe.

"I'm not through yet," Susan pouted. "We're only up to 1956—"

Too bad. Tough luck. Eat shit. Luther rudely hefted Lydia, who had rigor-mortised into her sitting position, and he carted her over that way to the edge of the grave, set her down like a bulimic Humpty-Dumpty, then unceremoniously kicked her in: *whoosh* . . . THUD! Lydia's wig popped off. Next, without pausing, Luther grabbed the shovel I'd been leaning on and began fanatically to fling in the clods. *"Fuck all of you adults!"* he grunted, working at double speed . . . then triple speed . . . then quadruple. *"You fucking miserable grown-ups!"* he groaned. *"You callous hyenas, you half-assed excuses for intelligent meat. I spit on your booze, your communism, your elections, your dead bodies, your . . . your . . ."* While this invective spewed from his mouth he dumped piles of dirt atop Lydia, and nobody dared intervene because that might have made Luther *truly* crazy, and then who knew what sort of excessive mayhem could have erupted?

Parents always try, though. "Hey, Luther—" I took one step forward.

"Touch me," he replied, "and I'll gut you like a dead elk."

When the grave was a third refilled, Luther dropped the shovel, fell to his knees, and projectile vomited into Lydia's final resting haven. I exclaimed, "Oh dear!" and, running forward, I reached again for my frothing boy.

"Touch me, Pop," he threatened between spasms, "and your hands will melt into useless protoplasm."

Then he reared up and staggered to a neutral corner near a mistletoe-riddled pine tree where he took a stand and braced himself as if for the charge of a Spanish fighting bull.

Miranda declared, "I'm starting to get one of those global headaches."

In search of guidance, or perhaps a clue on how to respond to the modern American teenager in a snit, Susan cast her querying perturbed eyes in my direction, but what was I suppposed to do at this late date, explain? Like Einstein with relativity? Watson with DNA? Gorbachev with Glasnost? Hey, forgedaboudit. Nevertheless, I've always been a plugger, so I raised my hands real slow in a pointedly flabbergasted gesture; then I delivered the mother of all shrugs. It's also possible that I cocked my head to no logical purpose whatever, completely rictified by latest events. In any case, time passed without the tick of a single clock, and in the end, finally, cautiously, Kelly stood up and brushed herself off, plucking pebbles from her hair.

After some hesitation, I ventured, "Well, folks, I guess that's about it." And I bent over gingerly to pick up Luther's shovel. "We might as well finish this job . . ."

Holy sunshine bathed us still, and the sky was delphinium blue, ultra-serene. I heard another bird call: *Chick-a-dee-dee.* The silence glowed literally golden, with lovely mountaintops throbbing in the background as I covered up Luther's mess, scraping the dirt in carefully so as not to be obscene. Soon enough Kelly quit staring over at Luther, picked up another shovel, and joined me. Susan even pushed some dirtballs into the hole with her feet.

"*Fuck you adults!*" Luther called over to us, though his interjection lacked considerably in vehemence this time around.

I consulted my watch: Uh-oh, it was almost four P.M.

Susan said, "Good-bye, Lydia. Sweet dreams. Don't be a bitch in heaven."

Weary to the max, we shoveled in the rest of the earth until her grave was filled to the brim. We raked smooth the dirt and used sage branches to whisk away our footprints. Lydia's FREE HUEY button had fallen off; I put it in my pocket. We arranged rocks, a rotting log, and handfuls of leaves and pine needles across the site until it would have been difficult for a casual stranger (or a reporter) to penetrate the camouflage, discovering a tomb. To all intents and purposes, Lydia's final resting place had disappeared. If FAGERBAN won, would we reveal it to halt the bypass? Or was the location more effective as a mystery?

Hey, we'd cross that bridge if we got there.

But before we could leave, catch this: Two tiny rare Phistic Copper butterflies arrived, the last of the season—and they began copulating in midair directly over the burial sight. I know that sounds hokey, but it's true: Who could make up such a wild story? Dishwater white in color and each no bigger than my thumbnail, they hovered eight inches above the ground, wings flapping in a rapid blur.

Kelly said, "*That's* a Phistic Copper?"

I reacted defensively: "Just because they're small and drab doesn't mean they're not special. The mere fact they exist at all is a miracle."

My voice sounded lackluster because I was tired. I was tired the way people feel tired after four years in a concentration camp, or seventy-two nonstop hours (at minimum wage) spent sorting, grading, and quality checking potatoes jiggling by at eight miles per hour on a rubber conveyor belt. But the heroes we read about in grammar school, like Martin Luther King or Sojourner Truth, were all folks who simply refused to throw in a towel. The relevant slogan is: "If you want to win you can't give in." And I guess that was a credo adhered to by us mourners at Lydia's gravesite. It's not easy to survive as an idealist in the barbarous nation we live in. Postmodern (dot.com) society mocks our simplistic gawky gestures against the slaughterhouse. Me, Luther, Kelly, Miranda, and Susan were clowns, ineffectual and deluded do-gooders, a quaint quintet of tiny monkeys dancing in a hot frying pan—lunatics to laugh at. Who in this world of Super Bowl halftimes, shopping channels, and cyber capital would ever lay a rose on our tombstones or shed a tear of thanks?...

Self-pity becomes not the revolutionary, however, so I turned my attention back to those fascinating Phistic Coppers, telling Susan, "Please take a picture of them for posterity."

My melodramatic reporter pal wrung her hands: "I wrecked my camera, it's useless."

Not to worry, I had one in my knapsack—a throwaway Kodak MAX Panoramic recently purchased at Smith's. While I retrieved it, Susan squatted low beside the minuscule insects, slipping her cupped hands underneath the bugs. Employing great caution, she began raising her hands so that the butterflies, hovering only about an inch above the palms, ascended also. Soon the ditsy reporter was standing upright, arms outstretched, hands cupping the two oblivious Coppers. Their oscillating shadows danced against her skin. Unperturbed at being lifted high, they remained perfectly balanced an inch away from Susan's kooky flesh, one petite abdomen joined to the other, Lilliputian wings beating furiously. Life on earth...the ecosystem in all its fragile glory...our universe in a grain of sand.

I aimed my camera, then moved around, up, down, sideways, poking the snout closer, searching for a perfect angle.

"Hurry up before they fly away."

"*Fuck you adults,*" Luther sobbed dispiritedly from over at his tree.

I squinted one eye, peering through the viewfinder at those two small and monumentally undistinguished critters fornicating against Susan's palms. The background was occupied by Kelly's face and Susan's, too, big, pink, blurry baubles in which enormous out-of-focus eyes gazed raptly at the itty-bitty bugs. Even Miranda's ghastly sweet oval shone like a pretty gemstone despite its sickening hues. This is what it was all about, our struggle against FAGERBAN, against the Greenhouse Effect, against worldwide inequality—

So I clicked the shutter, capturing infinity.

Then my wife reached forward grabbing the Phistic Coppers out of thin air; she squashed them in her fist.

What? I couldn't believe it. I stammered, "Why . . . why did you *do* that, Kelly?"

"Because I am jealous," she said.

THEN IT WAS truly over, rover, and we were all too pooped to pop.

Footsore, tired, and weary, the last upright remnants of our vast organization converged at Lydia's trailer, trudged inside, and clicked on the old black-and-white TV. We removed the corks on two bottles of champagne I'd stashed in the refrigerator yesterday and hungrily slashed open some bags of barbecued chips. Sagging into lopsided furniture too dazed for small talk or gossip, we glued our bleary eyes to the thirteen-inch screen's snowy reception, allowed to be zombies at last.

I was running on fumes. Kelly I was plumb out of words to describe, and yet: She looked as if her get up and go had got up and went about as far south as you can travel and still raise a T-wave. Luther snuggled into a slouch on the couch so perverse that if I hadn't known better I would have pegged him for an invertebrate. Susan arranged herself primly on the sofa arm, declaring, "Okay, here we are. And all's well that ends well." She was terribly pale, however, and seemed profoundly forlorn.

Miranda lit a cigarette, and, smoking it, she seemed so tough and vulnerable, gaunt and oddball, that I wanted to take her in my arms.

Lydia's filthy cats crept around getting on my nerves, fussing in geranium pots or squatting in foul tubs of Kitty Litter, starved for affection and ingratiatingly meowing to be petted like pintsized overweight Hollywood sitcom children, no doubt aware that with Lydia's departure their days on earth were numbered.

My head ached, my hand that had punched Kelly throbbed, I was bushed and ready for a nervous breakdown. I could barely concentrate on what the announcers and the expert analysts were saying. So-and-so here, such-and-such there, slim lead . . . already conceded . . . trouble counting the votes . . . District Attorney . . . Governor of Illinois . . . Proposition P . . . Amendment 111 . . . Resolution A . . .

Swish-pan to a squeaky clean blond woman showering with Zest deodorant soap.

Then I lost track of everything for a while . . . until suddenly we were on a different channel and Susan was saying, "Here it comes. Everybody pay attention. Wake up, Kelly! Wake up, Charley! Hey, *Luther!*"

"Here comes what?"

"They're talking about us."

We all gave the TV screen our rapt attention as an anchorman said, "Up north there really aren't many interesting races, but one controversial proposition on the ballot, a local initiative, has received wide attention because of the kooky campaigns waged both for and against a local highway bond issue. Now we go live to Kim Sweetwater at our Channel 7 Mobile Van, in—"

Jittery flashes of static were soon replaced by a lame remote feed featuring that tense but tony blond bombshell standing near what remained of the Channel 7 Mobile Van in the parking lot of an Exxon garage on Chambers Street.

Kelly belched impolitely and rearranged her features in a rubbery cockeyed manner, trying to focus. I could see it seep into her yet again, that mangled spark of light that touched some bizarre stray buoyancy in both her irises, causing an illusion of spunk. Kelly was so fucking wasted she almost seemed beautiful. My wife gleamed, she did, in all her dismal fury at the end of a broken road.

"Wow," she murmured respectfully at Kim Sweetwater, "look at those copious maracas."

"Watch out," Miranda cautioned. "You could get partitioned by God for that."

The sexy news anchor said, "Bob, you won't believe this, but we've been out of action almost since two P.M. when our van here, as you can see, was broadsided by the Butterfly Coalition's meatwagon. We have a Minicam canvassing town on foot or in taxis, but I'm afraid our reports are going to be fairly sketchy."

"Well, Kim," Bob said sympathetically, "can you at least give us a brief synopsis of the general mood up there now that the polls have been closed for a while?"

"The mood is chipper," Kelly answered, flushing from the sheer joy of repartee. "The Butterfly Coalition's sensational campaign to bring honesty and integrity back into American politics has changed the face of democracy and laid down the ground rules by which all of us will come to be judged in the future."

A ringing in my ears drowned out her prattle, yet Susan tried to buck up, answering Kelly: "You're right, sugar, even if you're mocking us."

Kelly glanced over at her with a piercingly wise yet uncomprehending look, but refrained from comment as a tiny squirrel parachuted off the tip of Susan's nose carrying a weentsy trombone. Did I mention Miranda was wearing black Doc Martens hiking boots that weighed fifteen pounds?

Apiece.

Kim said, "Actually, Bob, whereas most of the national and local races were decided much earlier, it still remains touch and go with the Prop X vote. At last count the race was unbelievably close. The Nays have four hundred ninety-two votes, the Ays four hundred eighty-nine. The only precinct outstanding is Precinct 4. But Chris Ledyard is at Central Command now waiting for the runner to bring him a final tally, which we expect at any minute."

"Kim, can you enlighten us further about the death of Sylvia Arlington Babcock this afternoon?"

"Well, Bob, at this point nobody knows exactly what happened after the Butterflies took her from the hospital. It's a lacuna we can't penetrate. Members of the Butterfly Coalition aren't talking. It appears the old lady was buried immediately, though, in a secret alcove nobody knows about. But the press was banned from the ceremony."

"Nobody 'bans' the press from a newsworthy funeral, Kim. Even as far back as in Journalism 101 no producer would have accepted that for an answer. We have cameras with telephoto lenses—"

"Bob, it's been a pretty long day up here. Lacking wheels, we seem to be arriving late at most of the appropriate venues. It's been hell bumming rides. So if you don't like my answer, I'd strongly suggest that you—"

"Okay, Kim. Great. We sure appreciate those fascinating reports you people up there have been channeling to us all evening. And now, let's—"

"Hold the phone, Bob. Here comes Chris! Maybe he has the P-4 numbers."

A disheveled mendicant entered from stage left, hair tousled, clothing askew, sweat glistening on all his exposed surfaces. I could sympathize—he looked like one of us. Unsteadily, he arranged himself beside Kim and ineffectually tucked in his shirt.

Kim said, "Bill, can you update us any further on the situation at Precinct 4 regarding the Prop X tally?"

"It's 'Chris,' Kim, not 'Bill.'"

"I meant 'Chris,' of course, Bill, I'm sorry."

"Well, yes, as a matter of fact I can."

"Great. *Dites moi.*"

He rummaged in his trousers, producing pieces of paper from various pockets, checking their scribbles, crumpling them up, tossing them aside. When he finally located the proper slip, he unrumpled it, smoothing out the wrinkles, and broke his heartstopping silence:

"Yeah, Kim, I got the figures right here. This turned out to be one hell of a dynamite election. I find it hard to believe myself. Guess what the final results are?"

Kim smiled painfully at Chris, then at the camera. "Chris, I haven't the faintest idea, believe me. Just read us the numbers."

"No, I'm serious, babe—guess. I mean, never in my wildest dreams would I have imagined. Lyndon Johnson's first legislative race was close, as I recall, but nothing like this. What we have here is one in a million, kid. Go ahead, take a stab."

"Chris, I'm not paid to hypothesize. My role is to report the facts. So if you'll kindly—"

"Aw c'mon, Kim, live it up a little. Be a sport. Don't be so darn uptight. Let the old hair down once every ten years."

Smiling desperately at the camera, Kim said, "Chris, I don't *want* to postulate. It's highly inappropriate on this important occasion—"

"Oh for crissakes, Kim, just one teensy guess won't hurt you. We're not talking rape, here, are we? I'm not gonna jump your withered bones."

Kelly grinned over at me both keenly and stupidly. "You know what, sweetcheeks? I kind of like this lardass."

My wife's head went into a funny elliptical loll and she halfway tipped sideways, but some internal mechanism rang a warning bell, I suppose, because she never toppled. Instead, she balanced precariously like a man hiking out on a racing sailboat to keep it from capsizing, then her flab constricted the way a snake's coils ripple, and her body, by magic or sheer effort of will, righted itself.

"Oh, all right," Kim said. "I'll say five-thirty-five 'Yes!' votes to five-twenty-six 'No!'s."

"Not even close. Try again."

"Chris, we're on the *air*. We're doing a *live remote*. Barney's camera's little red light is blinking. Now quit fooling around."

"What about you guys down there in Election Central?" Chris asked. "What do you think? Bob, what's the craziest election result you ever saw in your lifetime?"

Decidedly unhappy with the Ledyard deportment, Bob manfully maintained his composure. "I reckon Truman's 1948 victory over Dewey."

"How 'bout the Mets in '69?" Chris taunted.

A puzzled Kelly turned toward me and blinked rapidly, still

laboring to focus. "Remember Ron Swoboda in '69? And Terrific Tom Seaver and Jerry Koontz?"

Kim said, "Chris, I think we've kidded around enough here. Time is money. As I'm sure you know, we're covering the entire nation, hundreds of races in every state—"

"Doesn't anybody out there wanna make an educated guesstimate?" Chris said dispiritedly. "I mean, when I spill the beans you feebs are not gonna believe it."

"Oh please just read the figures," Kim whimpered, endeavoring to peek over his shoulder. But he was too cunning and sly for her, swiftly cupping a hand to the paper before she could decipher any information on it.

Loathe to capitulate, Chris said, "Just this once, tune up to *my* guitar. What's the most oddball, unexpected solution to an election where thousands of votes are cast? I mean, what's even more incredible than a hole-in-one in golf?"

Hesitantly—desperately—Kim said, "A tie?"

"You got it, baby. *A fuckin' humungous tie.*"

They were live, and nobody scrambled fast enough to bleep it.

"A tie?" Kim paled, convinced both of them were already as good as cashiered. "Incredible."

"It *would* be incredible if it was true," Chris said. "But guess what?"

"It's not true?"

"That is correct! It's *not* true. But guess what *is* true? Something even more fantastic than a tie."

In over her head anyway, Kim plowed blindly forward. "A one-point margin of victory?"

"BINGO!" Chris shouted deliriously. "Five-fifty-six to five-fifty-five. I never thought I'd live to see the day when it could happen. And to top it all off, how about those quintuple fives? It's a miracle, it really is. If you know anything about numerology, or about the random-chance philosophy of cybernetics as pioneered by Norbert Weiner at MIT, then you'll realize that the probability of something like this happening is—"

"Thanks, Kim and Chris," Bob said. "And now let's check in on the governor's race in American Samoa, where—"

"A one-point margin of victory?" Kelly faced me, drawling laconically, "What does that mean?"

"Five-fifty-six to five-fifty-five?" In bewilderment I contemplated my son.

Luther couldn't process the information: "Elections aren't won by a single point. That's impossible."

Susan said, "But as long as we won, what's the difference?"

According to Miranda, "One of affect, not effect."

Then I realized something. "*Who* won? He didn't say who *won*. Did anybody hear them say who won?"

According to Kelly, "We won."

"You heard them say that?"

"No, but it makes sense . . . doesn't it?"

Luther figured, "If FAGERBAN won we'll demand a recount."

And I peered at the dumb TV, utterly flummoxed. "I don't believe they didn't name the victor. That's absurd."

Susan said, "Ain't that the damned old truth?"

"'Truth'?" Kelly cackled. "What is 'truth' in this day and age? Truth is fleeting, Truth has many interpretations. Truth is a pagan, suckled on a creed outworn. When we say 'Truth,' do we mean, like, Everlasting Truth, or only some kind of Temporal Entity, here but for a moment on earth, buffeted by the winds of Time—"

Then that ludicrous woman swiveled sideways, screwing up her face in delirious mocking imitation of who knows what, and, as she extended her arms to embrace me, it hit her, like a ten-ton truck . . . like a big fat fist . . . like a sudden tornado. An enormous billow of air gusted free of Kelly, clearing out her lungs, and when she tried to suck the new air back in, nothing happened, nothing at all. Her throat didn't work, her lungs did not inflate, her body shuddered and she made a frantic gurgling sound, twisting and flinging up her arms as she fell over knocking apart cardboard boxes of Lydia's old newspaper clippings and smashing to pieces a fragile slatted chair. Her face puffed up, blushing crimson, and her eyes bugged out as she hit the floor sucking desperately for air. In a terminal panic, wild-eyed Kelly churned her legs, propelling herself across the stinking rug by jabbing her heels into the carpet and kicking hard, twisting and flopping and thumping as her scabby fingers tore at her own throat that unleashed terrible air-deprived, blocked-up grunting sounds, her entire body swelling from the effort to take in another fucking gulp of oxygen as Lydia's mangy cats leaped high and frizzed electrically, banging into each other hilariously in appalling midair collisions while they tried to escape among an *ack-ack* of flying potted plants, airborne books, and old mayonnaise jars full of dried apricots hopping off tables and shelves as Kelly went berserk.

Only a second elapsed before we reacted, and then Susan was the first to pounce. She sailed off the couch descending like a very odd bird into the turmoil of Kelly's flailing limbs and struggling body, and she clapped her lips over Kelly's mouth, blowing into my wife with all the energy at her disposal.

Kelly erupted, the entire contents of her stomach—liquor, junk food, bile, all the poisons she'd consumed for twenty years—splashing over Susan, over Kelly herself, over the apartment and TV screen and desperately scattering cats. "*Help me!*" Susan cried, and Luther dived onto his thrashing stepmom. "*Grab her legs!*" Susan ordered. "*Charley, come hit her chest!*" But by then I was there, grasping at Kelly, trying to latch on, already breathless myself and terrified because even without a split-second of reflection it was obvious, as Redd Foxx used to say, that this was "The Big One."

Miranda grabbed a fistful of Kelly's hair, banged her own forehead hard against the floor, but retained her grip.

Four of us fought to hold still Kelly's bouncing body making that hideous sucking sound. Her eyes popped out of their sockets double Rodney Dangerfield's, her cheeks were so red it seemed certain they'd burst into flame, then they turned blue. She kicked me in the chin, punched me in the chest, her elbow broke Luther's nose, a kneecap knocked out one of Susan's teeth, then Kelly sank her rotten choppers into my forearm and Christ Almighty I *screamed!* yanking my arm away so violently that I actually broke her jaw as one of Miranda's fruitboots caught me in the crotch. Riding that bronco, ducking her wild punches, Susan tried to blow in air; I thumped both hands against Kelly's sternum the way I'd seen it done in movies; Luther grappled to hold down her lunging frame so we could be of help; and Miranda simply latched on tight. But we slipped, losing our grips, we skidded in her vomit, it was impossible to pin her down, it was like trying to control a bucking Brahma or rein in a race car flipping end-over-end at Indianapolis or latch hold in midair of a powerful tail-dancing swordfish—

Then another eruption burst from her mouth and this time it was solid blood.

"OH MY GOD!" I yelled, "SOMEBODY STOP THIS PLEASE!"

Kelly threw us asunder like a movie monster getting rid of tiny people and propelled herself up off the floor, a veritable sounding whale, she was, roaring to her feet in an insane burst of energy shaking us all away again when we attacked back and she staggered sideways, making that horrible sucking sound, unable to get a single flake of oxygen into her lungs. Punch-drunk crazy, she knocked over the TV (which exploded, sparked, and sputtered), smashed trinkets off Lydia's shelves, broke glasses and kicked aside the kitchen table as we tried to tackle her and failed. She busted living room windows with her fist and tripped against the couch, losing her balance, toppling to earth once more like some huge, prehistoric, crippled predator made insane by a lightning bolt. Her shoulder flipped over a cat box that sprayed Kitty Litter all across her soggy torso, and the final huge nonnoise to break from her empty chest brought another massive spewing of upchuck and blood.

With that, Kelly's upheaval stopped on a dime as if a bullet had finally greased her between the eyes, and all the layers of flab beneath her shabby clothes shuddered in a final quivering before they came to rest. *"Oh No!"* I cried, but this time much too late. After years of

killing herself, my crazed and horribly disfigured wife had expired
justlikethat.

Thirty seconds, max, start to finish, and Kelly lay there dead,
saturated in red gunk and toxic vomit, garnished top to bottom in
millions of scented pebbles soaked in cat pee and kitty shit, the
most godawful mess I'd ever seen.

Surprise, surprise.

Susan kneeled in shattered glass by the TV heaving and gasping loudly. Luther had fallen against the overturned kitchen table,
both hands cupping his aching nose. Miranda's skinny tattooed
arms were lodged between the slats of a dismembered chair. I was in
a doorway, propping myself, coughing and dizzy from lack of air,
bruised all over as if from a professional football game. Aside from
our shocked panting noises, the silence was so scary I couldn't move
or breathe or think . . . and none of us were sobbing. Kelly released a
fart that lasted at least ten seconds, then her sphincter muscles
relaxed and the smell of shit swallowed up the trailer.

From the mess she had caused in the blink of a hellacious eye,
you would have thought a bomb had detonated in Lydia's trailer, or
an earthquake had transpired, or a space heater had exploded, or
some kind of low-level target-specific sonic boom had gone off.
Newspaper clippings and ravaged books lay everywhere among the
shards of jars, wrinkled apricot slices, tipped-over plants, smashed
chairs, champagne bottles, upturned tables, yanked-apart curtains,
clattery heaps of dismantled venetian blinds, and busted ceramic
mugs, crumpled lampshades, shattered lightbulbs, etcetera. All the
living room windows were somehow broken, twisted curtain rods lay
in the wreckage, cat boxes were upside down and their litter and turds
splashed about, the TV set (without a picture tube) was smoking,
and couch-cushions flung willy-nilly bled raggedy tufts of Holofil.
Several cheap prints of famous paintings knocked off the walls were
lodged in the rubble, their frames cracked, bent, massacred. And all
of the wreckage was plastered with the contents of Kelly's stomach
and her veins and arteries as if some kind of foaming painter/madman

had gone haywire with plastic restaurant squeeze bottles of ketchup, mustard, and pickle relish.

An English sparrow flew in through one of the windows, realized it had made a serious mistake, and fluttered deliriously around the room, desperately seeking escape. It banged into walls and fell down, launched itself up against the ceiling and somersaulted back into the wreckage, flung itself tipsily aloft again, banged into Susan's neck, flip-flapped dizzily right across Kelly's chest, plowed into the empty TV and somehow tumbled out again, then spun in circles for a moment on the floor until a grotesque, half-hairless calico cat sprang from nowhere, grabbed it, and leaped through a busted window to escape.

"Awesome," Miranda said.

After a long beat I became aware of Kelly's sour belly contents and blood all over me. Luther's face was splashed by a sticky red slime that matched the color of his Mohawk. Susan's drenched blouse was torn open, revealing her ribs, a comical black training bra, and a belly-button so *out* it could have been one of those thermometers in a self-basting turkey.

"Jeepers, creepers," Susan moaned, delicately pushing glass fragments off her soiled thigh. Then that awkward beanpole looked up at me, grave and beautiful, saying, "Poor Charley. . . *I am so sorry.*"

I staggered over to Kelly and fell to my knees by her side and lowered my forehead onto her filthy bloated belly, woozy and whispering bitterly, "You motherfucker. . ."

Luther crawled to the telephone and dialed 911.

Elvis had left the building.

AFTERWARD, NO ONE present at the debacle that took place on Nob Hill the night of Election Day was exactly able to describe what happened at the Fagerquist mansion. Perhaps my devoted and persistent reporter amigo, Susan Delgado, came closest when she summarized her sleuthing to me several days later:

"Suddenly there was a thunderclap, Charley, the ceiling blew out, a huge hole appeared in the floor where Jack Bannerman had been standing, a CLANG! sounded in the basement, and everybody screamed 'Earthquake!' as plaster bits and white dust rained down and boiled up everywhere, vigas began cracking, and most of the southside plate glass shattered. At first all the revelers at the FAGERBAN 'victory' celebration that was turning into a wake as the election results were announced thought it was a bad sonic boom. Then they figured a five-hundred-pound bomb had crashed through the house without exploding. But finally they realized that a single tiny vote, tallied on the screen of a computer miles away at Election Central, had actually done the damage."

Miraculously, Jack Bannerman was not killed by the lone (and lonely!) cipher that fell out of the sky and hit Clarence Fagerquist's obnoxious castle. But informed sources estimated that Jack came within four centimeters of being drilled into a mess of jellied meat with bone splinters in it no bigger than a mouse's clavicle. This might not have been a bad fate given the mauling that Bo Hrbyk had subjected him to behind closed doors in his S & L office that afternoon when the tough little federale laid down his cards for Jack to contemplate: insufficient collateral lending . . . phony cash-flow projections . . . too many short-term notes . . . a host of false evaluations . . . and letters of credit that had never showed up as loans on the books.

"If I need it I'll get reinforcements at the Fed Discount Window," Jack had countered brashly.

"When pigs fly," Bo had grinned.

"Touch my jug and I'll make you pay," Jack threatened.

"I hear you felons are hiding a loan viability ratio that's almost four to one," Bo malevolently replied.

In truth, Jack tumbled into the vote hole at the Fagerquists' faux chateau almost as if a trapdoor had opened directly beneath him— i.e., so fast the eye could not catch his act. He disappeared instantaneously, plummeting into the basement rec room, breaking his right ankle, incurring minor kidney damage, and suffering a moderate concussion. No guest realized Jack had survived (or even that he had flown the coop), however, largely because everybody else was running around squawking hysterically as billowing dust enveloped the large salon, adding to the drama and confusion.

FAGERBAN supporters floundered through the polluted atmosphere, ghostly, ghastly, bumping into each other, blubbering "Oof!" and reaching for their respective loved ones. Clarence's wife, Willa, pinned to the couch by a beam, frantically stretched her arms for hubby, fingers wriggling pathetically. Manjo, desperately seeking Eleanor (who'd dashed from the crash site without him), bled moderately from head wounds caused by flying detritus. Regal Lu Ann Bannerman scampered to safety with nary a hair out of place. Not Melody Kinderfink, however, who staggered from the wreckage in goofy plaster whiteface, clothes shredded, both her sneakers missing. And as Tammy Sue Clendennon, led by William Watrous (who was coughing, choking, and sneezing), hurdled numerous splintered obstructions, the ample bulges of flesh leaking from rips in her bonny outfit seemed astoundingly pink and succulent.

W. W. himself was mortified because even though he'd been unopposed, he had lost the election by a landslide to a write-in butterfly that wouldn't be seated until January, so we're talking a *cocoon* to boot.

Terrified celebrants escaped in all directions, out windows and doors, through arches, along carpeted hallways. The tipped-over fish tank sent tiny golden minnows flopping among stampeding feet that quickly squished them. Billions of feathers from upstairs pillows floated into the murky downstairs atmosphere, also pages from an old book—*Windmill of the Gods*—that seconds earlier had been sitting upon Willa's bedside table.

Four massive topside vigas had been shattered by the tiny missile, weakening the entire ceiling, which bowed and began to give way in the first thirty seconds. A half dozen floor joists had also bitten the dust along with a crucial lumber girder, hence the floor caved in, too, almost before the guests had fled. Sam Clendennon nearly broke his ankle; Billy Joe Bob Fagerquist banged into a mirror; Tallulah Moe barely escaped certain death when a chandelier crashed in front of her. All the children scooted away like startled bugs, reaching safety first. A Sikh security guard called an Immediate Response Team of city and state police simply by punching a red button. Then he flipped a switch to cut off the natural gas and ran toward open air with all the other Hollywood extras.

By any stretch the Fagerquist citadel was an imposing edifice, a homage to everything gross and greedy in America. Fluted columns in front, an elaborate widow's walk, parapets, porches, balconies, porticos, portcullises and porte cochères, gables galore and dormer windows and bay windows and fine brick chimneys, also a Jacuzzi and wading pool, and in the trophy room were lion heads, reebok antlers, elephant-foot wastebaskets, and a Steinway baby grand that nobody ever played displaying Willa's Troll collection on top—

But no more.

One mighty thunderclap, then a single wee "NO!" ballot fell through the roof . . . through the master bedroom . . . through the

Great Dining Hall of Mirrors . . . and into the billiard room/bar below, causing all hell to break loose. The straw had broken the camel's back; the torpedo had hit the *Lusitania*; King Duncan had been slain by Macbeth. Not all at once did that grandiloquent mega-structure crumble, of course, but as soon as the main floor caved in and a couple of water mains burst, the issue was never in doubt.

No sooner had the last petrified reveler fled into the Xeriscape garden or onto the thick green lawn, than the remaining vigas began to pop and crackle under duress and, as the horrified onlookers looked on, the sleazeball trophy manor began to quiver. "Jack, Jack!" Eleanor Poddubny called. Glass broke in all the upper floor windows as interior studs bent and sills buckled from the strain. Soon enough the walls were sucked inward, headers split in two, paneling shifted remarkably, and another key viga snapped.

Tristan Griffith had a premonition: "It's Mrs. O'Leary's cow!"

Cops arrived, sirens wailing. "Oh Jack where are you?" Tammy Sue sobbed, but Jack gave no response from down in that hellhole where he'd tumbled. Jack's secretary, Marbella Tremaine, repeatedly sprinted back toward the doomed hacienda, but friends, neighbors, and concerned public servants always tackled her short of the dangerously unstable house. "*Roast in hell, Jack!*" Clarence intoned as his home collapsed; "*you deserve the best!*"

At the stroke of midnight that weakened pleasure palazzo toppled into its own basement like an extinguished star sucking itself into a black hole. When the roof ridgepole went, the last of the load-bearing walls and joists underneath gave up the ghost. Out of the holocaust staggered Edna Poddubny, the last survivor to escape and every inch a symbol of defeat. Several emotionally disturbed guests pried loose bricks and chucked them at the Christian (turned commie!) newspaper editor, booing her vociferously. Lu Ann Bannerman put a stop to that, however, dashing forward and grabbing Edna's hand, leading the editor to safe harbor away from the dangerously unstable throng.

There followed a pretty quick finish. For days afterward witnesses spoke of appalling structural groans in the end and an enormous

amount of dust. But nobody saw the spark that caused the conflagration leading to the downright Biblical retribution that promptly
afflicted our town.

Perhaps it began in the electrical wiring. One theory had a flee-
ing flock of bees in the Fagerquist attic being ignited as all the
wiring tore loose, creating a sparkler effect that torched their wings.
And at least one bee traveled 80 feet into the neighbor's yard before
it expired, dive-bombing a tinder-dry pile of dead cosmos plants
Tammy Sue Clendennon had not yet bagged for the garbage trucks
on Wednesday.

Then again, it could have been just plain Fate, a heavenly (and
well deserved) accounting long overdue our ruling class.

Whatever, the minute Clarence Fagerquist's fanfaronade to
poor taste and deep pockets ate cheese, the Clendennon spread next
door went up in flames. Forget about the multiple sprinkler systems
and smoke alarms required by building inspectors and insurance
companies: In thirty seconds the structure was transformed into a
living torch. Carnivorous flames devoured the breakfast nook, the
cocktail pod, the billiards grotto, and the master bedroom with its
circular Magic Fingers waterworld monstrosity upon which the
Mayor and the Wet Dream had oft vented their libidinous excesses.

Only a hop, step, and a jump stood between that monument to
garbled architecture and the Manjo Poddubnys' Grecian hovel surrounded by topiaried ewe trees, a couple of aspen glades featuring
latticework gazebos, and a marble faun from Carrara, Italy. It all
started there when a guest cottage spontaneously combusted from
the sudden application of heat, landing fiery shingles atop the mansion's roof, which soon enough became an inferno that roared "as
loudly as a freight train" as it spread.

Nob Hill, that fabulous playland of our rich and famous, that
so-called "protected community" where all the cars had burglar
alarms and all the palatial estates positively quivered with seeing-eye
security apparati predicated on heat detection, first-strike capabilities,
and direct signals to Johnny Batrus, et al. (who remained on call

twenty-four hours a day only for that privileged section of town)—well, all the anti-gangster, pro-longevity technology functioned about as effectively, during this evening of pyrolatry, as tits on a boar hog.

I'm not sure if "firestorm" is the proper appellation for what transpired across our town's high muckety-muck Shangri-la. Calling it a "blow-up" is probably not far off the mark. Those fancy temples to almighty Mammon burned with remarkable gusto despite all the fireproof rugs and drapes, asbestos tiling, and years of accumulated Allstate premiums guaranteeing that No Harm would ever befall the indulgent bailiwicks at the top of our social, economic, and criminal food chain . . . or do I mean pyramid?

Do I delight in the rhetoric of destruction? Who—me? Charley McFarland, all-around Boy Scout, liberation ecologist, Compassion Personified? *You better believe it.* Hail to all meretricious rococo lingo! Such a fire as incinerated Nob Hill on the night of that Election Day deserves all the verbal embellishments I can muster. If Thomas Wolfe could have mated with William Burroughs to produce *Look Home-ward, Naked Lunch,* this chapter would've been it.

Yes, the entire Volunteer Fire Department arrived, but they could do very little. Take out their dicks and piss at Vesuvius about sums it up. The raging flames galloped from one hoity-toity posh lot to the next—*Snap! Crackle! Pop!* Trees exploded, flinging branches (trailing writhing snakes of fire) in all directions. The contents of swimming pools evaporated in seconds flat. Barking dogs, yapping toy poodles, shrieking mini-schnauzers and even asthmatically wheezing bulldogs fled in many directions, raising an awesome hub-bub. Shrilly piercing burglar alarms were strangled by hot air blasts. Mercedes, Jaguars, Cadillacs, and Range Rovers gave up their ghosts in loud salutes of noisy muffled gas explosions. All any owner could do was shout helplessly, retreat, flee.

At the height of the storm it seemed God was actually pour-ing gasoline onto the blaze—*goody for Her!* Yesterday, Park Place and Maple Drive had proudly displayed three-storey million-dollar stone mansions surrounded by thick green Weed Free rugs and

rhododendrons, peonies, and ornamental Japanese cherry trees up
the wazoo, also clay tennis courts and fabulous greenhouses (in
which rare and exotic orchids bloomed), goldfish ponds, and precision
evergreen copses shading their south lawns. And each lawn and
rooftop had displayed a VOTE "YES!" ON PROP X broadside. But all
of it now was ferociously consumed in a hot twinkle—flickety, flickety,
flick. Yes, Virginia, the ostentatious dwellings of bankers, lawyers,
insurance agents, mining czars, realtors, remittance men, artsy-fartsies
and other assorted heirs and heiresses, mergerers and acquisitators,
gambling figures and the like, all were consumed equally during that
brimstone-laden pandemonium: Democracy at last!

Chicago . . . San Francisco . . . Oakland . . . Hinkley, Minnesota:
Our town now joined those infamous cities of yore. *"Welcome!"* History yowled.

In retrospect, I'd like to think that some grand malevolent pay-
back of sorts incinerated Nob Hill, burning it so swiftly to the ground.
A revenge made inevitable by all the hideous inequalities driving the
machines of state in our town . . . and around the globe.

Shamelessly frolicking winds thundered up from the ghetto
inciting a destructive ardor that melodramatically cauterized everything in its path. So long, Jacuzzi Heaven! *Ciao,* Three-Car Garage!
Sayonara, all you dumbwaiters, tins of Beluga caviar, polo mallets,
and backyard putting greens. I'm told you could hear magnums of
Dom Perignon, Moët et Chandon, Pouilly-Fumé, Piper Heidsieck,
Chateau Margaux, and Chambolle-Musigny going *pop! pop! pop!* . . .
POP! as fiery dervishes danced among the happy detonations. Virtual
hurricanes of sparks whirled across the neighborhood, cyclonic,
exultant: *slam, bam, thank you, ma'am!*

Nobody died, mind you, not even a salivating Lhasa apso or a
parakeet. After all, we're talking "democracy" here, not some referen-
dum in Haiti or Sierra Leone. Of course, heaps of money safely
stashed in "guaranteed impregnable" safes were burned to cinders.
Paintings by Mondrian, Picasso, Pollock, and de Kooning were
vaporized in seconds. Coin collections melted, Purdy shotguns

bought the farm, and at least two dozen $50,000 Swiss Patek watches were barbecued in the mini-Hiroshima. To say nothing of all those big-screen TV sets, VCRs, high-end stereo concoctions, and elaborate personal computers: Meltdown—*doodle-y-op-bop!*—all gone . . . baby go bye-bye . . . *adios!*

The fire burned in a northeasterly direction, curling swiftly up and around Circle Drive, then racing downhill toward town like a speedy special-effects monster sucking up everything in its wake. That wonderful fire was Warren Buffet in the Heartland, Bill Gates in Seattle, Wilt Chamberlain in Philadelphia (and in bed)—an irresistible force, bigger than life, overpowering and unstoppable.

Also very selective and a speedy worker. And mighty short-lived into the bargain. To this day nobody understands why the monster died so prematurely, failing to wipe out our entire town. Full of energy, seemingly primed for bigger and better things, it roared four hundred feet lower to the northern base of Nob Hill where the Cruz Alta Subdivision began. But there, instead of leaping upon all those flimsy ticky-tacks, the fire stumbled, twisted in a most peculiar and virulent agony, then suddenly blew itself out in a great airy overheated WHOOSH! that scalded many an elm and poplar branch in that blue-collar bastion, but caused no further damage.

It's as if the disaster had a brain, a soul, an animated heart, also a mission clearly defined, methodically executed, meticulously controlled. Nob Hill lay in smoking ruins; but *no place else in town* was touched.

The black smoldering tree stumps of Nob Hill recalled etiolated photographs picturing the aftermath of bombardments at Khe Sanh or St. Malo. Of the Nob Hill dwellings only a few stone and adobe walls remained; all else had been consumed. When I bicycled up later, twisted pipes looked horrible in the charred landscape, and blackened auto hulks added to the air of desolation. Of course no birds sang. It was eradication, complete and irrevocable. That tony suburb existed no longer except as an insurance headache: Nob Hill had been wiped off the face of the earth.

By Wednesday morning, all water and electricity had been shut down and the press constituted a loudly murmuring throng hungry for gossip. Most of the Fourth Estate had gathered at the Fagerquist property where it had all begun.

"What happened?" Kim Sweetwater asked Susan Delgado.

"We won," Susan explained quietly. "Democracy carried the day."

"Where is Jack Bannerman?" Kim asked.

Susan pointed. "In there. Below that. Eating cat food."

"Egads, nobody could survive under such rubble!"

Guess again, Kim, and all you other purveyors of smut, false alarms, and the sexually explicit innuendoes so common to the generally irresponsible press. For indeed Jack Bannerman *had* survived as only a man of his innate character could have, huddled beneath a mountain of dripping debris between a television set, an overturned pool table, and a beer refrigerator leaking freon.

The rescue effort lasting a full day involved three D-7 bulldozers, twenty-five hardened volunteers, a construction crane, and Tristan Griffith's large Pyrenees/St. Bernard mix, Beowulf, who—it turns out—had been trained for bomb-blast rescue work back east in the wilds of Westchester, New Haven, and Queens.

The first words out of Jack's mouth when finally they lifted him free of the clutter were, "Thank God I'm alive."

Whereupon Lu Ann Bannerman's Capital City lawyer, Melody "The Bomber" Sheffield, served Jack with divorce papers that essentially demanded his money or his life.

But that's not all. A squad car traveling ninety swerved up Gaviota Drive, siren screaming, and raced through the charcoal-broiled streets of Nob Hill, churning up a furious wake of ashy dust that roiled behind it like the smoke from a volcano or an atomic explosion. Brakes began squealing forty yards below the Fagerquists' still smoking burnt-out shell, and the black and white skidded sideways, careening toward the crowd, which scattered like a prodigious quail covey flushing in a meadow of carbon char. When its tires met the curb broadside—WHUMP!—the cruiser left terra firma, rolling over two times in midair with a twist (degree of difficulty, 1.8) and landed upright, sinking so low onto its shocks that the oil pan, muffler, and differential were driven up through the frame and floorboards into the interior of the car itself.

A door flew open and Johnny Batrus touched down in full sprinting mode headed directly for Jack the Flak, who took one step backward and signaled for a fair catch. Johnny set his heels, screeching to a stop in the usual undulating cloud of gunk, drew his gun and twirled it rapidly five times before sticking the barrel up under Jack Bannerman's chin, cocking the hammer, and announcing, "You're under arrest!"

"Bullshit," Jack said. "Don't bother me, you two-bit poodle-brained Kojak, I got important things to do with my life."

WRONG.

Johnny brought the gun butt down hard on Jack's head, kicked his feet out from under, tackled him even before he struck the ground, flipped him over crudely, yanked Jack's arms behind his back, clamped on the Cheerios twins, leaped to his feet, flung his arms to the sky, and hollered, "*Time!*"

The Almighty Rodeo Announcer Up There said, "Four-point-three seconds. Nice job, cowboy."

A ND FINALLY:

On Election Night I did not even remotely possess enough strength to plant another fresh carcass (even though that one-vote victory belonged to us . . . and William Watrous had actually *lost* despite running unopposed!). So an ambulance arrived and Mimi Spitz and Dakota Namath came through the door carrying a stretcher, a body bag, and an old clean sweatsuit for Kelly. Those two women were considerate, professional, and very loving. The ambulance driver, Larry Boggs, gave Luther his Broncos windbreaker and a pair of too-tight cutoff jeans and a bag of ice for his swollen nose. We all washed ourselves in Lydia's shower. Miranda fit perfectly into the old lady's hazard-orange raincoat. Susan donned one of Lydia's tatty mink jobs that barely reached down to her midthigh. Me, I used an entire dress for a shirt, and wrapped a huge blue bath towel around my waist, safety-pinning it closed tight. We threw away our other soiled clothes. The three EMTs rolled Kelly into a body bag; Dakota zipped it up; then they slipped the stretcher underneath and carted out my wife. That's when Miranda embraced Luther and they kissed with an extraordinarily intimate gentleness, the first time I'd ever seen them touch each other.

By default Kelly fell victim to the undertaker's art. Luther and I took care of many funeral details at the Body Shoppe (with that human salamander, Elton Gaverdine, who had the last laugh after all). Then my kid and Susan Delgado and I drove out to the mesa together in my dying Buick, hankering for a moment of reprieve. Miranda stayed at the trailer, patiently cleaning up. It had been one helluva day.

We parked facing west away from town in the middle of a sagebrush ocean without a single artificial light burning in front of us. I turned off the ignition and slumped behind the wheel, my head tilted, staring at the Milky Way. Luther was beside me, Susan sat in back. Fatigue isn't what I felt, nor exhaustion, but rather a deadly lethargy, as if I had turned off my life. You overload the brain, you know what happens? It empties completely. The core problem of modern times: We can't evolve fast enough to incorporate all the meaningless information that clutters up our skulls.

So I sipped from a pint bottle of cheap blackberry brandy, then offered Luther a hit, but he declined, passing the bottle to Susan, who gave it back to me. My son's face was puffy from the broken nose, but he was macho and stoic and had an almost–Born Again glow modified by a terrorist gleam. From the far side of the front seat, leaning against the door, he contemplated the galaxies quietly. Dressed only in grubby jeans and a 10,000 Maniacs T-shirt with Lydia's FREE HUEY button on his chest, Luther clenched his teeth to forestall the shivers. The young *never* get cold. You could drop a teenager wearing flip-flops, shorts, and a T-shirt onto the North Pole in January, and they'd just laugh and start hacking away on their laptop.

My weary eyes roamed across the visible universe—twinkle twinkle, squared. Luther said, "Look, another shooting star." Yup, it was a clear bright night and every few minutes a glowing cinder zipped across the panorama. Coyotes fired off a fierce accolade of cries . . . but immediately their blood-curdling rowdiness subsided. Then it was silent and nothing stirred on the chilly mesa. Our breathing created billows of steam.

Oh woe. I savored each mouthful of sticky rotgut before letting it trickle into my body . . . you bet I was getting drunk. *Let the games begin.* Kelly's death had been so gross, so gauche, so visibly distressing, like watching a haggis explode. I wouldn't know what it's like to have an infant drown when your back is turned, but I felt that way. . . I think. The heart is a cruel black velvet monster with a relentless thirst for blood.

Luther asked, "Pop, are you okay?"

"Sure, no problem. I'm happy as a lark. So polite of you to ask."

"You don't sound happy," Luther said.

"I'll be tip-top in just a minute, son, as soon as I collect myself. Oops, there's another one." I nodded toward a blazing streak across the sky, instantly extinguished. Susan whispered, "Make a wish."

Luther said, "I wish Kelly wasn't dead."

"Gimme a break," I griped. "The only thing that pisses me off is, What took her so long?"

Luther shut his mouth and counted to five. Susan leaned forward and just her fingertip lightly touched my neck.

We all peered at the universe. I kept seeing Lydia in the bottom of our pit, bald without her wig, and Kelly dead on the trailer floor lathered in her own lethal puke, but the universe kept on twinkling loudly, bless its icy heart. I wondered if, after tonight, I would ever be able to stop drinking, taking up where my wife left off. Obviously, I was feeling a tad sorry for myself. You spend your life refusing to despair as a matter of principle, but every now and then the reality of the Shit Storm almost strikes you dumb.

At length I mumbled, "Luther, would you be willing to let me hold you for a minute?"

He balked, but then, incredibly, my boy shifted closer and tentatively gathered me in his arms the way you might embrace a sofa cushion drenched in adolescent sports sweat. With that, instantly—finally!—tears began gushing from my eyes. ("From where else would they gush?" my grammar school writing teacher Mrs. Annette Scarpitta would've harped.)

"Do you think you can ever forgive us?" I asked drunkenly, having passed through Astonishment, Guilt, and Anger into Maudlin.

"Shut up, Pop, or I'll hit you."

I don't care how many books you've read by Robert Bly, it's definitely embarrassing (and humiliating . . . and *spooky*) to be a man sobbing in the arms of your own formerly autistic son. I almost rather would have masturbated in front of Luther. Or asked him for a loan. Nevertheless, the water flowed out of me, though it was unaccompanied by noisy sobs or gurgles. No gasping, either, no heaving and choking . . . it was interesting. Like, turn on a spigot and watch the water flow. It poured clear of me and wouldn't stop for a long time. Imagine inadvertently peeing in your pants . . . for ten minutes. I would bet that nothing on earth is more discombobulating than asking your own offspring for absolution. No doubt Susan closed her eyes and bowed her head so as not to intrude.

Out on the mesa something fluttered, an invisible winged thing traveling through the dark. The smell of sage was faint. Luther's arms around me quivered, ready to take flight if I dared sink any deeper into my mawkish sniveling despair.

So my tears eventually ran dry and dissipated, and then gently I extricated myself from his self-conscious embrace. I wouldn't say "relief" took over my body, but something had drained away and I was fair exhausted in an almost erotic surrender. I'm not a Vietnam vet, but I reckon letting go of Kelly was like getting onto an American airliner at Ton Son Nhut after thirteen months on the line over there in a firefight every day with an invisible enemy who couldn't speak a word of English, always smeared feces on her punjii stakes, and gave you the clap every time you fucked her—

Something in that vein.

I had a final vision of Kelly, then, all alone back in her glory days bundled in dungarees and a puffy winter jacket. A bright knitted cap with earflaps was pulled half down over her gorgeous unruly hair. Don't ask me why this transition comes to mind, but think of Pamela Anderson Lee playing the Ingrid Bergman role in *Casablanca*. Kelly stood in a spotlight, self-consciously pigeon-toed, peering into the blackness toward her poor husband. That'd be me, the guy "who loved her despite everything." Peter Peter Punkin Eater. Kelly didn't move, or speak, or gesture in my direction. She merely stood there seeming beautiful and wistful for a moment and totally innocent like an animal from the Garden of Eden . . . until Scotty beamed her up.

"*Luther,*" I said in a whisper, "*I love you and I can't afford to lose you, too.*"

But by then he had turned his face northeast. "Hey, Pop," he said, "what do you think is happening in town?"

I cast an eye in that direction and exclaimed, "Oh my God!"

A spectacular rosy glow lit up Nob Hill. Billions of cinders zipped toward heaven like fireflies shot from mortar tubes. At certain locations the flames extended several hundred feet into the air; they wavered and doodled like diabolical hula dancers from Hades. The mountainous backdrop was illuminated and pulsing vividly, and roiling black smoke framed everything.

Faintly, we could hear the sirens of fire trucks and police officers humping to the scene.

When Luther found his voice again he murmured, undeniably awed, "Jesus, the Butterfly Coalition really kicked ass, didn't we?"

"Like troopers," Susan murmured on my behalf, scarcely audible.

"And now what is going to happen?" he asked.

I pondered the question a while but no bright ideas immediately came to mind. It was all, like, *duh.* Whatever. The struggle against Prop X had robbed my last harrowing ounce of vitality. I couldn't even get it up for the conflagration. I thought, *How pathetic it is to be made so weary by such a* small *k-fuffle.* Where did people like Gandhi and Ho Chi Minh and Joan of Arc get their *energy?* And I wondered, *How could we ever* feed *and clothe the hungry, and end racism, and save the environment, and build sustainable economies, and redistribute the wealth if it took so much effort just to stop* one . . . idiotic . . . highway . . . bypass?

But the way it works for any person who wants to live in a better world is like this: *The Eleventh Commandment is hope.*

So taking a deep breath, Susan Delgado said, "Okay, guys, I'll lay it out for you: My vision of the New Millennium." She paused, thinking, but not for long. "It goes without saying that Lydia's property will be protected in perpetuity as an internationally famous wildlife refuge with particular emphasis on endangered species. Farragut will set it up, airtight, forever. Her trailer will become the first building of the Rachel Carson Institute for Politically Correct Minority Environmentalists. And the Phistic Copper will appear on a U.S. postage stamp that outsells Elvis and Marilyn. They'll never build the highway bypass, hence Biogard, Genetavil, and Citi-Mag will come a cropper in our town. Thanks to Bo Hrbyk and his boys, First State S & L is sure to collapse, the attendant lawsuits falling like a meteor shower on all the major players' heads. Manjo, Clarence, Jack, and Sam should wind up in a federal country club playing golf for a couple of months, at least. Naturally, having been burned out of their Stygian roosts, all our rich and greedy citizens are going to move elsewhere, allowing the ghetto to relocate itself on Nob Hill. Eleanor Poddubny will wake up one morning *fat* and Edna P. will shrink until she's thin. Then, to every poor family in our town the government will extend a Fanny Mae housing allowance, three acres, and a registered mule. Providing the family accepts complimentary Blue Cross/Blue Shield health care coverage, a generous pension at fifty-five, and, for the kiddies, full scholarships to a four-year college (with open admission policies) thanks to Tío Sam."

She halted, catching her breath.

Luther said, "Is that all?"

"No," I chimed in, suddenly feeling a spark down deep. "The Butterfly Coalition has so raised the collective consciousness of our community that soon every ticky-tack in Cruz Alta will be retrofitted with Trombe walls, solar panels, composting toilets, and thermal (or wind-driven) hot-water heaters. The hospital will accept, free of charge, all women needing abortions up through the second trimester. When the ligtonite mine shuts down for good, Superfund dollars will rehabilitate the land. And the racism that plagues us all will miraculously go away. The Butterfly Coalition will start its own four-year college where most classes will be held in several native languages, and students will be encouraged to major in Environmental

Law, Ecology Studies, Minority Civil Rights, Liberation Theology, Native Cultures, or Marxist Feminism from the African-American Standpoint. Susan will teach revolutionary journalism; Randy Featherstone will broadcast the lectures."

Luther smirked, "I can't wait to go to your college, Pop."

"Hey, there's more," Susan added, her voice stronger now, almost glowing. "Our town is going to become the first minicity in America to *abolish* the automobile. It'll be replaced by an efficient public transportation system of ethanol buses, solar trams, and free battery-powered shuttle vans for the elderly. At the same time crime should disappear, thanks to collective bargaining, the equal redistribution of wealth, and summer jobs for all teens at twice the minimum wage. Plus free family and alcohol counseling for everybody, regardless of race, creed, color, or financial bracket. Am I going too fast for you?"

Luther asked, "What about Willow Road?"

I fielded that grounder easily. "We're gonna form a neighborhood association and elect me to run it."

"And what will you *do?*" Luther asked.

"We'll pass laws that lawns must be allowed to go to seed for the benefit of birds and other wildlife, also to conserve water. We'll ban insecticides, pesticides, and herbicides, and all new landscaping activity will be Xeriscapic in nature. Bug Lites will come down as martin houses go up. Charity Gingivitis will lead the neighborhood recycling effort; Ethan Chambers can head our Big Brother program with orphan kids from the ghetto; and Butchie Maelstorm will lobby the County Commission for bicycle paths that'll soon extend along either side of the picturesque road. Mildred Olney-Florissant will organize study groups on heart-friendly diets, creative exercises, and 'Democracy Instead of Capitalism.' Others from our street will lead the Phistic Volunteers who, in season, will work as para-scientists in the lab at the Rachel Carson Institute implanting butterfly sperm on the underside of *Calexis trifida* leaves, artificially inseminating almost all Phistic Coppers, and thus increasing reproduction to the point where, within three years, the bug can be moved from an 'endangered' to a merely 'threatened' status."

I paused. Luther said, "Is that all?"

Not according to Susan. "Well, even Tristan Griffith will join us, running socially responsible investment workshops, and selling butterfly T-shirts in the Carson Institute gift shop on Saturday afternoons, and also—"

Luther interrupted: "T-shirts? God, that's so lame, Susan. That's like trying to kill an elephant with a fly swatter."

"Excuse me?" His declaration startled us because we hadn't seen it coming. I said, "What did you just say?"

Luther took off like a thoroughbred hayburner. "It's a new millennium but most of the world is still starving to death," he sputtered angrily. "One sixth of the population on earth controls five sixths of the wealth. Half the people in American prisons are black even though blacks are only a sixth of our population. Antarctica is melting. And there aren't any trees left in Haiti."

He halted, sucking for air. His cheeks were flushed, and suddenly his whole body was trembling.

"Yes, I know," I agreed, in shock. "But—"

Luther cut me off. "You can't stop hot lava by putting a Band-Aid on a volcano, dude. You can't cure capitalist ills by using bourgeois solutions, either. That only compounds the problem."

I squinted at him. He was not being derisive, he was serious. Towering flames from the Nob Hill fires flickered against his eyeballs, giving him the look of a deranged fanatic about to toss a bomb into a cop convention or a KKK rally, and his teeth—exposed in a grimace—positively glistened.

Gently, Susan's fingertip touched my neck again. She said, "He's not talking about Band-Aids on a volcano, Luther. But it *is* important to realize that every small positive action has infinite positive repercussions—"

"Oh fuck that Mickey Mouse bullshit," Luther grunted contemptuously. "I just want to kill all the slimeball oligarchs tomorrow. I'm tired of futzing around. If we don't stop GM, the Amazon jungle is doomed. The only man I admire is Fidel Castro. And the Pope's birth control policies are insane, so we need to eradicate the Catholic

Church immediately, except for Father Benny Wombat."

Cautiously, I reached over and touched *his* shoulder. He tensed so quickly I jumped. I said, "Luther, lots of stuff needs to be done. But even the most modest decent gesture is important. You don't count out anything. And I don't think violence—"

"I want to be Eco-Rambo," he interrupted fiercely. "I want to blow up the market economy and slaughter bankers and slumlords and replace them with a compassionate socialism based on full employment and sustainable agriculture. I hate planned obsolescence and conspicuous consumption: Death to Wal-Mart and Coca-Cola! I want to give homes to the homeless, make millionaires illegal, and quit logging in the National Forests. And anybody who kills a Willow Flycatcher gets strangled to death in a metal garroting device. *Twice.*"

I leaned back and regarded him, flabbergasted. I couldn't decide if a bright halo had begun to shine above his bald Mohawked cranium, or whether the nubbins of incipient horns were sprouting at the top of each temple. Had he evolved at last into my idealized creation . . . my long yearned-for political apparatchik . . . my darling little Marxist-Leninist *Frankenstein?*

Or did I suddenly have on my hands a berserk ideologue who'd spend the rest of his born days mired down in anarchical demagogic zealotry?

Fearing the worst, hoping for the best, I asked, "Are you through?"

"No."

"Okay, what else?"

"All political power comes from the barrel of a gun. I hate namby-pamby liberals. I wish I had a flamethrower screwed into my left arm so I could barbecue everyone I catch drinking Coors beer. If I had a plane I'd drop napalm canisters on the headquarters of Ligget & Meyers. And furthermore—"

One vote, and all the world (and all the life upon it) hangs by that slender thread.